THE CURSE AND THE PRINCE

KINGDOM OF CURSES AND SHADOWS II

DAY LEITAO

To everyone who believes in love.

CONTENTS

1

———

FACING THE MONSTER

Zora had imagined her return many times. In some versions, she'd be ashamed of her loss, dreading facing her family, her friends, her students. In others, she would come home as a winner, bathed in glory, proud to have represented the Dark Valley. Her valley.

But she had never imagined she would be running away, wounded, with Prince Griffin. Until a few days before, she thought he wanted her dead. To be honest, she still wasn't perfectly sure he had never tried to scare her, and yet, here they were, sitting together on a horse-drawn cart. For all her fears that he could be trying to kill her, she had been the one who'd almost got him killed.

Griffin was accompanying her to the Dark Valley, which meant he would eventually learn that she had cheated her way into the Royal Games. The thought gave her chills. And yet, she had no idea where else to go, even if she was getting more and more anxious about how people back home would judge her. Now that it was about to become a reality, she wasn't that sure if technically winning the games would make up for taking Seth's place, for representing the valley without their consent. Well, actions had consequences, and soon she'd face hers.

But none of that compared to Griffin's strange news.

"I'm the monster," he said.

Zora stared at him for a moment. He was serious, head down, with a pained expression on his face.

She waited for him to say something more, to tell her it was a joke, to explain and make it make sense, but he didn't.

Zora shuddered, but she still had a faint hope that perhaps she had misheard or misunderstood him. "Are you going to elaborate on that? Or should I just try to guess?"

He took a deep breath. Trembling and staring at a distance, he spoke quickly. "Midnight fever. Only when the moon is completely dark. I... become something. Not myself." He turned to her. "We need to get back to the castle. I have a safe room where I can be shackled."

So... it wasn't some kind of weird joke. Zora caught a breath. But this was time for planning and action, not fear. Returning to the castle would be problematic, considering Griffin's brother, Kiran, who also happened to be Gravel's king, wanted him dead. But that wasn't even the main issue.

"Night's falling. We'd take some two hours to get back to Gravel City. Is there... a specific time you become *not yourself*?" She tried to keep a neutral expression and not show any shock, fear, or worry.

He buried his face in his hands and sighed. "As soon as it's night."

Zora glanced at the setting sun. "You mean in some thirty, forty minutes?"

"Yes." His hands still covered his face.

Griffin looked so wretched that Zora extended a hand to

caress his head, but then retreated as soon as she touched his dark hair, remembering what that touch and their kiss had done to her mind.

She touched his shoulder instead. "Hey. Hey. We'll find a solution. There's a fix for everything. What's going to happen when night falls?"

His eyes were misty and wide with fear. "I... don't know."

This was getting more complicated than she had expected. But they needed to act fast, even if she had no clue what was happening or going to happen. "All right. First thing, let's get far from the road."

Zora pushed the cart into the forest as far as she could, then untied the horse and pulled it through the trees. As they walked, she turned to him. "If you don't know what happens, how come you shackle yourself? And how is it that you can't open the shackles?"

"I..." He bit his lip. "Get violent and break things, but I can't use a key. I can't do anything that requires precision. I do try to get free." He pulled one of his leather bands on his wrist and showed red scars, as if the skin had been pressed against metal. He then stopped walking. "Get away. Get away from me. Run. Zora, please run."

"I don't run from monsters." Then the image of that book with a person turning into a strange horned creature came to her mind and brought chills to her spine. "Do you... change your appearance?"

"I don't know. I never remember what happens."

That was odd. "But nobody told you?"

"My mother was the only person who knew about it. All she did was lock me up in those nights. She said she never saw me."

"Not even your brothers know about it?"

He shook his head. "They have no idea."

She took that in, then added, "And you're saying it's only when there's no moonlight."

"Yes." His voice was dry.

She tried to think, tried to find a solution. "Maybe it has to do with the dark. Like the shadow creatures in our valley." An idea hit her. "We'll find a meadow, light it, and maybe things will be different."

"Zora, you don't know it! I could kill you."

She kept walking. "I'm not that easy to kill, in case you haven't noticed. I'll tie you. I'll take the horse's, uh, rope thingy."

"The harness."

"Exactly." She figured it would be enough to tie him. "And we'll make a bright fire. It will be fine."

He stepped in front of her and took her hands. Her heart skipped a beat. "Please," he pleaded. "Leave. Go as far as you can."

Zora pulled her hands. "No. We'll tie you and light a fire. If I notice you're getting weird, I promise I'll run. But not before that."

Griffin closed his eyes and took a deep breath, but didn't say anything and kept walking with her. Zora followed the sound of running water and found a thin stream, where they drank and also watered the horse. Zora tied the animal and gathered wood as fast as she could. Griffin helped her despite his protests that she should run. His eyes were distant, lost.

Zora lit a fire, then proceeded to tie Griffin to a tree.

"This won't hold me," he said even as he sat quietly and let her tie the knot.

"I doubt you'll transform in one second, and I doubt you'll break free at the first sign of transformation. This is just so I have time to run." In truth she was pretty sure it would hold him, but she didn't want to argue. "I still think the fire might help."

His breathing was heavy. "Can you... go away? I'd rather you didn't see me."

"Someone has to tell you what you look like." She said it as a joke, but he didn't smile or look amused, so she changed her tone. "If every time it happened, you were alone in the dark, maybe it will be different now."

He looked away. "This is the most shameful moment of my life."

That didn't sound right. "Really? But this isn't your fault. I mean, I would be more ashamed of stuff that was my own doing." She had been thinking of her own mistakes, her own lies, but he looked down and bit his lip as if her words had been about him. True that he had made mistakes too.

He then faced her. "You're right. There are other things I should be ashamed of. If it helps, I *am* ashamed." He closed his eyes and sighed. "But... admitting this..."

Zora smiled, trying to reassure him. "Look at the bright side. I'm not anyone important. And my word is worthless. It's the same as if nobody knew about it."

He snorted and shook his head, then paused as if about to say something, but ended up looking away.

Those were not Prince Griffin's eyes, at least not the ones she had seen before. Those were eyes she saw in children when they were afraid. Young children. It was such a contrast to his strong, even intimidating physique. She wished she could hug and comfort him, but the idea of hugging him reminded her of the touch of his lips, which she'd better forget.

"Look at me," she said. He did. She continued, "I'm here

with you. Give me your hands." She held them, doing her best to ignore the spark she felt, the softness of his skin, his dark eyes on her. Why did it have to be so complicated? All she wanted was to comfort him. "I'll let you know if anything happens, but I think this night will be different."

He swallowed. "Can you promise to run if I tell you to? Run far away? Don't try to interact with whatever I become?"

She didn't want to leave him there, helpless. Perhaps it was still her guilt. Guilt for having told his brother about him, guilt for the potion she'd given him, which almost got him shredded to pieces by a lion. "You're not going to say 'run' for no reason, are you?"

He shook his head. "I won't." He glanced at the fire and at her hands. "But I'm not sure this is going to work."

Zora smiled. "It's worth a try. Remember I'm from the Dark Valley. We never cower."

He shrugged. "Sometimes crouching can help you avoid a blow."

It was good to see him being playful. "Oh. I'll rethink my strategy, then."

He looked at her hands, holding his, then looked in her eyes. "Thank you."

"For what?"

"Uh, let me see..." His eyebrows furrowed as if he were concentrated, thinking. "Maybe jumping in front of a lion?"

Zora trembled. He didn't know that she'd been the one to brew the potion that made him unfit to face the beast, and she wasn't sure she was ready to tell him. She decided to be playful. "Nah. That was nothing."

Griffin's breathing was heavy as he looked at the sky. Zora glanced too, noticing its last purple fading to dark blue. Perhaps Zora should be afraid of the so-called monster that he would turn into, but she wasn't. All she wanted was to comfort Griffin, perhaps make sure he'd never have to suffer again. She wanted to be with him in his dark moment. Perhaps it was still guilt. Perhaps it was something else, one of those unidentifiable feelings from a strange, hard-to-reach place that she couldn't really translate into words. Or maybe it was just a normal urge to help someone in need. An urge to smile and give him hope. Make him believe that everything would be fine, that everything was possible. Even if it wasn't.

Larzen had been sitting for hours in that meeting room. A lavishly decorated room, with a heavy mahogany table and gold-foiled chairs, with barred doors, nonetheless. A prison for people too important for the dungeons. He'd thought Kiran had sent him there to greet a visitor, just to be surprised when the room was empty and the heavy iron doors were shut behind him. Now there he was, trying to guess the reason he'd been put there.

Gravel had no threats of war with any neighbor, no rebellion, and even if there was any of that, he should be helping his brother make decisions. He should. He should have watched the Royal Games. Except that perhaps something else was happening and he'd been left out. Quite annoying, frankly. For someone who always strived to be one step ahead, Larzen had fallen way behind.

He was wondering if he'd been left there to starve to death for some mysterious reason when the door finally opened.

Kiran stood at the threshold. "Sorry." He shook his head. "I... I had forgotten you."

Larzen walked towards his brother. "So, am I supposed to guess the reason I was locked here?"

"Nothing much. I just wanted to make sure you wouldn't meddle." Kiran's jaw was tense. He turned around and walked away.

Larzen rushed to catch up with his brother, then stepped in front of him and put his hands on his shoulders. "What's happening?"

Kiran pushed his hands away and raised an eyebrow. "Careful. Remember who's king here. I don't owe you an explanation."

"Remember who's your brother!" Larzen protested. "I'm worried about you."

Kiran scoffed. "Brother. As if it meant anything. But I'll tell you. Griffin has been sentenced to death for treason. My men are looking for him right now. They don't need to bring him alive."

The words took a while to sink in. Griffin? Treason? That made no sense. He felt as if someone had stabbed his stomach. Kiran sounded serious, though. Larzen had better keep the same tone and not show any of his horror. "What... are the accusations?"

"Personal issues."

That made even less sense. He had to get the truth out of Kiran. "So you're telling our guards, meaning Griffin's men, to hunt him without giving them a reason?"

He waved a hand. "All they need is motivation. Anyone who disobeys me will be sentenced to death."

Sentenced to death? Like that? It was like staring at a stranger. A monstrous stranger. One small consolation was that Kiran definitely didn't understand how motivation worked. His strategy would only assure that guards *pretended* to follow his orders. Which was a relief.

Larzen nodded. "Of course, of course." It was always better to agree with people who had given up on reason. "Now, can you tell me, brother to brother, what happened?"

Kiran fiddled with one of his rings. "I'm not... feeling... very fraternal." He then faced Larzen. "But I'll tell you. He attempted against Alegra's honor. Manipulated her. Tried to steal her from me."

Larzen trembled. He'd always thought that Kiran didn't care for the Linaria princess, that he saw her as an unwelcome burden and would give up on her easily. He'd better bury those thoughts and all the wishes now poisoned with this new reality.

Now, Griffin and Alegra? That made no sense. "Kiran, our brother is interested in the Dark Valley champion. Didn't you notice it at the picnic?" That day Larzen had realized how much he'd miscalculated, thinking she'd catch Kiran's attention, when it was Griffin who was enthralled by her. "He couldn't get his eyes off her. Until he decided to have a scorned lover outburst. Which was quite dreadful."

Kiran shrugged. "Possible. That slut protected him."

Larzen was horrified at his brother's choice of word. Still, he shoved down the feeling and tried to push his point. "See? That's who Griffin is interested in. Anything else must be some misunderstanding."

His brother shook his head. "I've got my sources. More than one, in fact. Plus, I interrogated some guards. It doesn't matter. It's in the past. My beloved is safe now." He then looked at Larzen in the eye. "All I ask of you is not to meddle with it. Allow a man the honor of his revenge. If you help Griffin, you'll join him against me. Don't make me lose another brother."

Kiran turned around and went on his way. Larzen was frozen, trying to understand what was happening. Trying to make sense out of this insanity. Seeing his brothers broken apart like that was like his worst nightmare.

He'd need to get to the bottom of it. Larzen took a deep breath and tried to gather his thoughts. Griffin manipulating Alegra? Absurd. The only thing Griffin could manipulate was his sword. It was as if someone had brainwashed Kiran.

Could it be the princess? Larzen felt as if someone were squeezing his heart. Alegra had been a spark of joy in the castle, a spark of hope. He was feeling like a fool now.

THIS WAS WRONG. Griffin should be telling Zora to run away, should offend her if that was what it took. And yet here he was, holding her hands, looking in her eyes. Looking at those calm, honey-colored eyes reflecting the fire, it was as if there were no curse. Staring for so long into someone's eyes was like ripping himself open, letting them see all that he was. And yet it didn't feel strange or uncomfortable. It rather felt reassuring to let that steady stare peer into him.

Those were loving eyes, but if it was not romantic then it was some other kind of love so great he was ready to let it swallow him whole. Their kiss came to his mind, that desperate kiss. Which she reciprocated—and then pushed him away. And yet here she was, holding his hands, as if she were ready to go down to the depths of the kingdom with him.

She glanced at the first visible stars, then back at him, and smiled. "You're still you, Griffin."

He squeezed her hands. "I guess."

Griffin wasn't sure he wanted to tell her that he didn't know at what time the transformation occurred, and that they were far from safe. He just wanted to keep her there with him, keep looking in her eyes and holding her hands.

Almost unintentionally, his thumbs circled the inside of her wrists. Zora let out a breath and her lips parted. That was surprising. He'd thought she'd glare at him or make some playful comment that he was supposed to hold her hands, not distract her. But she didn't. He kept at it, silently telling her how much it mattered that she was there with him in a soft, innocent caress. A hint of fear crossed her eyes just for a second. Or perhaps surprise. Then she exhaled and closed her eyes letting her hands relax as if surrendering.

His heart sped up. Still caressing her wrists, he wanted to lean over and kiss her. More than kiss her, he wanted to touch, see, and taste every part of her. He wanted to rip out the harness holding him and lay her down. The strength to rip out the leather was coming to him—and the realization that he was about to lose control.

It took all his effort to let go of her hands and mutter, "Run."

She hesitated for a second, then got up and did what she'd promised.

A tiny part of him tried to remain leaning on the tree, while his entire body ripped the harness.

THESE CAVES WERE SAID to be haunted. Haunted by the ghosts of the people who had lived here hundreds of years before. Tris had accepted that she'd probably end up stuck here forever. Appropriate, since she was no more than a ghost of her former self.

But the brown eyes staring at Tris were curious—and certainly not dead. For hours and hours, the guy with dark auburn hair leaned on a rock and looked at her, perhaps with the same fascination she once watched colorful carps in the castle's pond. He had long legs and arms, and always wore leather pants and a light tunic, similar to what many commoners wore in Linaria.

She'd told him. So many times. He'd never listened. No way her parents would come looking for her or pay whatever ransom these people expected. No way. As to Gravel, it was unlikely that they worried about guests who didn't show up. Nobody from Linaria had ever come to watch their brutal games, and it wasn't as if Gravel ever sent a note asking why. Plus, Tris had no reason to want to run. Or fight the weird mountain people, even if they would never tell her their names. She'd named them by their hair colors. The guy was Purple because of his dark auburn hair. But he didn't listen.

At least her cage was large enough that she could stand up and walk while looking through the opening at the forest below. A cage in a cave on a mountain. Some exaggeration for a worthless hostage who wasn't even planning on escaping. If only the guy listened to her half as much as he watched her.

But there was still some fight in her. Fight for the things that mattered. The things that were worth living for. A bit insane to leave someone in a wooden cage unwatched. She had a splinter. Sharp and long, she hid it under her skirt.

Nirus, the captain of her father's guard, had also been imprisoned, but they kept him away from her, probably afraid they would conspire together or some other ridiculous idea. In the beginning she'd told them they could kill him for all she cared, but they obviously didn't listen. Which was good, considering she didn't truly want these mountain people to kill him. No. There was a part of her heart still alive. It still cared for something. These people hadn't shown any intention of harming her, but her mortality stared at her from the gaps between the wooden bars. Would they keep her alive once they realized she was worthless?

That was why she begged and begged and begged to see Nirus one last time. Perhaps her heart no longer knew what it was like to feel annoyed, but she still had a vague memory of how to annoy people out of their mind. Purple had asked her if she loved Nirus. She'd never given an answer, but that didn't stop him from coming to his conclusions. Apparently, love was something the mountain people understood. And her wish was about to be granted.

2

―――――

RISING SUN

Griffin found himself lying down on green moss, staring at a blue and pink sky. He sat up. It had been his first cursed night while not restrained. There was something sticky in his hands. Something brownish red. Blood. Not only on his hands, but on his clothes too. Everywhere, blood that wasn't his, as he felt no wounds. There were some entrails by him. Then he remembered the last thing he'd seen the previous night. Those calm eyes. A cold chill ran through his body.

"Zora?" he tried.

There was only silence. He called again—and got no answer. It was as if ice was prickling him from beneath his skin.

"Zora!" he called again. A thin hope in his heart. She had to answer, she had to be around.

He didn't care if he got defiant, distant Zora or Zora with the calm eyes and soothing hands. He didn't care if she never kissed him again. All he wanted was to make sure she was all right. He called again. Was it useless to hang onto hope?

"Zora!" His voice was ragged, desperate.

He tried and tried, barely able to breathe. It couldn't be. Couldn't be, and yet... It was as if all his insides had turned to nothingness, a cold hollowness that would hopefully kill him. Her calm eyes came to his mind, but all they brought was the despair of maybe never seeing them again. He should check the entrails, he should check if there was a body. Perhaps his answer was there, but it was an answer he couldn't face. Defeated, he fell to the ground and slammed his fists against it, a grunt of pain coming out of his throat, tears running down his eyes.

He wished the earth could swallow him whole and end his suffering once and for all.

"Griffin?" a strange voice called him, as if from a dream.

He looked up and saw what looked like a vision, a miracle washing away his pain. "Zora?"

She tilted her head as if examining him, "Are you normal?"

Relief turned into mortification as he realized he must have looked ridiculous crying. Did she really let him think she died? That was heartless. "It's day. And I was calling you. Didn't you hear it?"

Zora frowned. "Well, you were yelling and grunting. And you called me all night."

That didn't make sense. "I called your name?"

"Yes. That's why I didn't know you were you when the sun came up. You were here screaming 'Zora, Zora', and I wasn't sure."

He glared at her. "It's me. And you gave me the greatest scare of my life. I thought I had killed you."

"I'm not that easy to kill." She swallowed.

He shook his head, unwilling to argue, then approached the entrails and saw a large carcass. He didn't even want to know what animal it was. "I killed this thing?"

"And ate it. At least one of us is not hungry."

He wasn't. Just grossed out. He closed his eyes and put his hand on his face, but then felt its stickiness and grunted in disgust.

"Don't worry," she said. "Your face… uh, was already dirty. Let's clean it in the stream. Come."

He followed her, then washed his hands and his face. Even his hair was full of blood and his mouth was sticky with it. At least if she never wanted to kiss him again, he'd know why. Her calm eyes didn't look at him with disgust or horror, though.

There was a question he had to ask, even if it was painful. "Did you… did you see me?"

She looked at him for a moment, as if hesitating, then said, "Yes. You looked normal, sort of, just didn't stand as straight, and… you got disheveled. And your eyes turned green."

He frowned, surprised. "Green eyes? What kind of curse makes someone's eyes prettier?"

"I mean green, the whole thing." She made a circle in the air with a finger. "Glowy. I prefer your brown eyes."

He took that in. "And that's it? No horns, or, I don't know…"

"You sound disappointed."

"No, just… surprised. Me with glowing eyes. That you don't like."

"Not my style." She smiled.

"How did you escape?"

"I crossed the spring and climbed a tree. I think you lost the trace."

Trace. Like an animal. He closed his eyes and sighed, then looked at her. "So you didn't sleep."

"Neither did you. But we'll get there soon."

"We'd better not take the road. I'm afraid…" It was hard to

say these words. "My brother." He looked at her. "How's your shoulder wound?"

"I washed it with water, but…"

"I'll get you to the Dark Valley. Let's just take the horse. And I'm sorry for tonight."

She shook her head. "I'm the one who's sorry. I thought I could, somehow, stop your… is it a curse?"

"I suppose so."

"I thought I could stop your curse." She looked down.

He lifted her chin. "Thank you for trying." These words were weak for what he wanted to express, for how much it meant that she had stuck with him, that she had held his hands in his worst hour. But then, perhaps it had been stupid and dangerous. He'd never forgive himself if he had killed her. And yet, for a moment she had made him believe that everything would be different. And even now, after seeing him bloodied and disgusting, she didn't treat him differently, didn't run, didn't reject him. He touched her face. *Oh, no.* "You're hot."

She blinked. "Excuse me?"

"You're burning with fever."

"My wound." She pointed to her shoulder. "My parents can fix it."

"We'll get there soon. Do you know where the horse is?" He hoped he hadn't eaten it.

She nodded, then took him to where it was tied. It was jumpy when it saw Griffin, perhaps remembering whatever he'd been at night.

"But it has no saddle," she said.

"Don't worry." He put Zora on the horse, then mounted after her, one of his arms around her waist. "I won't let you fall."

They rode by the stream then a river. It was not the straight path to the valley, but it was the best he could do while avoiding the main roads. Her body was so hot that he could feel it even through her leather clothes. All that mattered now was to get her to her parents soon. Later he would need to come to terms with his own guilt and shame, his betrayal, and how it had ripped him and his brother apart. For now, he just focused on riding fast and getting to the Dark Valley.

Zora broke the silence, her voice weak. "The Blood Cup... You think it can cure you?"

That was a big question. So much hope had hinged on that, and it could be all lost. "If I had won it. Probably."

She was silent for a while, then said, "Are you sure I won it? Has the competition been completed?"

"What seals it is the final sacrifice. You killed the lion, you won it."

"I'm so sorry. If I had known why you wanted it..."

That made no sense. "You did nothing wrong, Zora."

She exhaled. "I'll get it for you, I promise. I'll make up for everything."

He didn't understand why she was acting guilty, but then she was feverish and maybe delirious. True that she shouldn't have gotten the cup, but that wasn't her fault. Griffin wasn't sure if another person wielding the Blood Cup would be able to help him, but he didn't want to talk about it now. "We'll see. First we need to get you patched up."

She scoffed. "Shoulder. A little lower it would have been the heart. In the end it all comes down to luck."

That was true. And horrifying. Horrifying that she could have died for him, horrifying that his brother had ordered their archers to shoot her. Even more horrifying that they would obey that insane request.

It was dreadful to realize how much his brother had been shaken because of that princess. How much it had affected him. That had to be the reason; Alegra. He shuddered thinking about what had happened between them, something that didn't make any sense now, and yet, caused so much pain. Even Zora knew about it. About his horrible mistake, his betrayal. He'd been aware of his downward path, but had never realized how much, and had never considered that he could be hurting people other than himself and Kiran. He had never imagined he'd hurt a girl who was nothing but brave, honorable, sweet, and kind; who certainly didn't deserve to suffer because of his mistakes.

Griffin held her close. "I'll get you to your valley."

She leaned back on him, perhaps sleeping. He had no right to notice how close they were. In fact, he shouldn't have kissed her when everything with Alegra had been so recent. But the worst was that now he didn't think he had ever been truly in love with the princess. Mystified, attracted, entranced, perhaps. And now this mistake cost him his title, his life as he'd known, even his brother's love. Perhaps rather than trying to break his curse, he should just get it over with. Let it consume him. But then, he could feel the heat of the girl leaning back on him, trusting him, willing to risk her life for him. Perhaps there *was* something to look forward to.

TRIS COULD FEEL her heart accelerating with the anticipation of seeing her father's captain.

"They should be coming soon," Purple said.

He never gave her any useful information and never talked about his people or himself, but somehow, he was now trying to comfort her. Maybe he only allowed her to see Nirus because of his curiosity, perhaps interested in seeing her reaction. Hopefully it would be entertaining enough.

Soon she saw two mountain people dragging something. Nirus. He had legs and arms bound on a net made of rope. One of the people pulling it was a red-haired girl who sometimes watched Tris, but watching in that case meant standing close by, not staring at her for hours. Then there was another guy she rarely saw. But Tris's eyes were focused on the man lying down. He was her aim. Her goal.

His head was bound and he was gagged, which explained why he was so inert. Still, he was awake. Awake enough to look at Tris. His expression was unreadable, thoughtful.

Once he was close enough to her, lying still, with their captors far from him, Tris threw her splinter. For a second she feared she would miss her only chance, but it was pointless fear. The splinter reached him between his eyebrows, its trajectory long enough for her to register fear on his face. Good.

Like that, Nirus was dead. Her only regret was that it had been too fast, too quick, too painless. Purple and the rest of the mountain people were agitated, yelling stuff she didn't bother paying attention to. Tris didn't care. Revenge was the only satisfying feeling left for her in this world.

ZORA WAS asleep in Griffin's arms when they approached the Dark Valley. All he could see were the tall stone walls and the top of a hill inside them. There was a valley outpost near the gates, where guards were stationed to make sure no creatures escaped. In truth, they were there to make sure nobody escaped, as if the Dark Valley citizens were a threat to the king-dom. Well, if nobody lived there and fought the creatures, then the valley would be a threat. Not that anyone recognized the work the people there did. Treated as prisoners or as a nuisance, the sole reward the Dark Valley citizens got was some leather, metals, and other supplies that couldn't be culti-vated in the valley, given like some huge favor. The stories claimed that it had been their own ancestors that had released the magic of the shadow creatures. But still.

As Griffin got close to the stone wall and building, he real-ized that the outpost would have medicine and healers to treat Zora, so there was no need to enter the valley. But then, she had specifically asked for her parents. And if his brother were searching for them, the outpost wouldn't be safe. The valley, on the other hand, was a place where even trained soldiers didn't dare enter, and the fear and superstitions about it would keep them protected.

There was nobody outside the building or near the gates when he approached them, until a soldier came running from the outpost. A young kid, sixteen or so, probably on his first assignment.

"Who's there?" The boy asked, then glanced at Griffin on his horse. "Your highness. Sorry. I was just taking a break."

"It's fine. I just need to get in."

The soldier's young eyes were wide. "In? In there? With the monsters?"

Strange how a soldier could fear so much a place that Zora called her home. "There's people living there, you know?"

"Yes, but... what about when you want to get out? They'll say you never got in."

Griffin sighed. "You've recognized me. I'm sure someone else will recognize me too. Just open the gate."

"What about the girl?" The soldier pointed.

"She's from the valley. The champion. I'm bringing her back."

"The real champion?"

Griffin frowned. "Why? There was a fake one?"

"Yes," the boy said. "He was brought back a few days ago."

Strange. Griffin knew nothing about it, and the games had been under his jurisdiction. Used to be, in any case.

"Well, she's the real deal, and I need to bring her home."

The young soldier shrugged.

Griffin nudged Zora. "We're here."

She babbled something while still half-asleep, so he decided to carry her. He got off his horse and took her. She wrapped her arms around his neck and leaned on his chest. The feeling was strangely comforting. The young soldier stared after them and it annoyed Griffin. "What are you looking at?"

"Nothing."

"Take care of the horse. If anyone asks, say it was lost."

The soldier nodded, then moved to the side of the gates, where he pulled a chain. Thick bars moved up and Griffin went under them, finding himself in a walled corridor without a ceiling, facing an even heavier gate which was soon raised. This was it. He was crossing the threshold, stepping into the Dark Valley for the first time in his life. On a first look, nothing about it was spooky, mysterious, dark, or scary. There were green fields and many, many stone houses in the distance, in what was a huge village, then, further down, a forest and a hill.

His hands were both busy holding Zora, but he didn't think they'd be attacked out in the open, in plain daylight. Still, he kept his ears sharp for any unusual sound. With no weapon, he figured he could pull the sword from her back if the need came. Hopefully he wouldn't have to fight while holding her. That would be a bit much even for him.

He crossed the fields thinking that it was strange that people feared that valley, when it was beautiful and even peaceful. A stone path led to the village where he also saw some gardens and chicken pens. Everything was cute and calm, which was not something anyone would think about the Dark Valley. The truth was, outsiders didn't think about that place at all, as it was easier to ignore the people living there. Griffin had known that inviting one of them to the games could change the way that valley was perceived, he just hadn't imagined how much it would affect him.

He came across a small orchard, and three people came running at him. Like Zora, they all had swords on their backs and wore leather attires, looking more like warriors than farmers. Well, they probably had to be both.

"That's Zora!" an older woman said.

"Is she hurt?" a man asked.

Griffin wasn't sure what to say. "She's fine. Just a... uh... sprained ankle."

"But she's unconscious," the woman said.

"Some fever." Griffin realized how alarming it must be for them to see her like that. He pointed at the village with his head. "Her house is that way?"

"Yes, I can walk you there," the woman offered.

"It's fine. I can get there."

"You're unarmed!" She sounded horrified. "Don't worry, it's no trouble."

Well, Griffin didn't want to be rude. "Thanks." It was funny that an old lady was walking with him as if to offer protection, but then, she probably knew a ton more about shadow creatures than he did.

"How well did she do?" the woman asked.

Griffin smiled. "She won." Strange that he could still smile even though his chance at getting the cup was gone. But Zora had no fault in it, and she'd done something she should be proud of.

"I knew it," the woman chuckled. "Some people didn't like that Zora went, but I was sure she would be wonderful. She's saved my grandson, you know? Very brave girl."

"Definitely brave."

She raised an eyebrow. "You're the first stranger to set foot in our valley in years. Generations, maybe. Who are you?"

He didn't want to get into the whole prince thing, especially when there were people looking for him. "Part of the Royal Guard." Technically, it was true. At least it used to be.

The woman glanced at Zora. "Dear me, her lips are white."

"Fever. Why I'm taking her to her parents."

The woman frowned, as if confused. "Don't you have doctors in the city?"

"She got hurt on the way back." Those questions were making him uncomfortable, and he was even more uncomfortable imagining what he'd tell her mother and father.

"Oh, poor thing. They said she did it to run away. I doubted it. I knew she'd come back."

"She loves this valley." That was one of the few things he knew about her.

"Oh, she does. She's our best teacher."

He knew she was a teacher, having heard the motivational cry she'd made for her students, and now feeling guilty for having mocked her. And still, he had never tried to imagine what her life was like, never tried to understand her.

They followed a wider path into the village. A sight impressed him. Some thirty kids, with real swords, practiced various forms and stances in front of a large building. That was an interesting way to train, but Griffin didn't get to see much more of that, as one girl screamed, "It's Zora!"

The kids sheathed their swords and ran to Griffin, swarming him with questions: *Is Zora well? Did she do it, did she win? Who are you?*

"She's sleeping," Griffin said. "She won the Royal Games and winning those games can be quite tiring."

There was some murmur of cheer about the news, but a girl with a scar across her face asked, "Why are you carrying her?"

He shrugged. "Winner privileges. She can nap when she wants to."

"Now leave him. He's taking Zora home," the woman said, then she turned to him and pointed to a heavy metal door in front of a large stone house just across from where they were. "There."

Suddenly Griffin felt wholly inadequate at showing up like that, considering Zora was hurt and had an untreated infection. Her parents would think he was worthless. Perhaps he should have gone to the outpost. But then, it wasn't what she had asked. What a pitiful spectacle he was making of himself, not to count the fact he was running away without money, supplies, anything. Showing up on their door like a beggar. It wasn't what she deserved.

The woman knocked on the door, then left. The children watched him from a distance as a teacher called for them.

Griffin stood there, feeling small and unworthy. The door opened to reveal a blond woman in her late thirties at most.

"Zora!" She covered her mouth with her hands. "Come in, come in. Put her there." She pointed to a bed beside a counter covered with bottles and other supplies. She closed the door and yelled, "Zanel! Hurry here."

The bed where Griffin laid Zora had a solid structure with no legs. No shadows. Her first room redecoration came to his mind and he wished he had been more understanding.

A dark-haired man with some streaks of gray came running in and examined Zora.

"What's wrong with her?" the woman asked.

"She was hit by an arrow." Griffin pointed to a hole in her top. "Here. That was yesterday. We haven't had a chance to clean or treat it properly. She has a fever." He bit his lip.

"Anything else?" the man asked. "When was the last time she ate?"

Giffin sighed. "Yesterday. I don't know what time." What a disaster.

"Do you mind waiting outside? Or in the other room?" the woman asked.

He didn't want to leave Zora. "I can help. I know how to patch wounds. When I have the tools."

"We'll have to remove her clothes. Don't worry. We'll keep you updated."

The man led him to another room, and Griffin had an odd ache in his chest as he stared back at the door closing behind him. At least it was better than going outside, as he didn't want to face those kids and tell them he had let their teacher down. This room had a table and many chairs, none of them with legs, which made sense, if anything could spawn in dark spots and they wanted to avoid shadows.

He sat down, thinking. Zora should have gotten home in glory, not like this. He leaned his head on his hands. What a mess. He'd ruined his life and hurt everyone around him, including the girl lying down in the other room, who didn't deserve any of that.

A CHILD'S voice snapped him awake. "You get spider like that."

Griffin sat up and saw a young girl, around three years-old. "What?"

A dark-haired young woman holding a baby boy pointed at him. "Your hair was creating shadows. It could spawn a spider underneath it. But then, there's a lot of sunlight coming from the windows."

He rubbed his eyes and leaned back. "How's Zora?"

"My parents are treating her." She sat in another chair, while the little girl stood staring at him. "What happened?" the young woman asked.

Griffin had no idea where to start, and in fact didn't want to start. "She'll tell you everything. But she won the games." Then something she said hit him. Parents. Right. "You're her sister?"

She smiled and extended a hand. "Kala." He shook it. Then she pointed to the girl. "This is my daughter, Eneida."

Griffin smiled. "A nice name for a nice girl."

"Don't want nice." The girl crossed her arms and frowned.

"Brave, then, like your aunt." He shrugged. "But she's nice too."

"Zora sneaky." The girl giggled.

"Don't mind her," Kala said. "And you, are you going to introduce yourself?"

He should say he was just a guard to avoid the attention, but he didn't want to lie. "I'm Griffin." He looked away.

"You mean Prince Griffin?"

"I... believe I lost my title."

She raised an eyebrow. "You can *lose* that?"

He sighed. "It's a complicated story."

Kala got up. "Well, I'll see how my sister is."

The little girl turned to him. "You lost yourself?"

"Eneida!" Kala yelled. She then turned to Griffin. "I'm sorry, P-, uh, Griffin, she's just a child." She pulled the girl and went to the other room.

There was something odd about seeing this normality, a family, in the Dark Valley. That said, he noticed that Kala had a sword on her back. Even the little girl had a sword, or play-sword. Probably one more of the children for whom Zora wanted to have hope.

After some time, Zanel, Zora's father, allowed Griffin to see Zora. She had been moved to her own room and slept deeply, a side effect of whatever healing potion they had given her. Her shoulder was bandaged and she wore a light camisole. Her face was peaceful, and yet...

"How is she?"

"She'll heal," her father said.

Griffin wanted to ask when, but that would be a bold question from someone who hadn't taken care of her wound in over one day. True that he'd been unconscious or mindless most of the time, which wasn't something he was going to explain right then. Still, he wondered how long it would take for his brother to send someone looking for him in the valley. He sighed. At least Zora was getting the attention she should, and it was better than whatever he could have improvised or that they would have done in the outpost. Plus, perhaps nobody would dare cross the gates, and she would be safe for the time needed for her to heal.

Her father then invited Griffin for lunch. They brought food from the school kitchen and he sat with Zora's mother and father to eat chicken and potatoes with some vegetables. Somehow he had never wondered what they ate in the Dark Valley. Griffin wasn't hungry but didn't want to decline the invitation, especially considering he would never be able to explain why he was still somewhat full. Ugh. He had no clue how come he hadn't gotten sick yet.

It was so awkward to sit at that table with Zora's parents. First, there was no place for his legs and he had to sit sideways, but that was obviously not the issue. Griffin had been thinking that they would grill him with questions, demand explanations, and all he got were polite smiles. Perhaps they didn't want to bother him because he was a prince. Disgraced prince, they should know, but Griffin just told them he had a disagreement with his brother. Technically, it was true.

He wanted to muster the courage to apologize, apologize for getting their daughter almost killed, but what was the point in saying "sorry" when it didn't change anything? Perhaps it was good just to let them know how much he regretted what had happened. "Sorry" could be such a pathetic word. And yet he ended up saying it, together with more words admitting that Zora being hurt was partly his fault, even if he couldn't explain why, and more words trying to convey how much he wished things had been different.

He felt better when he was left alone with Lorena, Zora's mother, and she asked him how her daughter had done in the Games. That part brought him no regrets, even if he had to confess that he had been worried about her daughter's safety at first. Lorena nodded, as if approving his caution. It encouraged Griffin to tell her how he'd been careful and made sure none of the challenges were dangerous, to which she nodded even more. Fine that he had omitted the part where he also tried to get her daughter eliminated, but perhaps the important thing was the overall intention. He wished he could shake Zora awake and tell her, "See? See? Your mother agrees with me."

He kept talking about the games, and Lorena had a sparkle in her eyes when he told her how her daughter had been brave, smart, and resourceful in the competition. She laughed when she heard about Zora bringing down a cage and was interested in hearing how her daughter had won a competition in the dark. He mentioned how stunning Zora had looked in a gold and blue dress and how gracious she'd been at the balls.

Griffin stopped, realizing he was gushing. And the woman's bright eyes, full of pride for her daughter, got him in a different way. For so long he had wished, dreamed that one day his mother would have those approving eyes, without that shade of distrust that had always colored her look. He'd always thought he would recover the Blood Cup and tell her he was no longer a threat, that she would no longer need to fear him. But he'd never tell her anything. Thinking back, he'd rather have that mistrustful look than no look at all.

He felt something heavy in his heart, compounded with the uncertainty of what was going to happen to him and so much emptiness and confusion, and changed his tone. "Your valley did well in choosing her."

Lorena raised her eyebrows in surprise, paused, then had a small smile. "Sure." She sighed. "It's actually somewhat… complicated."

"How so?" He'd always wondered how exactly the champions were chosen, and obviously wondered how a girl not that strong had been picked.

"Zora will tell you better than me."

He'd need to ask. There was something odd in this story.

Griffin didn't leave the house or do much other than take a very welcome bath and then sit by Zora, as her parents and her sister came in and out of the room. In a rare moment alone, he stood up and took her hand, the hand that had held him even when he was about to turn into something else, the hand that had wielded a sword to save him, the hand of someone who had almost given her life for him.

The sky was darkening outside, but he didn't move away even as her mother came in to light lamps all around the room. The window faced some of the forest and the hill. As the sun set, hundreds, maybe thousands of points of light appeared from among trees, as if there was another sky, but with yellow-orange stars, beneath the real sky. The landscape was scintillating, almost glimmery, making up one of the most beautiful sights he'd ever seen. This was more like the Bright Valley.

Griffin sat down, thinking. Only Zora could get the cup, and here she was, comfortable at home with her loving family. Would she be willing to go on a foolish quest that might not even work? That was the girl who had risked her life for him— but who had also pushed him away. He sighed and leaned back on the chair, lest his hair cast shadows again. His thoughts were cloudy with uncertainty.

A hand on his shoulder awoke him. It was Zora's mother, who directed him to a small room with a bed. The worst was having to sleep without sheets or any covers, with a lit lamp, and with light coming from the window. It wasn't that he felt cold, just that it felt odd; he always slept with at least a thin sheet. Eventually slumber took him anyway.

THE FIRST THING she noticed was the familiar smell. And it wasn't a certain food, fruit, or any kind of tree. It was the opposite; the absence of any peculiar or different scent, but rather just the way air normally smelled, the way it smelled... home. Zora opened her eyes and found herself in her room. Her room. Back to her world. Fuzzy memories of her mother caring for her, her sister bathing her, a hand holding hers. Had that last part been true? Had everything been some kind of dream? Then there had been Griffin looking crazed, yelling, and running around, then killing something with his bare hands, while she watched from a tree, hoping he didn't find her, regretting not having run away. That had been like some very strange and frightening nightmare.

But this, *this* was real. This was the life and the world where she was just a teacher. She'd always thought she'd be happy to be home, but instead, she felt a strange pang in her chest.

"Finally awake?" A familiar voice. Kala was sitting by her and smiled.

Zora sat up, glad to see her sister, but also worried. "What day—time—is it? How long have I slept?"

Kala mussed her hair. "Since yesterday. Apparently, you didn't rest last night. It's normal."

She was wondering whether Griffin was still there, but afraid to ask and get an answer she dreaded. "How's everything?"

"You mean some people hating what you did?"

Zora swallowed. She knew that replacing Seth without anyone knowing wouldn't go down that well.

Kala shook her head. "Some do, and it won't be easy for you, sister. Some think it was destiny. Some hate Seth too and think it was deserved. What is done is done. Now you need to think about your future." Her face then changed from concern to sternness. "Also, are you being careful?"

She didn't understand. "Careful of what?"

Kala grunted. "What every girl has to be careful about. I hope you're not under the delusion that being in love will prevent you from getting pregnant."

Zora blinked. "What? No. I'm not... I'm not in love or involved in any, uh, baby-making activity." She remembered she had been taking the monthly potion, though. "But I am being careful. Just in case."

"Good. Because these things can happen when you least expect. And you don't want to be a mother before you're ready. But I'll get you some food. And our parents."

Ugh. That was mortifying. Zora had almost argued that in her case she had planned it quite carefully and taken all necessary precautions, but then she remembered who she'd planned it all with and her stomach turned.

A strange thought occurred to her then, wondering if that had been how Eneida had been conceived, and if Kala resented that. Her sister was young, just twenty-two. Still, Zora had always thought she was a model of happiness. Well, she could be perfectly happy and still wish she had waited a little more, or maybe Kala wasn't sure Zora would find someone to be as happy with. Zora wasn't sure either, and didn't dare hope.

The door opened and her eyes lit up when she saw her parents. They were bringing some soup and didn't look angry or disappointed. And that was what mattered.

While she ate, they asked what had happened. Strange that Griffin hadn't said anything. Perhaps he'd left quickly. She buried the thought and the heaviness it brought to her chest.

Zora talked about the competition, the lion, Kiran telling

his guards to kill Griffin. Of course her story was quite nonsensical since she had to omit the reason the king wanted his brother dead, how she had known Griffin wasn't fit to face the lion, and how exactly they had escaped. That last part she was omitting not because she wanted to protect Alegra, but rather because a woman singing and everyone stopping would be too weird to explain. Oh, she also had to omit glowy-eyed Griffin, and it didn't make sense why they had taken so long to get to the valley if they hadn't slept. She just said they had avoided the roads. If their parents realized that her story had some huge, glaring gaps, they didn't say anything.

Her father was thoughtful, then looked at her. "Well, that was quite an ordeal. But you did well. That part. Now, about you going—"

Yes, the tricky part. "I'm not sorry," she interrupted him. "And I don't regret it. Seth doesn't have any honor to represent our people, our valley. I know the way I did it was wrong, but it saved us from even greater shame before the kingdom."

"I guess he isn't honorable," her father said. "You could have told us. We'd find someone else."

"In less than one day? There wouldn't have been time. And I didn't want him thinking he was better than me, or everyone thinking that the only things that matter are violence and stuff that they deem manly. I'm worthy. And I took my chance to prove it."

Her mother sighed. "You should have signed up to represent our valley, Zora."

"I thought Seth..." She looked down. There were so many things she had thought about Seth, so much hope she had placed on him. Stupid hope.

"It's done," her father said. "Now, I want you to think about something. Why would you need to prove your worth to other people? Even to someone you think is dishonorable?"

Zora exhaled. "I know my worth, but it sucks not to be recognized."

Her father stared at her. "You are recognized. By the people who matter the most. The future of our valley."

"The kids? Nobody cares what they think, nobody cares what I do, if I'm not out there fighting shadow creatures."

Her father shook his head. "If you want to change what is considered important, first change whose opinions you give importance to."

Zora stared. Perhaps it hadn't even been that she wanted to prove herself, just pure pettiness, and strangely, she still did not regret any of it. On the other hand, she hadn't considered what kind of punishment she'd face and what it could mean for her life. "Do you know what's going to happen to me?"

Her father shook his head. "Not yet. The other leaders weren't even sure you were coming back."

"Of course I was coming back!" Even if the valley now felt too small to her, even if she'd yearn forever for a bigger, wider, freer world outside. Even then, she'd never leave them.

"We know, darling." Her mother held her hand, then added, "You even brought a prince with you."

Griffin. The thought made her heart speed up. He still had to help her find the Blood Cup, she still had to find a way to end his curse, and yet, she had one fear. "Did he leave?"

"He's outside," her father said. "I believe you have things to discuss. We'll send him in and catch up later."

Like that, her parents left her room. She wanted to tell them not to leave, that she didn't have any secret to discuss with the prince, that it wasn't what they were thinking, if ever they were thinking anything, which, depending on the type of anything, would be insanely awkward, but before she protested, the door was open and Griffin was walking into her room; a strange, beautiful sight that didn't belong there.

He grinned when he saw her. "You're better." His smile was magical.

"You didn't leave!" She then regretted saying it, it sounded so eager, so... Plus she felt a chill in her stomach and would need a serious talk to her inner organs that they were not supposed to react to him like that. He was like a shooting star, something beautiful and magical but that wasn't going to last in her life. Or perhaps like a real star, way beyond her reach. A prince. A prince in love with someone else, and she had to remember that.

Griffin chuckled. "Why? You thought I was going to sneak out while you were sleeping or something?"

"I don't know." He was standing beside her bed, and she became aware of their closeness. Not that they were even that close, but it was as if there was a tight cord between them, tugging her towards him, clearly unaware that there was a world of difference between them.

The previous night came to her mind and instinctively she put her hands behind her back as she recalled feeling as if her wrists were intimate parts. As she recalled what she had felt then. What she had, for a brief moment, wanted to happen—even if it were to really happen, she'd probably freak out and change her mind. One consolation. But the feeling had been there. And it hadn't been about him, but about her, what she'd wanted for herself, but now that she saw him, it was embarrassing. She shouldn't feel these things for a prince in love with someone else.

Zora had to get her mind elsewhere, quickly. She smiled. "I

believe I have a prize to claim, don't I?" Then she became serious. "Do you think it could help you?"

"Maybe. Or else..." He looked down. "I was thinking. Perhaps the Blood Cup could undo the magic or curse of this valley."

That was more than she'd dreamed. "You think so?"

"It can undo magic, so it's worth a try."

"But we have to fix your curse too," she said.

He smiled, but it wasn't his amazing smile, as it didn't reach his eyes. "Sure."

"We should leave soon. Tomorrow, maybe." She'd sneak out if she had to, but this time not without first telling her parents. Well, that wouldn't be sneaking out. Regardless, she was leaving.

Griffin took a deep breath, as if getting ready to say something difficult.

It made her anxious. "What?"

He scratched his head. "Zora, I don't know how soon my brother will come looking for me in this valley. It could be any time now. Then I won't be able to claim my status as a prince to get you through the gates. I know you might still not be feeling well, but I could maybe carry you, put you on a horse..."

"Why didn't you wake me up earlier?"

"You were feverish."

She didn't even remember anything after climbing on that horse. "How did I get here?"

"I carried you."

Yikes. Awkward. "I was that bad?"

He nodded. "I had no choice. And I agree your parents are great healers. You wouldn't have recovered so fast in the castle, for example."

She sat on the side of the bed, as if to get up. "I'll tell my parents. We'll also need some supplies. I'm sure they'll help us. We could leave in half an hour or so."

"I'm sorry you don't have more time to catch up."

Zora shook her head. She wanted to see her students, her family, but she wanted to get that cup and fix Griffin's curse. And to have a chance to fix her valley! That was what she'd always dreamed. "This is more important." She then got up and walked to the door. "Mom, Dad!"

It took a lot less convincing and explaining than she'd expected. It was almost as if they knew she was going to leave again, and they seemed relieved rather than worried, perhaps still fearing whatever punishment Zora could face, perhaps happy that she would have the opportunity to leave this valley. Right away they were offering to pack supplies for them. She was stunned that they had agreed to let her go so easily, but happy too, glad that they trusted her, glad that they wanted what was best for her.

Still, there was one thing she wanted to do before leaving. "Where are Eneida and Raphael?"

"At Kala's. She went back home when you woke up," her mother said.

"Can you finish packing while I run there real quick?" She looked at Griffin. "I just want to see my niece and nephew. It won't take long."

"Go," her mother said. "We'll make sure you have all you need."

"I'll come with you," Griffin said.

"No, it's five minutes. That way you can check our supplies. I'll be right back."

Zora dashed outside, threading that familiar path, a

shortcut behind the line of houses. Before she knew it, she was knocking at her sister's door.

Little Eneida opened it. "Where's the prince?"

"He's waiting." Zora then lifted the little girl. "And how's my little warrior?"

Her niece took her wooden sword and brandished it in the air. "Strong."

"Always." Zora kissed the girl's forehead. "And where's your brother?"

"Sleeping."

Kala came out of the room. "I just put him in bed."

"Can I see him? I have to leave again."

"Come in," Kala said.

Raphael was lying down, eyes open, his little boy lips in a pout. Zora put her finger in his hand and he held it. Such a strong hold, as if babies came with a natural urge to attach.

Zora almost told her sister that she could have a solution for the valley, but she didn't want to bring up that much hope. Even to her parents, she'd just said they'd find a magical object, without explaining what it could be used for.

Holding her nephew's hand, Zora turned to her sister. "I love you all. And I'll be back."

Kala shook her head. "Don't worry about us. Find your own happiness."

"Turning my back to my family would never make me happy."

"You should rather leave. Take your opportunity, leave and don't ever come back, Zora." Her sister's eyes were sad, almost pleading. "Especially now that some people are upset at you. Find a better future. We'll be happy for you."

"We'll see," Zora said.

Kala was probably afraid of what could happen to Zora in

the valley, and also thought she'd have a better future outside the walls that had always surrounded them. There was no point in trying to explain or argue, or in telling her that she wanted to see Raphael and Eneida grow up. She wanted to see her students too. But she would do anything to find a solution for the valley—and to rid Griffin of his curse—no matter what it took.

Her heart was full after seeing those innocent little faces, especially now, when, for the first time in her life, she had a sliver of real hope for their future. She was going to run back to her house, to Griffin, and then out of the valley, to find the Blood Cup: his cure, and hopefully, the salvation for her people with it.

Zora was on the path leading to her house when she heard steps, not like shadow creature steps, but human, and yet, rushed. Before she could turn to look, two people had grabbed her arms. She elbowed one of them, but felt something sharp against her throat.

3

———

HOME

"We'd rather not kill you, sweetie." It was Razi's raspy voice. He was Seth's friend, and this couldn't be good.

"Stop it," Zora said. "We can find a solution."

Seth was there, and his brown hair with golden highlights reminded her of the straw he'd once slept on and how she'd been dumb to pity him. He looked so obnoxious Zora couldn't believe she'd ever been interested in him.

Holding a shovel, he smirked. "So you thought you'd just get away with it, huh?"

The knife was still on her throat. She tried to argue, "You won't gain anything by killing me. The village leaders will punish you."

"Oh, I don't think so." He chuckled. "You know what your father said to the other leaders? *What's done is done.* It will be the same after we break your bones. Or kill you, if you don't behave."

Zora's sword was on her back, but her two hands were being held, and she had no clue how to escape other than begging. She might have mocked Seth for not knowing how to read, but that also meant he'd spent a lot more time training than her. Same thing with Razi and whoever else was holding her. "Please, you're a good person, Seth." She had been in love with him once, he couldn't be a complete monster. "Don't do this."

Seth sneered. "More than good. Great. Except that you took my victory, you took everything I had."

"Just smack her," a girl said.

The voice was familiar. "Cecile?" It was the girl Seth had been seeing while still pretending to be with Zora. "He's not worth it."

"You're the one who's not worth it. Just because he didn't want you anymore," the girl said.

"That was not how it went. Please. Don't do this." Then she yelled as loud as she could, "Help!"

She felt a hand on her mouth, the knife pressing harder against her throat, and for a second saw her life before her. A life focused on surviving, with very little hopes, goals, and dreams. Seth had been her dream once. Now he moved towards her with the shovel and it was a nightmare.

But Zora still had fight in her, and wasn't going to be defeated like that. She headbutted Razi, who was behind her, and elbowed Cecile, but still they held her. Seth's shovel was about to hit her, but she dodged at the last second. It hit Cecile, who fell back. Still, Zora couldn't break free from Razi, and Seth was advancing again.

For some miracle the hands holding her let go and allowed her to duck. Seth hit Razi, who fell back. Someone pushed Cecile. Griffin. He was there. He then jumped on Seth and had his hands around his throat, as if about to strangle him. She then noticed Griffin's eyes. Glowing green. In plain daylight?

He was definitely about to kill Seth—and maybe even disembowel and eat him.

"Don't!" Zora yelled.

Cecile moved towards Griffin, or whatever he was, but he just pushed her away again and turned back to Seth, who was fallen and now unconscious. The prince would probably feel guilty if he killed someone in that state. She remembered how he had called her that night, and had an idea.

"Griffin!" He looked at her. Good. "Here!"

Zora ran as fast as she could towards the forest. She heard steps following her, and kept running without looking back, racing like her heart, especially considering the small possibility that he would kill her. But then, it wasn't as if she could outrun him. She stopped and turned. He bumped into her and they both fell on the ground. His eyes were lost, crazed, and had that eerie green glow. His hands moved to her neck and she closed her eyes, regretting the decisions in the last minutes of her life. She felt his teeth on her lower lip and was about to kick his groins and try to escape, when the bite turned into a kiss. A strange kiss. The same soft lips, the same feel, and yet, it lacked some of Griffin's gentleness, some of what had made that first kiss so incredibly amazing. Not that she hated it, which was much stranger.

To her relief, he moved his lips away from her. "Zora?"

She opened her eyes and stared at normal brown eyes.

"What's happening?" he asked.

She swallowed, still trying to process what had just happened. "You were... the green-eyed version of you." She had no intention of mentioning that weird kiss, which she planned to forget.

He got up, horror in his eyes. "Zora, it's day. You know what it means?"

"We're in the Dark Valley. The magic here is messed up. It must be what's happening."

He put his hands on his head. "No. Near the end, I'll start having this... midnight fever at other times, then I'm gonna turn forever." He sighed and looked away. "It has started."

Zora got up too and put a hand on his shoulder. "It's the valley, Griffin. Shadow creatures survive in daylight. Think about it."

Griffin was still staring, and swallowed. "Why were we..."

She'd better explain everything. Or almost everything. "Some people were attacking me. You, or maybe the other version of you, saved me. But you were going to kill them. I thought you would regret it, I feared for you, so I called you and ran. It worked. You ran after me."

His eyes flashed something like anger. Or fury. "It could have killed you."

"I..." How was she even going to explain it? "Didn't think that thing wanted me dead, Griffin."

His face was somber. "And what do you think now?"

"I... don't know." She was relieved he had no idea he'd kissed her.

"Please never do that again, please. Run if it happens again."

Zora nodded, unsure what to say.

He shook his head and touched her neck. There was blood coming from a cut, but it wasn't deep. This had been close. He frowned. "I did this?"

"No. The people who attacked me."

His frown deepened, "Why were they doing that?"

Zora felt a chill down her spine, wondering how much he knew. "Seth wished he had been the champion. He wanted to hurt me, he said he wanted to break my bones."

Griffin was silent, thoughtful. "I'm not sure I would have regretted killing him." His voice had a dark edge.

Zora swallowed, surprised at this confession, perhaps surprised that he had this penchant for violence, but glad he didn't inquire about Seth or why he wished he'd been the champion. Postponing the truth would only make it worse, but she wasn't sure she was ready to tell him how much she had lied. And taking that idiot's place was nothing compared to everything else she'd done.

They took a long turn through the forest to avoid the village. When they were approaching her house, a sight made her tremble. Some twenty or thirty men in the crown's green uniform. Guards. In the valley? Already?

"We took too long," Griffin said. "I can't believe they finally had the nerve to cross these gates."

Zora took a deep breath. "We'll find a way." At least she hoped so. "Let's go to my house through the back and get our supplies. I don't think they'll see us."

When they got there, Zora tapped on the window. Soon her mother opened it and handed her two bags and a sword for Griffin. "Hide," she said, then looked at her and her eyes widened. "What happened?"

She must have seen her cuts. "Seth tried to attack me. For revenge. With Cecile and Razi. Griffin saved me."

Her mother caught a breath. "Go. And stay safe."

"I will." These words didn't convey how much it mattered that they were helping her, supporting her, letting her go. The window closed and Zora's mother disappeared inside the house. An odd goodbye. But at least there had been one.

Zora and Griffin walked back to the edge of the forest. From there, they observed the village. Soldiers were opening doors and pulling people for questioning.

Griffin had a serious, worried expression. "Too many people saw me. I'll have to let them take me."

"No." She held his arm. "Your brother might kill you. And I want that cup. I have no clue how to get it on my own. You have to help me. And I'll help you with your... you know." She didn't want to mention the curse.

He held her hand and locked his brown eyes on hers. "They'll start interrogating people. I'm sure you don't want that to happen."

She didn't understand why he was so worried. "Well, if they want to waste time asking questions, let them waste time."

His look was a mix of pity and sadness. "Oh, Zora."

"What?"

"You don't know what they do when they interrogate people?" He was serious. It sounded bad.

Zora tried to think. "They... torture?" Griffin closed his eyes and nodded. He was probably thinking she was a naïve idiot, which was exactly her opinion right now. But still, it didn't make sense. "But these people are innocent. Aren't they your men?"

"Some of these people are twice my age. I have control over the Royal Guard in the city. The rest of the army, well, they were already soldiers when I was crawling."

Zora swallowed, a bitter taste in her mouth. Her mother had told her to hide, probably well aware of the risk. People knew there had been a foreigner staying at her house. They'd soon figure it was Griffin. They'd soon detain and interrogate her parents, perhaps even her sister. But then...

"We can all fight. They'd be outnumbered."

"True." His eyes were on the village, then he faced her.

"Can you imagine the disastrous consequence of a confrontation, though? What could happen to the valley?"

Zora tried to think. "Hang on. They want you, right? If they see you, and if they get us through the gates, they'll stop bothering the valley. The issue is escaping after that."

He nodded "I can pretend to surrender, and then we'll make a run for it." He stared at her. "But if they catch me, you have to promise you'll run."

"I won't leave you."

"Think of it this way; they'll probably take me to the castle." He smiled. "I'll meet you there."

Zora nodded, even if she knew she wouldn't leave him, but she didn't want to argue. They walked close to the wall, which was the longest way to the gates. When they were almost there, a sound made her insides curl. Three gongs. A warning. Not only any warning, the worst of all.

"What is it?" Griffin asked.

"Shadow creatures. Lots of them."

He frowned. "They can show up during the day, like that?"

Zora looked at the mostly blue sky. "It's a little cloudy. Still, it shouldn't happen."

"Maybe the gongs are just to scare the soldiers." He shrugged.

Could it be? No, that didn't make sense. "But they wouldn't even know what these gongs mean."

He cocked his head. "True."

"Maybe the creatures spawned last night and only now are getting near us. Let's keep our ears perked."

They crouched behind a bush by the gate, waiting to see if someone opened it, but there was nobody around. The guards were probably all in the village, hopefully not interrogating them in the way Griffin had suggested.

They waited in silence, watching for any movement by the gate. Zora had her ears perked for any sound of shadow creatures. If they were indeed in the valley, they would probably head towards the village, where there were more people, but they could still come to where they were.

Griffin got up. "This is taking too long. I'll just go to the gate and pretend to surrender. They'll surely be happy to get me out of here."

"I'm coming with you."

He paused for a moment, then said, "Very well."

If most of the soldiers were down in the village, perhaps this could work and they could try to escape. At this point she was also wondering if there were truly any shadow creatures in the valley.

But then her answer came. Five soldiers were running towards the gates, yelling for help. Zora crouched again, and Griffin did the same. A shadow wolf was chasing the soldiers, who, instead of turning and getting ready to fight, were banging on the bars, hoping to escape. This was a huge mistake.

"I can't watch this," she told Griffin. She then ran in front of the guards, sword in hand.

When the shadow wolf was close enough, she hit it twice, and it disappeared. Further down, she saw some five human shadows walking in their direction. Griffin was by her side, holding the sword he'd been given.

Zora yelled at the guards. "You! Turn around and get your swords out. Stand in a semicircle around the gate. If you don't fight, you'll die."

She glanced at them, so young, looking lost, scared. None of them did what she asked. They'd all be doomed.

4

———

ROCKY PATH

Zora roared, "Semi-circle and swords in hand. NOW!"

The tone she used with her students did the trick and the guards got in position. Four human shadows approached first, their rugged gray skin dull even in the bright sunlight. It was odd to see them like that, in such an open space, when it wasn't night and wasn't even raining. Somehow it made them look more real, and yet so out of place in that bright landscape. Even their claws, sharp as knives, didn't shine. Grey tunics covered their malformed ugliness that she could barely call bodies.

Zora's sword was drawn. When the creatures got close, she stepped forward and landed two blows on one of them, which disappeared. She swung her sword for a finishing blow on a creature that was about to bury its claws in a soldier, and then two more blows on another creature.

Griffin had his sword out and eyes wide as he finished another one. It looked like she and he had done most of the work. It didn't matter, they were all alive, even if a couple soldiers had cuts on their arms, a common occurrence when

51

trying to fight creatures with sharp claws. Against the horizon, she saw some ten more creatures heading towards them. They were all human shadows, which were the easiest to deal with.

"Swords drawn, don't break formation," she yelled again, and wished she had some of her eleven-year-old students instead of those clueless soldiers who were too scared to fight decently. They had never learned to replace fear with focus—but she couldn't worry about them, as they were slightly outnumbered as it was. At least Griffin was calm, but he had a simple sword, not yet enchanted. On the other hand, he was an exceptional fighter.

As the creatures approached, a sight made her shudder. It looked like a dust ball, rolling and getting bigger and bigger. It was larger than a human head, now. And if it got close to anyone, it would explode in a matter of seconds.

She ran towards the shadow ball, avoiding a human shadow. Thankfully, Griffin stepped right in and covered for her. She wasn't sure if he knew what she was going to do or if it was just an instinctive move. Zora grabbed the ball. For a split second, she considered throwing it against the first gate, that gate that had kept her people locked in for so long. But that would only mean nobody would open the second gate, and she had to get out. She threw it at a group of human shadows coming at a distance. It landed with a loud boom, scattering rocks and earth.

Griffin stepped in front of her, as if to protect her from the debris, which was exaggerated since they were far away. "Stay here. I'll try to open the gate," he said.

She wasn't sure what he was going to do, but didn't argue. Either way, the remaining creatures were distant. When two more came, she destroyed them both with swift blows.

"Here!" Griffin yelled.

Zora turned and couldn't believe her eyes. Two bars had been bent in such a way that a person could go through, and he was letting the soldiers out. Zora crossed the gate. Griffin followed her and then bent the bars back with his arms.

She would need to ask him how he did that. But then, she probably knew: a side effect of his curse.

"You're Prince Griffin," one of the guards said.

"You're welcome," he replied. "Now, do you want me to open the other gate or not?"

"Let him open it," another guard said.

Griffin went to the other gate and bent two bars. He asked Zora to cross first, crossed it, but then he closed back the bars.

"Hey! Let us out!" a soldier yelled.

"Ask your friends to open it," he said.

Two soldiers were outside the gates and approached Zora and Griffin. She couldn't believe that they'd just been watching their colleagues and doing nothing for them. Lack of compassion. But then, perhaps it had been fear. Odd how it made people selfish.

Griffin glanced at her, sheathed his sword, then extended both arms. "I'm handing myself in. You can call back the soldiers in the valley. I'm here. Just let her go."

Zora put her sword back too.

"We're taking you both," one of the soldiers said.

"Your choice," Griffin shrugged.

They were two against two and could try to make a run for it, but Griffin still had his arms extended. Of course, he wanted to lure him in. Indeed, when the soldier approached him with a manacle, the prince pulled him and caught the soldier's wrist instead. The other soldier ran towards Griffin, but with a swift movement, Zora put her sword on his neck.

"I wouldn't if I were you," she warned.

Griffin put a manacle on this other guard, then attached them both to one of the bars in the gate. He turned to Zora. "Let's go."

He took a horse, pulled her behind him, and they were soon galloping away from the valley, Zora's hands tight on Griffin's waist, as she was still afraid of falling. But then, going in front of him would be quite awkward. Hang on. If her memory was not failing her, he'd ridden behind her on the way to the valley. So embarrassing. Still, the memory of his arms around her was still with her, a pleasant soothing feeling —that she'd better forget if she wanted to stay sane.

They had ridden for some ten minutes when Griffin stopped. He got off the horse then extended his hand to help her. Of course. They'd better go where horses and carriages couldn't follow them.

"Can you walk?" he asked.

Her shoulder still hurt, but she rolled her eyes. "I just fought shadow creatures. What do you think?"

"Just want to make sure you're feeling well."

He had that concerned look she'd seen so many times before. The one that used to unnerve her with the hint that he underestimated her. It hit her differently now, as if he cared. She'd better not dwell on it. He needed her to get the cup and was probably still in love with Alegra. "I'm fine."

Griffin nodded, then sent the horse away. "I know where we can go."

They walked in the forest, then came across a shallow river. He told her to walk in it in the direction of the valley. She took off her boots and raised her pants. The cool water felt good against her feet, and the rocks were mostly smooth, with just a few small and somewhat prickly exceptions here and there.

"You fought well back there." She broke the silence. "With

me. You gave me space, covered when I needed…" What she actually wanted to say was that he didn't underestimate her or get in her way.

"I just took your lead and did my best to support you, since you know those creatures better than I do." He smiled. "You could be a general, you know?"

Zora laughed.

They got off the river on the other side, then walked to some rocky hills.

It was a good place to run from pursuers, but had its downside too. "We'll take a long time to get to the city, won't we?"

He chuckled. "Let's give them a chance to spread out and try to wonder where we are. And the important thing is to get there. Better to take long than to be caught."

"It makes sense. And do you know where the Blood Cup is?"

He took a deep breath. "I have some clues in my bedroom. We'll have to go there."

Zora felt uneasy. "Clues. But you have no idea."

"There's a magical contract. Only the winner of the competition for the Blood Cup can find it."

Her stomach was lurching. "So… am I going to be able to guess where it is or something? Because I wouldn't even know where to start."

He shook his head. "You'll find it. I know what you need to do."

If only she could be half as certain as he was. "What if… the way I won it, it wasn't how it should have been?" In more ways than she was ready to tell him. "Won't it invalidate my claim?"

"The important part is the sacrifice and a competition

open to many champions. The contract doesn't specify any details."

Zora sighed. Everything about her participation in that competition had been so wrong.

Griffin looked at her. "Why are you worried?"

No way she was going to mention what was bothering her. Instead, she said, "It's not gonna be easy to try to find it while being chased by your brother."

"We'll manage it."

"And you think I could also find a way to reverse the magic of the valley?"

He swallowed. "Sure. We'll find the answer there."

His tone, his voice... There was something odd about it. "Is there something you're not telling me?"

"A lot." Griffin smiled. "You know very little about me, right? For example, I haven't told you my favorite fruit, my favorite season, the kind of books I like to read—"

"Dark magic. Right?"

"For research. Not for fun. Regardless, 'dark magic' is a misnomer. And you know why I do it."

"To find a cure."

He nodded. Zora remembered the dreadful book she'd seen in his bedroom when he was sick. And the dreadful hypothesis she had come up with. She then said, "If people knew why it was that you are interested in dark magic or whatever magic it is, they wouldn't judge you."

"Of course not. They'd kill me."

That didn't make any sense. "Why?"

"It's a prophecy."

"Prophecies are stupid."

"People are stupider." He shrugged, then added, "It's said

that a cursed son will dismantle the kingdom. Do you know what some kings and queens used to do?"

Zora shook her head.

"Check if the babies had the curse. At the first sign, they'd kill them."

"That's horrible."

"Smart mothers, like mine, hid the curse. But..." He paused.

"But what?"

He looked down. "It's hard."

"We'll fix it. If you're saying the Blood Cup can cure you, there's nothing to worry about."

Griffin had a sad smile. "True."

That sadness... Well, it was normal, considering his own brother had tried to kill him, considering everything. And yet, it was as if there was something else going on, something he was hiding. Perhaps it was a good reminder that, despite appearances, they weren't close, and that she shouldn't trust him completely.

TRUTH. People claimed it was hidden. More like it always stood in plain sight, but everyone looked away. Unfortunately, Larzen had been no exception. Until he decided to look. It hadn't taken long to cross-examine and compare whispers about where Griffin and Alegra had been, and times when they had left the castle alone. So yes, they'd been together, unless for some unfathomable coincidence they had always decided to be alone at the same time. The news shocked Larzen.

Griffin was many things, but he was not a ladies' guy, always too busy with his questionable magic books, training, or else stuck in his room by himself. Larzen had never seen him being flirty or playful or doing anything at all to attract feminine attention. And then, perhaps showing off his strong arms was all it took. No, that made no sense. Wouldn't they prefer someone charming like Larzen? Pointless thoughts. It was pointless to wonder why Alegra had picked his younger brother. Strategically, it made no sense. So many unanswered whys. So many ruined plans, lost hopes. And now it didn't even matter.

Still no news from Griffin, except that now his older brother had a reward for bringing him, and had Stavos as head of the Royal Guard, replacing him. The man was probably happy to get the position he'd always coveted. Quite annoying that Kiran finally decided to understand the need for motivation.

Larzen crouched and took turns petting Tempest, Wind, and Storm, his hand running through three different sets of black fur, their eyes wide and eager for attention, affection, their tails wagging. He rarely came here, but at least this was something he could do for Griffin. The dogs were huge now, even menacing, and yet he remembered when they'd been nothing but tiny pups, fitting on the small palms of Griffin's hands. His brother had found them almost dying by the forest and brought them to the castle. At the time, he was in that in-between period, almost no longer a child, still not yet a teenager. His eyes had been bright as he suggested that each of them take care of one dog. Larzen was given Tempest. Or Wind? He wasn't sure and couldn't even tell which was which anymore.

All he remembered was that the puppies were newborns, badly hurt, and took a lot of work. Kiran refused his puppy and Larzen ended up giving up after one day, tired of having to give them milk every few hours. He regretted it now, regretted the time he could have shared with Griffin, the support he could have given him. All he saw was his little brother almost falling asleep during meals, tired from coming in the middle of the night to care for the pups.

The one thing Larzen did was talk to his parents, reveal his brother's secret, but also convince them that it would be good for him. He didn't even remember what he'd said. His mother had always looked at Griffin with some fear or mistrust, perhaps worry because he was so small. As to Kiran, she'd always made an effort to treat him like her own son, with emphasis on "effort".

His parents made no secret that Larzen had been their favorite, which brought a bitter taste to his mouth. More than that, his memories of his parents were dark and poisoned now. So poisoned. But gone and he'd better forget it all.

Larzen had never asked to be more loved than his brothers, never wanted that, and yet, he knew how to use it to his advantage. In this case, he convinced his parents to let his younger brother keep the puppies. That had been right before Griffin started training more, exercising, perhaps realizing that even if he could not be tall, he could still be big. Like him, his dogs grew to be menacing. And yet he had been just a small boy who wanted to take care of puppies. And now this boy was somewhere far away, hunted like a criminal.

Meanwhile, Kiran had completely shut out Larzen. It made sense that he would be upset, offended. But, to want to *kill* Griffin? For Larzen, watching this happen to his brothers was a nightmare. After everything. He sighed.

Steps on the path outside caught his attention. When he saw a flash of red hair, Larzen clenched his fists. She might be the key to everything, and he had to talk to her, and yet just looking at her altered his temper. "Alegra!" he called her.

There were two guards following her from a close distance as she approached. "I can't talk much. My dear future husband doesn't want me having private conversations with his brothers."

The dogs growled and barked. Larzen narrowed his eyes. "Why? Just explain why you were involved with both of my brothers."

"Malicious whispers. How is it my fault?"

He scoffed. "Don't. Don't give me that 'whispers' talk. You know what you did."

She raised an eyebrow. "Go on. Look at me with those accusing eyes. You've made your mind, right? You're so honorable. And yet Kiran was flirting back and forth with other girls. Why don't you go talk to him?"

"If you saw it, you should have dissolved the engagement. Easy."

"Soooo simple." She chuckled. "It's not as if I have obligations with my people."

"An alliance with Griffin would have worked, it would still be an alliance between the kingdoms. You should have picked one brother."

She tilted her head. "What if I wanted a crown too?"

"Then you were playing with Griffin. Why would you do it?"

Alegra shrugged. "Perhaps for the same reason he played with me. I'm pretty sure you are acquainted as to why people do it."

Larzen was actually stunned. He hadn't expected to hear her confess it. "Why, though? Why Griffin? Because he's young, impressionable?"

She didn't even flinch, show any remorse, nothing. "I'm sorry to say that he knew very well what he was doing."

"I doubt it. I doubt he knew you were playing with him. Griffin wears his heart in his sleeve."

"He never wears sleeves." She rolled her eyes.

One of the dogs growled, and he wanted to do the same, glad for the kennel bars separating him from Alegra. "It's not funny. It's my brother's life at stake."

"I'm not the one threatening his life, Larzen. You want to get angry, get angry at your other brother. Now, you can't do anything to him because he's king. I get it. But don't come yelling at me. Kiran threw me in the dungeon too, in case you didn't know."

"How come he forgave you?"

"My kingdom's gold. And my charms. I don't know how long this will last. If it helps, I am afraid." Her brown eyes were wide.

"Should have been afraid earlier."

"You're so honorable. I saw you exchanging whispers with the Dark Valley champion. And yet you weren't interested in her. Are you going to deny you were throwing her at Kiran?"

Well observed. Larzen had no choice but to be honest. "Perhaps I wanted you to see who he was before it was too late."

"And you didn't think about her for a moment."

"Why? Are you gonna tell me you care for her?"

Alegra shook her head. "I do not. It doesn't mean I want to see a young girl being manipulated and taken advantage of."

"Much better than trying to kill her." He stared at her, waiting for a reaction, waiting to see if his suspicions were true.

She paused, then laughed. "You can't be implying that I was trying to kill her. Tell me it isn't so."

"What do you think?"

She approached the bars. "Your assumption is insulting. If I wanted that girl dead, she wouldn't be breathing anymore. I'm not *that* incompetent." Her eyes were hard staring at him, as if in a warning.

"Well, I'm not incompetent either. You should be careful, there are many accidents that can happen even to princesses."

Her expression was placid. "And?"

"I don't care who you play with. If you have charms, as you say, incredible but whatever, use them. Get Kiran to forget Griffin, leave him alone. That's all."

She put her hands on her hips and glanced at the guards approaching her, then back at him. "So disappointed. I thought you were the brains, Larzen. Do you really want me to go to Kiran and tell him I'm worried about Griffin? How's that gonna work out?"

"Distract him. Do something. I don't care."

"It's clear you don't. I have to interrupt our delightful conversation, but I'd better go before your lovely older brother decides he wants to kill you too."

She walked away, trailed closely by two guards, her red hair shining in the sun. His eyes followed her until she disappeared from his view.

Only then he could collect his thoughts. He was still stunned by how coldly and matter-of-factly she had acted, without a single effort in denying anything. True that it would only paint her as a liar. He used to enjoy her dry humor, wit, and sarcasm, but now it made her seem callous and cruel. There was an odd coldness there. While princesses could be cold and deceiving, he felt that there was something off about her. Larzen had to figure out what. It was time for a plan. A decent plan this time, not a plan based on foolish dreams and whims.

WHO WOULD HAVE GUESSED that it took murder to be freed of that cage?

Purple led Tris to the border of the cave, overlooking the forest and the kingdom below. Perhaps he was considering pushing her down from that height. She wasn't sure if she would have any fight left in her if that were the case.

He sat on a rock. "I'd like to talk."

"That's quite impressive, considering I've been here for over a month and never even got a reply to my questions." Still, she sat beside him.

"You could have killed us all. Why didn't you?"

She scratched her chin and looked up. "Hum... let me see... Killing the people who can open your cage." She narrowed her eyes. "That would be dumb."

"We let you out sometimes."

Tris took a deep breath. "I don't want you dead."

His eyes were attentive on her, and there was more than curiosity this time, perhaps some admiration. Odd. "What is it you want, then?" he asked.

Tris shrugged. "Your name would be nice. Or do you like Purple?"

He tilted his head. "I don't mind it. But I'm Lukas."

Such a common name. She'd been expecting something a lot more exotic. Then again, it wasn't as if they even spoke a different language or anything. "I'm Tris, as you should know by now."

Lukas nodded. "I wish we could let you go, but we can't. Soon, maybe, you'll be able to return to your kingdom. I apologize for what you've been through."

Tris snorted. "You think this is suffering? A cage is suffering? It isn't. This won't give me nightmares. This is nothing."

He looked down, then back at her. "You've suffered, then."

She looked away, feeling uncomfortable, unwilling to bring back those memories.

"That was why you killed that man," Lukas said. "He made you suffer. I'm sorry. I wish... I can't imagine what he did. I'm sorry you went through whatever happened."

Tris shook her head. "It wasn't me. Not directly. Have you ever loved anyone?"

He was startled, then said, "My sisters."

"I used to love my brother too. Now... But I'm talking about romantic love, the one that gives you heart palpitations, that makes you feel like you're flying."

His eyebrows raised in surprise. "You wish you could fly?"

"I wish I could love. Or... maybe not. Maybe it truly is like flying, except you don't have wings, and then the fall crushes you."

He frowned and looked away. Perhaps he knew what she was talking about.

She continued, "You think I want to go back home? I don't. My parents are monsters. My brother is a monster."

He stared at her, his face hard. "What did they do?"

She looked down. "I was in love." She had to talk about this as if it were someone else, disconnect herself from what had happened, or else the grief and horror would overwhelm her. "My parents found out. They killed him." She swallowed, taking courage to tell the rest, realizing she was shaking.

"Slowly." With a deep breath, she swallowed back her tears. "And made me watch."

Lukas stared at her with misty eyes. She looked away, afraid of allowing her own tears to fall, afraid of drowning in them.

"They are monsters," he said after some time. "Is there anything I could do to help you?"

She stared at him. "What difference does it make to you?"

He had indeed tears running down his face. "I don't like to see grief. Our lives are so short, sometimes so meaningless. I need to care about something."

Hopefully he didn't want to care about her. "Well, I'll never care about anyone again."

"It makes sense. Now tell me, is there a way I can help you?"

She had never considered that these people could help her in any way, but now that she thought about it, perhaps it could work. Revenge. Wasn't it the only thing left for her?

Tris stared at him with a smirk. "I have a proposal for you."

5

NIGHT

They'd been walking for a while in difficult terrain. Griffin observed Zora. She didn't complain or ask for them to stop, even if she sometimes grimaced as if in pain. He worried about her wound, but she said it was nothing and he didn't want to keep asking, afraid of upsetting her. It would be two days of walking like that, until they got near Gravel City, and from there, they'd need to sneak in the castle.

At least all the walking gave them some time to talk. He told her how he'd been interested in swords since he was a kid. Part of it had been to learn to be brave enough to face the lonely nights when he was shackled, part of it to try to be strong enough for his brothers and other people to stop mocking him. But he didn't tell her that. Still, just talking about his youth gave him a feeling of peace, comfort.

Zora told him then how they all practiced since they were little. He could imagine that, having seen her niece with her toy sword. At five, Zora had gotten her real sword. No wonder she had named it Butterfly, at such a young age.

But in her case, learning to fight was not for bravery, honor, or wanting to show off; it was a basic need for survival. She told him some stories about her students, how she encouraged them to fight, and he felt guilty that he had never, in his entire life, wondered what it would be like to live in the Dark Valley. To grow up there. And yet Zora told all that without any bitterness or anger. In fact, since he had mentioned she could perhaps use the Blood Cup for the valley, her eyes had a brilliant spark of hope. It made him nauseous.

But then, what was worrying him were her wounds. By mid-afternoon, when he heard her moaning in pain for the third time, he decided it was enough and said he was tired and wanted to stop to rest.

"How are your wounds?" he asked as they sat under a tree.

"Better."

There was some healing potion in the supplies and Zora applied it to her neck, which had scrapes from her fight with the people from the valley; and to her shoulder, which was still healing from the arrow. Griffin wanted to help, but at the same time wasn't sure how she'd take it or if she'd think he just wanted to touch her. Well, he did want to touch her—and had better forget it.

They ate some of the bread they were given.

Zora finished her loaf and asked, "So, who hid the Blood Cup and tied it to a weird contract for a competition?"

"I'm not sure." That was true. "All we have are ancient documents stating what it can do and that it can be found by the winner of a contest sealed with a blood sacrifice."

She nodded. "I see. And how come... how come nobody ever got the cup?"

"They had to take part in the competition, right? The last step is the sacrifice against a much bigger animal. They all died."

"But it doesn't make sense. Wouldn't they be unnaturally strong? Like you?"

Thinking about his past ancestors who hadn't survived did cause him dread. "Maybe some of them weren't skilled. Some of them died after winning the competition, though. I'm not sure why. With royalty, our death records always claim it was some natural cause even when there was foul play." And then maybe there was something else and he wondered if he was leading her to her end, leading them both to their doom and death. But he tried to sound more cheerful. "It's nothing to be sorry about. Like I said, this line is cursed. Some sons were killed when they were babies. Some grew up to try to find a way out. The cup was their way out. At least they tried, they lived, they hoped." That was what he often told himself, even if he wondered if it would all be useless.

"You think it's better to die than to live with your curse?"

"It will eventually get worse. Eventually it will consume me, Zora. It has happened before. Some eighty years ago, one of us had to be put down like a crazed beast. It could happen to me." He had to tell her that.

She had an encouraging smile. "Not anymore. We'll get the cup, remember?"

"True." He made an effort to smile.

Griffin wasn't going to tell her that as far as he knew, it had to be him wielding the cup. He wasn't going to tell her everything he knew about it. Perhaps he just wanted to see hope in those calm eyes for a while. Perhaps he wanted to make sure she'd follow him in this hopeless quest. If ever they found the cup. There was that too.

"And how do you think it can help the valley?"

He sighed. "It undoes magic. We'll look into it."

Zora looked down, as if worried, then chuckled. "You think your dear brother will let us conduct research in the library?"

"I have some books and other tools." He'd better change the subject. "Maybe we should set up camp. Your father said there was a tent here."

"Tent? We don't have those."

Griffin opened his bag and pulled out the contents. There was a large thing that looked like a net, with rope, and another large fabric. "I'm assuming this..." He had no idea how to set it up, though.

Zora took a look at it. "Hammock. We tie it in a tree. That way it's safer."

"You know how to use it?"

"Well, I teach kids how to use it. It's for long ranging patrols. We need to find a tree with branches that we can climb to, then we can tie the hammock up high, away from potential dangers." Zora opened her own bag, as if looking for something, then asked him, "Do you have the other one?"

He stretched the hammock he had in his hand, to see if there was another, then looked in his bag. Nothing. "This is it."

Her eyes widened in surprise or maybe even fear.

Griffin understood the issue, and offered, "I can just find a place on the ground. Don't worry."

"But it's not as safe." She shrugged. "It's fine. It fits two people." She looked down. "It's just... I thought... My parents wouldn't want us... But I guess they trust you. What did you do to them?"

He didn't even know. "Apologized. A lot." Was she afraid of sleeping in a hammock with him? "What about you? You don't trust me?"

"I..." She thought for a second. "Do." It didn't sound convincing. Then she shrugged. "I'm just surprised that my parents would send only one hammock, that's all." She took it. "I'll set it up."

ZORA HAD NEVER SLEPT in a traveling hammock, which was what they called it in the valley. She had set it up before, yes, but never for real, as she had never slept outside her house when living in the valley.

Ignoring her pain, she attached the hammock to two branches, with a foundation attached to the trunk, then pulled the edges up and attached them to upper branches. The traveling hammock was made in a way that someone could sleep in it and not fall, and made to be hung on a tree for safety reasons, as shadow creatures weren't great climbers.

It was meant for two people, again for safety. But still, it meant she'd spend the night beside Griffin. Her parents either thought they were already together or... Or what? Her sister's words about being careful came to her mind. They obviously thought Zora and the prince were pretty close by now. They didn't know about Alegra, though, and didn't know so many things.

Griffin was still down on the ground, wiping their footsteps and getting water. This was a good respite, as she could no longer disguise her pain. Dreadful, all-consuming pain, as if someone were taking her insides, pulling them out, then stuffing them in again. It made it hard to think. She had drunk an analgesic potion, but all it did was make her cramps slightly bearable, but still horrific. The worst was Griffin staring at her with that worried, concerned expression, likely thinking her wounds were not healing properly or that she was severely hurt. And yet the pain had nothing to do with any of that. It was "normal" pain, as every month feeling that someone was disemboweling her was part of life. Somehow she'd always forgotten it made her want to die and hurl and scream and crawl, knowing well nobody could do any of that at the same time, knowing well it would pass, knowing well she should have gotten used to the pain by now.

At least she was lying down now. And up in the trees, they'd probably be safe from pursuers. Alone in her sleeping hammock, she was wondering why Griffin was taking so long. But it hadn't been that long. Did she miss him? That was a horrifying thought. How many times would she have to tell herself that he was in love with someone else and was a prince? He would want nothing with Zora. And how had she gone from hating him to feeling like that? Perhaps it was just his breathtaking smile, or the fact he was so attentive to her, even if it could be annoying sometimes.

She sighed and took the opportunity to grunt in pain, since nobody was around to hear it. All she had to focus now was on getting the cup, reversing his curse, saving her valley, then saying goodbye to Griffin. He would be just a memory. Oh, just a memory. It reminded her of Seth. Her anger towards him had subsided a lot, and yet, there was still a bitter taste in her mouth. It got much more bitter when she imagined she'd just be a memory for Griffin. If he remembered her. The thought hurt, but it was better to be prepared for the worst than to be caught unaware.

Right then, she heard him climbing the tree. He had that smile. "This is great."

Zora sat. Perhaps the potion was taking effect, as she was able to talk. "Yes." A question came to her mind. "Do you miss her?"

"Who?"

She rolled her eyes. "Alegra."

"Ah." Griffin then looked down. "For a moment I thought… you were talking about my mother."

Zora had forgotten about that. "It's been two years, right? I bet you miss her a lot. I'm so sorry." She couldn't even imagine what it would be like to lose her parents at her age. "It must have been hard to see them getting sick." Black fever, she'd heard. Highly contagious and caused a lot of suffering.

He looked at her for a long moment, then said, "They weren't sick."

It hit her. "They were…" She put a hand over her mouth.

"Murdered." He closed his eyes. "We just… never wanted people to learn what had happened."

Her mind gravitated towards Kiran. "Do you know who did it?"

He nodded while looking away. "Yes. He was caught and sentenced to death. But it doesn't… It didn't fix anything, right?"

Zora was at a loss as to what to say.

Griffin had a half smile, as if wanting to change the subject. "It happened. At least I have my brothers. Or had. Zora, I have a question. Was Larzen… Did Larzen…" He seemed to have trouble wording what he wanted to know. "Where was Larzen when Kiran ordered the guards to kill me?"

Zora tried to remember. "He wasn't there. But…" She recalled he had told her that something was going to happen involving Griffin. "I don't know. I don't know how much he knew."

"Do you know who suggested we go to the ruins? For the picnic?"

Just remembering it still got on her nerves, the way he'd been looking at Alegra like a puppy, how he'd humiliated

Zora. But this was a time for truth. "I chose it. I had seen you and Alegra the day before. I mean, not you." She looked away. "Your clothes."

He took a moment as if letting the information sink. "I'm sorry. I'm so sorry, Zora."

"For what?"

"For getting you almost killed. I shouldn't have gotten you involved in any of that."

Zora took a deep breath. He had to know at least some part of her guilt. "There's something you should know. The day before the challenge, I mean, night. After the dogs. I spoke to you in your office, remember?"

"Sort of. I wasn't feeling well. I had this headache, couldn't remember things."

"Well, I told you that I had seen you two. I thought it was either you, Alegra, or both trying to kill me because of what I saw."

"You thought I was trying to kill you?" He sounded aghast.

"I did."

His eyes were wide, horror on his face. "Do you still think that?"

Zora tried to ignore his dramatic overreaction. "I don't know. I think it could have been Alegra and you did nothing to stop her." She wasn't sure anymore, though. Still, the fact he had never investigated the princess or her attendants was one more reason why she shouldn't be falling for him. His smile be damned.

"I tried to," he said. "That's why I met her that other day at the ruins. It was to tell her not to mess with you. I thought she'd done something to your horse. But..." He looked down. "I don't remember much, but yes, I do remember the part where our clothes came off. But it wasn't why I went there. I wanted to put a stop to that." He shook his head. "I… I don't know what happened. And I agree I should have done more for you. I'm sorry."

Zora rolled her eyes. "It's not a mystery, Griffin. People in love ignore reason."

He was serious. "I was not in love."

Perhaps he believed that. Zora wasn't sure. "That only makes it all worse, then."

He fiddled with his wristbands. "I know."

She took a deep breath. "But… what I wanted to tell you is that, somehow, people can hear what happens in your office from the outside." Those words were hard. "Kiran heard our conversation. He made me explain who I was talking about, who I'd seen you with. He said he would find out, he…"

Griffin's eyes locked on hers. "You told him."

"I did. But he said it was no problem. He said it was fine, Griffin, that he didn't love Alegra and it was a relief to hear that. I… I had no idea he was going to do what he did. I didn't know it. I'm so sorry. You have no idea how sorry I am."

He shook his head. "It was my fault, not yours. If not you, someone else would have told him. I'm the one who shouldn't be doing what I was doing." He had his arms crossed and looked away.

"Well, now you know how your brother learned about it." There was more she should tell, but she wasn't sure she was ready.

He looked in her eyes. "Zora, what do you think of me?"

"What?" She wasn't sure she understood.

"Do you think I'm a terrible person?"

"No. You saved me. You carried me to the Dark Valley, and you didn't have to. You're here."

"I'm just wondering if Kiran will ever forgive me. If there even is any room for forgiveness."

Right. So it wasn't her opinion he was worried about. Which made sense. "I don't know. To be fair, what he did wasn't right either. It was way worse."

"He shouldn't have threatened you. Or ordered the soldiers to shoot you. I... I don't know if I can forgive that. I made the first mistake, though. But I swear, I didn't know it. When I started with Alegra, I thought they would break apart, cancel the engagement, that they didn't even care about each other. I had no clue. Then they announced it. And I realized she'd been lying to me. I understood the lies and deceptions. I wanted to put an end to it. I tried." He exhaled and shook his head. "Clearly didn't try hard enough."

Zora shivered at the way he mentioned the princess' lies. He would probably hate her too if she didn't tell him the truth soon. Well, he would probably hate her regardless, which at least would make it easier to avoid him. But she tried to say something to console him. "Well, people are irrational when they are guided by their hearts, so..."

"I wasn't in love. I thought I was, but I wasn't. And you're right that it only makes it worse."

"Then it was not the heart. Another body part. Still irrational."

He stared at her. "That's what you think of me, then. That I'm guided by my... desires. That I'll let them ruin everything else. Yes?"

In truth Zora hated the idea that he'd been blinded by the princess. But it was true. "You're the one saying it. It's the only explanation. And what difference does it make what I think or not?"

He scoffed. "What difference? Yeah, no difference whatsoever, I'm glad you think... whatever you think." He paused, stared at his wristbands, and bit his lip. "The worst, the worst of all is that I'm not sure that princess ever gave a damn for me. So add stupid on top of all that."

Zora felt a knot in her stomach. She hated that princess who had ruined a family. But she had to tell him the truth. "Griffin, I didn't exactly explain how I escaped the arena."

"You said Mauro helped you."

She nodded. "Yes. He's a fantastic fighter, but do you think me and him could face all the soldiers doing security for the games?"

"I doubt all those soldiers would attack you."

"They didn't. At first. Kiran told them to kill you and arrest me or kill me and they just stood there, unsure what to do. I can see how the order didn't make sense to them. But then your brother said he'd kill anyone who disobeyed him. I think they were afraid. They advanced on us. Some archers shot. I was surrounded. You were unconscious. I was trying to protect you."

Griffin frowned. "Why didn't you just step away? Let them take me?"

"Let them kill you?" The thought was horrifying. "For a mistake that shouldn't warrant anyone's death? No. How would I live with myself?"

"Better than dying with me." His eyes were hard, and there was anger in his voice.

Was he really upset that she had saved him? Wacko. "Right." Zora exhaled and rolled her eyes. "Can I continue? Or do you want to discuss the hypothetical version where I leave you for dead?"

"Go on."

Zora swallowed. It was uncomfortable to talk about his

former lover, but she owed him the truth. "When I thought all was lost, Alegra showed up. She was not wearing her beautiful clothes, but some strange burlap thing. And she started to sing. When she did that, everyone stopped what they were doing and stared at her, as if entranced. For some reason Mauro and Sam, his friend, weren't affected. He carried you and got me the carriage where I escaped. But..." she looked down, hating what she was about to say. "Alegra also saved you."

She was ready to see his eyes brightening with the news that the princess cared for him. Instead, Griffin frowned. "Singing? What did it sound like?"

"Some beautiful melody, but without words."

He exhaled and put his hands on his head. "That's it. That's it, Zora. I remember. Not very well, but I do remember seeing her singing, and it was strange, I didn't understand why she'd do that out of nowhere. Then I forgot everything that happened afterwards. It happened after she announced her engagement, when I didn't want to see her again, at least not in those conditions." He blinked, as if confused or coming out of a trance.

At first it sounded like one more excuse, but then, it was true that she had some strange power. Could she have used it to ensorcell Griffin? Zora shook the idea away because it also brought her hope that he had never cared for the princess.

She looked at him. "So you think she put a spell on you or something? I mean, she's quite beautiful, I'm not sure she'd have to—"

"No. Not at first, no. At least that's what I think. But later, when I started to see who she was. It was also when I got some blackouts, times without my memory."

Could it be that she had been controlling him? It would

explain so much of his behavior. But then, he could be using it as an excuse.

He added, "It all fits. I just don't understand why..."

Really? He didn't understand it? If Zora had the magic power to make someone fall in love with her, she wasn't sure she'd be above using it on Griffin. That was a horrible thought. Still. "You do realize you're good looking, right? I mean... It's not that hard to see—" She stopped when she noticed his smile.

"You think it was my dashing good looks?" He sounded sarcastic.

His eyes were on her and she had to turn away. "I'm sure you're aware what you look like and can come to your own conclusions."

"But Kiran is better-looking than me. And he's the king. She already had him. You see how it makes no sense?"

Ugh. Kiran better looking? After everything that happened, just recalling his face made Zora sick. "Maybe she wanted the title but also wanted you." It hurt to say those words, but they were the truth. "Men do that sometimes. They have a wonderful woman and still look elsewhere."

Griffin shook his head. "There was something else happening, Zora. I know it. And this singing... I think I read about creatures who could do that. But they haven't been around for hundreds of years. Unless it's a different magical skill common in Linaria. Still, it sounds unhuman, as if..." He snapped his fingers a few times, as if trying to recall something. "We'll get to the castle and check in my books. There's something that doesn't click in this story."

"And you'll find the answer in books?"

He laughed. "About her magic. We'll find out what she is."

Maybe. One thing still didn't make sense. "Why do you think she saved you?"

He shrugged. "How can I know? Perhaps she felt guilty, perhaps she still has some use for me. It's all her doing. Saving me is not exactly heroic."

Not all Alegra's doing. Some of it had been Zora's. *Not exactly heroic.* Now she feared he wouldn't even help her get the cup if he learned all that she'd done. No, he had to, for his curse. But he could still despise her.

"You look troubled." Griffin's voice was so soft, and he stared at her with those concerned eyes.

She smiled. "It's been a lot."

"I know. I'll make up for everything, I promise."

He touched her hand, oblivious to what it did to her. It was certainly more powerful than any supernatural singing. And at the same time, so awkward, when they'd just been talking about his former lover. Ensorcelled or not, he'd been attracted to Alegra. Well, who wouldn't be attracted to her? And then maybe he had kissed Zora to forget the princess. And maybe if he saw Alegra again, he'd realize it had been no magic singing.

He moved his hand away from hers. "I'm sorry."

"It's fine. It's not as if you were..." All the things she wanted. "Something."

"Try to rest."

Zora did. And yet every part of her body was aware that Griffin was beside her. She wished she could stop feeling that way. Perhaps she was going down the path of a broken heart regardless.

Zora was walking *in a dark forest at night. There wasn't even any moonlight to guide her path. Something bright caught her eye, like a*

6

ILLUSTRIOUS VISITORS

Before he opened his eyes, Griffin felt the scent. That calming, comforting scent. Clean hair, steel and leather and then something else, but together it was like the best perfume in the world. He dared look, and realized he was hugging Zora. The faint dawn illuminated her through the tree leaves. She slept peacefully and looked so small and fragile. And yet this was the girl who had jumped in front of a lion to save him, who somehow had guessed he wasn't feeling like himself, who had risked her life for him.

He exhaled and held her close. Perhaps he shouldn't be doing that. He had no right. At least not yet, when he wasn't sure if the curse would consume him.

"Griffin?" She still sounded half-asleep, but there was something special about hearing his name in her lips.

"Yes?"

"It's you." Then she was quiet and sounded as if she'd fallen back asleep.

He ran his hand through her hair, wishing he could stay

there for many long hours. But they were on the run and he'd better get moving.

RIADNE FEARED that everything would fall apart. Griffin was gone, Kiran wasn't responding to her magic, and Larzen, Larzen was dangerous. She'd come to Gravel to squash these brothers, end the royal line, save her people, and was feeling as if walls were closing in on her.

Now she'd been assigned the king's quarters. Not Kiran's room, fortunately, but the room the previous queen and king occupied, where they had been found dead. Quite morbid and she wondered if their spirits would maybe show up to spook her or try to scare her away. Of course she hadn't said anything or protested. She rolled her eyes. Such an honor, to be placed in these death chambers.

The upside was that Kiran was chasing Griffin but somehow still believed her innocent. Sort of, as he had her watched twenty-four hours. It made no sense but worked for her. That way she could still influence the remaining brothers, hope that maybe Kiran got the youngest, and hope for them to destroy each other. Of course, then what she'd done at the arena made no sense. Strange that she should have saved Griffin and Zora. She sighed and closed her eyes. Had the youngest brother ensnared her instead of the other way around? No, that made no sense. She didn't even miss him. It wasn't that. It was her misplaced compassion. Powerful as her magic was, she hadn't been prepared to be ruthless. All the suffering and pain she'd seen and felt somehow had softened her. It couldn't be. If she wanted to do something, she had to be stronger.

At least nobody seemed to remember what she had done at the arena. Out of the hundreds of people there, many must have been unaffected by her magic, but they didn't talk about it. People were afraid of looking crazy and avoided talking about experiences they couldn't explain logically. Good for her. That had been too much power. If people got hold of what she could do, no doubt some kingdom would come and try to enslave her, try to use her magic to win wars, unaware that magic was shifty and unpredictable like the winds over the mountains. Even she had no idea how she'd managed to save Griffin, and feared her feat had weakened her, as she was feeling her magic slipping away more and more, her body feeling more tired than usual.

One of the guards knocked on the door.

"Yes?" The lack of privacy and freedom in this castle was getting to her nerves and she made no effort in disguising it in the tone of her voice.

"There are visitors for your highness," the voice from outside the room announced.

Visitors? That made no sense. She opened the door.

The tall guard said, "Your presence is required in the reception hall."

Her heart sped up, but then she told herself to calm down. It could be just some merchant from another region or someone deemed important enough to bother Gravel's future queen. "May I know who it is?"

"Your brother and his fiancée, your highness."

She froze for half a second, then recomposed herself and smiled. "Delightful. Unfortunately, I'm afraid I'm too indisposed to meet them right away."

The guard nodded. "We'll pass on the message."

Riadne closed the door and had to sit down. No, no, no, no,

no. That couldn't be. Linaria's crown prince there? No, no, no. Her people were watching the roads. Not even a letter from that kingdom could have reached them, let alone the prince and his entourage. She would at least have been warned. Now she was trapped and her farce was about to be uncovered.

No, no need to panic. Perhaps she could sing to the prince, make him confused. If ever her singing worked on him and on his fiancée, whoever that was. Or maybe she could make a run for it before they found out she wasn't Alegra. She clenched her fists. Why hadn't she done her work faster? So much hesitation, as if she had unlimited time—and now it was all about to be lost. There had to be a solution. Quick, quick, quick, she had to think. Singing. Yes. She had to hope the recently arrived couple were not really in love, which was in fact quite common among nobility, and then she could sway them with her magic.

Someone knocked on the door again.

"Yes?" she yelled, not worried about hiding the fury in her tone.

"Your brother is here to see your highness," the guard said.

"I know!" she roared. "I'll come down later."

"Can they come in?"

They were in the hallway? This was getting worse by the minute. "Not now!"

"Sister?" a voice called her.

She recognized that voice, and then a different worry made her open the door. Her brother, her real brother Lukas, stood there. His auburn hair had been dyed black, and he stood beside a girl wearing a hooded cloak over her dress, covering her hair and most of her face. Riadne wondered what dreadful incident had happened to bring him all the way here.

"Come in."

Her brother and the hooded girl stepped in and a guard followed.

Riadne turned to him. "Some privacy, please? This is my family."

"Orders, your highness," the guard said after closing the door behind him.

She gave Lukas a meaningful look. He approached the man, touched his neck, and the huge guard fell on the ground. Her brother didn't even bother to break his fall, and grinned. "There." He couldn't sing and enchant people like Riadne could, but had other interesting skills.

His mood was too light for someone bearing sad news. Still, Riadne was wary. "What's wrong?"

He had a huge smile. "Your brother coming to visit is wrong? Since when?" He knocked softly on the wall and whispered, "Can they hear us?"

"Come in." Riadne directed them to the main office in her quarters, away from the antechamber by the door. That was one advantage of having the former king and queen's abundant space, as morbid as it was.

She sat at a table and her brother and the girl did the same. "Here we're safe," Riadne said. "Spill it. And introduce your companion."

The girl lowered her hood revealing long, straight black hair, light brown skin, and brown eyes with long lashes. Riadne knew who she was, and glared at her brother. "What's the meaning of this?"

"Calm down," Lukas said. "She's a friend." He turned to the girl. "Tris, this is my sister."

Tris? No, that was Alegra, Linaria's princess, and her being here could ruin Riadne's plan, but she smiled. "I thought your name was Alegra."

The girl rolled her eyes. "Like a cute, adorable little thing. No. I refuse to be called by that ridiculous name." She took a long look at Riadne then frowned. "You don't look anything like me."

She shrugged. "They only checked the gold. It matched, so they didn't care for the rest." The Linaria delegation had been bringing gold, precious stones, and gifts, which Riadne had brought with her. That made it easy for the people in Gravel to believe she was the princess. As to looks, Linaria was such an isolated kingdom and the princess so recluse, she doubted anyone would know her appearance. Her guess turned out to be right. Nobody had ever doubted Riadne's claim that she was Alegra. But with the real princess here, things could soon get complicated.

What was her brother thinking? Oh, one glance at the way he looked at the princess explained everything. What a fool. As much as Riadne could entrance with her singing, she'd seen women doing that without any magical power. That was the case here, as her brother was completely hypnotized by the princess, who was either oblivious or pretending not to notice it.

Riadne smiled while at the same time wringing her hands under the table. "And to what do I owe the honor of this visit? Is there something wrong?"

The question had been rhetorical, as there was obviously something insanely wrong for Lukas to bring the real Alegra here.

He shook his head. "Everything is fine. Tris is a friend, sis, she knows our plan and understands the meaning of revenge. We can trust her."

Gre-a-t. Now the princess who decided her name was no longer Alegra also knew their plan. Riadne was going to smack

Lukas. Instead, she leaned back and crossed her arms. "Yeah, I can see how she's your *friend*." The emphasis on the last word was intended, to see if Lukas got a clue.

The real princess faced Riadne. "If I understand well, you're here to destroy the royal family."

"Make them destroy themselves. Quite trickier."

Lukas nodded. "How has that been going?"

"One prince is on the run, his brother intent on killing him. The others... it's just a matter of time." Not really. More and more she was having difficulties influencing Kiran, and Larzen, she had no clue where he stood. But she wasn't going to tell her brother that.

"How come he escaped?"

Riadne shrugged. "No idea. But if we look at it strategically, it works for us. If the king kills the others, he'll still be alive, and we won't accomplish our goal. We need to get them all against each other." Technically, that was one of the excuses she'd given herself for helping Griffin escape. Not that she was going to tell Lukas what she'd done.

Her brother smiled. "You're skilled. And you're engaged to the king, right?"

"Yes. But he thinks I'm Alegra." Riadne glanced at the girl.

Alegra, or Tris, or whatever she was called, looked at her. "I'm not here to ruin your plan and I won't jeopardize your secret, don't worry. It's just that I need help, and I can give you something in exchange for this help. I have a deal to propose."

Her voice was soft but firm, and something in her expression made her seem trustworthy. Riadne wasn't totally convinced, though. What if the girl used some form of magic? She raised an eyebrow. "I'm listening."

"Linaria is rich," the real princess said. "We're not strong, but we have enough gold to buy defenses if needed. With the help of Gravel and your magic, I want to conquer it."

That made no sense. "Aren't you already the princess? The kingdom is yours."

She shook her head. "It's my parents' and my brother. I want them dead."

Riadne was wondering if she had to clean her ears better. Or maybe the real princess would laugh at some insanely weird joke. Or maybe... the girl meant it. "Hum. Dead. I'm sure you've heard of something called poison? Or some professionals called assassins. Not hard to get."

The real Alegra, or rather, Tris, shook her head. "I want them to know it was me, to know I came for them, to know they are paying for what they've done. I don't care for power, but I can make your brother king. Your people can have a kingdom."

Oh, that explained it. Riadne was sure Lukas didn't care for a kingdom either, but for the idea of being king beside the beautiful Linaria princess. Fool. Men were such idiots, sometimes. Had he forgotten there was a huge possibility he wouldn't live long? Had he told her? Probably not.

Riadne raised her hands. "I give you my blessing. Go home, commit familicide, make my brother king. It all sounds delightful."

"We need support," the princess said. "An army. Lukas says you can convince people to do what you want. Convince the young Gravel king to take Linaria."

Right. Or else maybe the girl would take matters into her own hands, uncover Riadne's deception, and convince Kiran herself. The thought of not being engaged to him anymore did sound tempting, except for the part where she had to make the Gravel royal brothers kill each other.

"Maybe *you* could get engaged to him and do all the convincing?" Riadne asked the question as a test.

"Don't say nonsense," Lukas protested. "Tris doesn't need any more suffering or an arranged marriage. And she wants to help us."

Riadne sighed. "Right. An arranged marriage, what a terrible thing. You seem so concerned about me, Lukas."

"You're different, sis. You have your magic, you can influence them instead of being under their control."

Lukas was so convinced... Riadne shook her head. "It's not that easy. Regardless, about Linaria, what are we going to do with a kingdom full of gold? It won't help us live longer, Lukas."

"That depends on the other plan," her brother said. "Get the Gravel Royal line to destroy itself. We can do both at once."

Riadne rolled her eyes. "Well, I guess I *am* good at multitasking."

Lukas smiled. "You are amazing."

Right. Now he no longer understood sarcasm. She wanted to bang her head on the table. No, his head.

The real princess added, "Instead of hiding in the mountains your people will be able to live in the Linaria castle, use our riches."

"We don't *hide* in the mountains, we live there."

Lukas shrugged. "Linaria is among mountains, sis. I think it can work."

Tris looked at him and smiled. A simple smile, and his face lit up as if he'd learned he was able to fly. Fool, fool, fool. As to the princess, she wasn't in love, that was clear, but Riadne wasn't sure how much she was tricking her brother. It was an added complication to a task that was already complex. Not to mention that Riadne had no clue how to make the brothers destroy each other and feared she wasn't made of resilient enough stuff to cause people to suffer, even horrible people.

"Maybe. Yes, sure." Riadne turned to Tris. "Would you mind letting me talk to my brother in private—"

"No," Lukas interrupted. "We have no secrets. Whatever you want to say, you can say in front of her."

Riadne waved a hand. "Oh, it was just some boring family talk, but we can catch up later. Leave me, then. Both of you. I need to rest." And think. Perhaps she could convince them to go to Linaria and exchange the grand revenge plans for some simple murder.

"We will continue planning this," Lukas said as he got up.

"For sure."

He noticed the unconscious guard, knelt, and unstunned him. The man opened his eyes. Lukas was kneeling by him. "Are you all right?"

The man got up, confused.

"I think you fell," Lukas added. "Might want to see a healer. We just need directions back to our quarters."

Tris turned back to Riadne. "Delighted to meet you."

She pulled the princess's hand and jerked her forward, so that their faces were close. "Don't play with my brother," she whispered.

"I'm being honest with him," the girl replied.

It sounded right. She had never returned his warm gaze or given him any flirty smile. And yet, his eyes were full of hope and adoration. Empty hope. But perhaps it would be better for her if she never fell for her brother. Doomed love could rip your heart and break you apart, and Riadne was not that selfish to wish that upon anyone, not even a princess intent on non-immediate familicide. She nodded and squeezed the girl's hand. "All right."

When they closed the door Riadne was left with her mind whirling. Right. Getting three brothers to destroy themselves, nevermind the mathematical impossibility, was not hard enough. *Let's also take a kingdom.* Lukas, Lukas. What a complete fool. Riadne had been missing him, thinking he could help her, but no, instead, he came only to complicate her already complicated life.

A sound caught her attention, and a movement behind a curtain. Larzen stepped out of it. His blue eyes were pure fire.

"So, on top of everything, you're an impostor."

As he advanced towards her, Riadne had seconds to think. She could scream for help, but that would not make him forget what he'd heard. Her only option was to enchant him. Riadne focused on the sound for confusion and memory loss, and opened her mouth letting it fill the room, hoping it would have effect in such short seconds.

It didn't affect him. In two steps he was upon her and had his arm over her mouth, preventing her from screaming or singing. Plan A had flopped, so she had to try something else. Riadne could affect animals, just cause confusion, unease, like she'd done with the Dark Valley girl's horse. She'd never tried it on a human, and it could backfire, but still, she reached a hand and touched his hip. Nothing happened. Why was Larzen immune to her magic? She'd have to fight him, but even as she elbowed his stomach, he didn't seem to feel anything and put a hood over her head. She wriggled in his hold but couldn't get free. This was it: she was dead.

"I'm not gonna hurt you," he whispered. An incongruous, pleasant chill ran down her spine. Maybe it was the relief that he wasn't going to kill her? He continued, "At least not yet. Now, you can struggle and get hurt, or you can do it nicely."

Riadne stopped wiggling and fighting. It was better to

pretend to comply, let him lower his guard, then surprise him later. He made her turn a few times, probably to lose her sense of direction, then directed her to what she assumed was a secret door, as he wouldn't dare step in the hallway and pass the guards with her in that state.

She was pushed down a hallway then a set of descending stairs. At some point, when she felt his hold loosen, she pulled her hood, elbowed his ribs—and stumbled on the steps.

He caught her by the arms and broke her fall. "I need you alive, *Riadne*, so please don't roll down the stairs. Lovely name, by the way."

She was in a staircase so dark that she couldn't see anything except a faint light coming from down below. "Let me go."

"Everything in its time. Go, keep walking." He didn't even bother putting back the hood on her.

Riadne descended and found herself in some sort of empty underground dungeon with stone walls and a single lamp lighting it. She couldn't fight her way out of this, so she sang. This had to work, had to make him compliant, obedient, confused.

He smiled instead. "You're very talented. Is that a famous tune or something?"

She raised her hand to slap him, but he blocked it, then pointed to a cell. "Now, be nice, or I won't be nice. There's a lovely pile of straw there, so you can make yourself comfortable, and I'll be back soon, so we can talk." He opened the door. "Will you do the honors or do I have to push you?"

Riadne rolled her eyes and walked in. The upside was that she wouldn't feel guilty when she made Kiran or Griffin kill him. If she ever had the opportunity to get close to them and finish her plan, of course. That was another problem.

"You don't know what you're dealing with. You'll pay for this," she yelled.

He closed the door of the cell and held the bars. "I'm absolutely certain I have no clue what I'm dealing with, my dear Riadne. And I'll need your help to figure it out."

"Let me go and I'll help you."

He was already walking away, but then he turned. "Oh, don't worry about that. I'm sure you will."

His tone chilled her to her bones. Riadne kicked the bars —and regretted it. All she did was hurt her own foot.

7

BREAKFAST

Zora woke up alone in the hammock. The sun was up, so it wasn't that Griffin wasn't himself and was killing some defenseless animal. She went down and saw him throwing dirt over ashes.

"You made a fire?" she asked in surprise.

"Very small, and I fanned the smoke, don't worry." He smiled at her. "This was meant to be a surprise. I got some fish."

She was almost asking if it was a good idea to make a fire and perhaps alert their pursuers, but on the other hand, this was such a sweet thing to do. Other than her parents, nobody had ever prepared any food for her. She returned the smile but looked away quickly before he got any wrong impression. More like right impression, but he didn't need to know how she felt.

He gave her a grilled fish. Zora took it and sat on the log by him. "Thanks."

"It's also for me." He chuckled. "I know this is not time for fish, but..." He shrugged.

"I was hungry, so it is an excellent time." Zora put the fish inside the bread, in a weird sandwich, as it made it easier to eat. She was still stunned that he had gotten up earlier than her to get them food. Because he was hungry. Zora shouldn't read anything into it. She had to remember he was a prince and she wasn't even close to being any type of noble. But still, his gesture had been nice.

He looked at her. "Are you feeling better?"

Considering the dreadful disemboweling feeling usually lasted only one day, she was feeling much, much better. But that wasn't what he was asking about. "The wounds are healing well."

Griffin shook his head. "I still can't believe how close it was."

"Perhaps destiny plays a hand."

"Do you believe in it? That our path is set?"

"I don't know. Maybe it's luck, who knows... What about you?"

He looked away, thoughtful. "I often fear to peer into the future. I grew up with the thought that..." His voice cracked. "Perhaps... Perhaps there's no way out."

"Isn't the Blood Cup your way out?"

"It's not like we have it with us, is it? Or that we used it and it worked."

"Griffin." That got his attention, as he looked at her. "I'll do everything I can to help you reverse this curse, I promise you. I'm not one to quit or to be dissuaded by difficulties or fear. Trust me. It's going to be fine."

He bit his lip and looked away.

"What is it?" Zora asked. "What is it you aren't telling me?" At this point she was sure he was hiding something.

He looked away, then his stare fixed on her. "Why don't you

start? They talked about a fake champion returning to the valley. Nobody told me how you got chosen. This other guy, Seth, apparently was willing to kill you or hurt you. There's more in this story, isn't there, Zora? And while I can make tons of assumptions, I'd rather hear it from your mouth."

He eyed her intently, and while it felt like his usual concerned look, there was also a challenge there.

Zora picked a twig from the ground and examined its texture. She didn't have to tell him anything. Lucky that she was, somehow he hadn't figured it all out yet, unless it was included in what he called "assumptions". On the other hand, if she didn't tell him the truth, she'd always have that nagging feeling, that unease. But what made her mind was what she'd told her father: that she wasn't sorry. And now, after everything, she was even less sorry than before and found that taking that idiot's place had been one of the best decisions in her life.

She looked back at Griffin. "What do you think?"

"I have no clue. I'm asking." His expression was neutral. It was indeed a question.

Zora glanced at the twig and rolled it between her fingers. "I was never chosen as the Dark Valley champion." She looked at Griffin, whose chin had dropped. "Seth was our champion. We did have a small competition, but it was just a formality; he was our best ranger."

Griffin's expression was one of disbelief. "You lost the competition."

Zora snorted. "I didn't even enter. I... I wasn't sure my parents would let me leave. I wasn't even sure it was for me. See, since the announcement, Seth had been excited about it. I was happy for him. We were..." Her hands stopped rolling the twig and she stared at it. "He was... I thought we were together." Why did it hurt to say those things? Now she was being vulnerable and she didn't want Griffin to see it. Zora shrugged. "But it turns out we weren't. He was an asshole, so I stole his letter and the rod and pretended it was me." She faced him. "There, happy?"

He rested his chin on his hand. "I have no words, Zora. No words."

It was ridiculous that he'd be angry about the whole Seth thing. "Why? You're feeling sorry for the scumbag who just attacked me?"

"Oh, no. No doubt he deserved way worse than what he got."

"Then what's wrong?"

"Wrong?" He scoffed. "What about, 'I was chosen to be here and I earned my right fair and square,'" he mimicked her voice.

Great. Now he was making fun of her. Zora got up. "I won my right. I stole the letter and wrote my name in it."

He shook his hands. "Zora, I knew it. I knew it the moment you said you were the champion, I knew there was something odd, but 'no, if you doubt I'm a champion it's because you hate women.'" Again that stupid voice.

She wanted to punch him when he tried to imitate her. "Well, tell me, how did you suspect I wasn't the champion? What exactly tipped you off?"

"Your size, for one."

"Ooh, look at the giant speaking." This time she almost sounded the way he did when he imitated her.

Griffin looked away, then laughed and shook his head. "How creative, Zora."

Perhaps that had been a low blow and unnecessary. But still. He wasn't listening to her. "Not only you said I shouldn't compete, you said I should get a husband. You humiliated me."

He grimaced. "Right. Now saying you're a desirable match is humiliating. What else, fire is cold?"

"Would you say it to a guy?"

He shrugged. "Maybe. Some champions do go to the games to find partners."

Zora waved a finger. "You wouldn't say that's *all* they can do. You wouldn't. I doubt you would."

He waved a hand. "Oh, please. I opened our guard for female soldiers. I'm the last person you can say has anything against women."

Zora put her hands on her waist. "Oh, by the Light, would you look at that? He has done *one* thing for women and therefore nothing he says or thinks can ever be sexist."

He put his hand on his chest. "I did something. And I faced criticism for it. As to you, I had a feeling that something was off." He got up and stood so close to her that their faces were less than a palm apart. "You can say whatever you want; you weren't the Dark Valley Champion. I was right. I was right, Zora!"

Zora stepped back. "Congratulations. Do you want me to make a sign or something? *Griffin was right.* Will that make you happy?"

"If you put the sign in your head and try to understand my point, it might."

"You wanted me to quit. You tried to make me lose."

He waved his hands in the air. "Cause I was worried about you!"

"Cause you thought I wasn't capable. Say it. Say why you were so worried about me and not worried about any of the other champions. What was the big difference? Say it."

"We'll circle back." His voice was quiet now, and he had an arrogant smile. "You were not a real champion."

"But I proved I was capable and I know how to fight. How I came to Gravel city makes no difference."

He took a deep breath, then looked away from her, at some point far in the distance. "All that time, saying you'd disappoint your people, claiming you were the champion..." He turned to her and narrowed his eyes. "You were lying, lying without any remorse, without any difficulty. You are a liar."

Liar. Maybe. She could accept that without shame. "So what? Of course I can lie well. I'm a teacher. I have to tell the kids never to give up hope, to believe in their dreams, blah, blah, blah. I have to say it with a straight face, knowing well they'll never leave that disgraced valley. Knowing well they'll have to deal with shadow creatures their entire lives. Of course I'm a good liar."

He snorted. "Is that your excuse for everything? Oh, the kids in the valley, the kids in the valley... Sounds so selfless, I'm almost convinced that's all you think about. I'm almost convinced the reason you insisted on staying in the games wasn't a frivolous need for validation."

Zora threw the twig aside before it landed on his face by accident. She smiled and mustered the calmest voice she could. "Frivolous. Absolutely. You nailed it. My motivation for being in those games was fri-vo-lous." She paused as he took those words in, perhaps stunned that she had agreed with him. Then she raised her voice. "And so was everyone's motivation there. Proving you're strong or fast or whatever in some stupid game won't accomplish anything or change the world. Every single champion was there for some frivolous motivation. But you won't say that about them, will you? They are men. Nothing they do is frivolous."

Griffin exhaled as if exasperated. "There you go again. You think I hate women."

"Not at all. I think you find women desirable even if they are sometimes silly and frivolous."

He grimaced. "It's none of that. None of that. Frivolous, silly, pointless, call it what you want. My motivation for being in those games was important. Unlike yours."

"Unlike everyone's and yet you didn't try to convince them to quit."

"Because I knew I would win. For the record, I should have beaten you too, if things had gone as planned."

"Why though? If you wanted that cup so much, why make those games?"

"It's the rules," he said softly.

That made no sense. "Why not skew the challenges towards you?"

Griffin shrugged. "I didn't have to. I'm stronger and faster than everyone."

"But not smarter. You ended up tricked."

"By my own brother. That was the issue."

"Anyone could have slipped a slowness and confusion potion in your drink and you wouldn't be none the wiser, smart ass."

Griffin frowned, as if thoughtful. "Potion? I thought it was... I wasn't sure what it was. How do you know?"

This was it, the question she feared, and there was no going around it this time. "I brewed it. I thought we would duel and wanted to make sure I'd win." It was weird how she'd feared so much confessing this, and now it gave her a strange pleasure to admit she'd tricked him—and great relief in finally getting it out of her chest.

"You..." His eyes dulled like a lamp going out. "So that's

why... It was guilt, not..." Griffin looked down. There was no anger, just disappointment, sadness.

Zora hadn't expected this reaction and she regretted the way she'd said it, even if she knew it was something he'd eventually have to find out. She reached out a hand to his face. "I had no idea your brother was going to do what he did. I had no idea."

He pushed her hand away and she felt as if he had slapped her. He stared at her. "That part isn't your fault. You know what kills me? I told you. I told you, Zora, that winning this cup was my life, I told you how much it meant to me. And yet you were willing to cheat and trick to win it, even though your reasons for winning it were... what? To prove yourself?"

"How could I know what it really meant for you?" She realized she had yelled, and then toned down her voice. "People exaggerate. I know you said it was your life, but I thought it was a manner of speaking. I never thought you had any valid reason for needing that cup. I couldn't have known. Was I trying to prove myself? Yes. But I had something to prove. You, you're a prince, Griffin, and everyone knows you're strong and skilled. You had nothing, absolutely nothing to prove."

He crossed his arms and looked away, then suddenly turned to her. "I'm sure you noticed I'm not that tall. You just mocked me, in fact."

"I didn't mean... You're taller than me, I can't—"

"You did, Zora, and we both know that damn well. When I was a kid and a young teen, people mocked me in my face. After I grew up, at least people waited for me to turn around. Most people, not you." He looked down. "Not that I wanted that cup to prove myself."

With that amazing face, it was weird that he'd feel he had something to prove. "Guys are stupid. I doubt you ever had any problem with the ladies." They'd probably be like Zora, too enraptured by his looks to bother checking how tall he was.

He had a quick half smile, then got serious again and rolled his eyes. "I was a prince. I could be hideous and there would still be some that would want me."

"You know you're anything but hideous."

He shrugged, his jaw set, looking away from her.

Then something hit her. "Except Alegra. She was a princess and would have chosen you over your brother."

His eyes were set on her, but with a dark glint. "Right." He scoffed. "I pick my companions based on piss contests. I don't know how you can still manage to surprise me with your opinion of me, I really don't. You, and your... complete lack of honor."

"I *am* honorable."

He snorted. "Right. To trick your adversary, so honorable."

"Honor stops where self-preservation starts."

"Then it's not honor!" He waved his hands in front of him.

She glared at him. "You mistake honor for stupidity. You should have rigged those games for you, if winning was so important. Now don't blame me for using every means at my disposal."

"Yeah, I'm quite stupid. Trusting people like you, what am I thinking? But at least I'll pay with my life. You won your cup. Congratulations." He took a small vial from his pocket. "Know what this is?"

Zora wasn't sure she was following him. Such small vials usually carried one thing, but it couldn't be. "Poison?"

"For when my transformation starts for good. But hey, at least you won the games."

Zora was almost dizzy seeing that, but no, he'd never need to drink it, ever, she'd make sure of that. "It makes no difference if it was me instead of you. I'll get the cup and we'll reverse your curse. I owe you that. Even if I hadn't made any mistake, I would—"

"We can try," he interrupted her. "I mean, that's what we're doing, isn't it?" He lowered his voice. "Except that, as far as I know, it won't work if someone else wields the cup." He shook the vial. "At least I have this."

Zora felt a horrible knot in her heart. "Don't you ever drink it."

He put it back in his pocket. "Not yet, I won't. Now just... leave me. I need... Leave me alone for a while."

Before she could even think about something to say, Griffin turned his back and walked away from her. Zora felt a bitter taste in her mouth that spread to her entire body. Everything was bitter.

8

CAPTIVE

Riadne sat on the hay as she tried to collect her thoughts. There wasn't much point trying to understand how this had happened, how Larzen had overheard her conversation. There were secret passages in the castle, and from the looks of it, one of them led directly into her previous room.

How could she have been so careless? She sighed. There was no point lamenting the past; she had to fix her future. If Larzen had heard their entire conversation... she tried to recall it. Well, she had said she wanted the three brothers to kill each other, Lukas had implied she had some magic, but a lot of things had not been revealed. But then, Larzen knew she wasn't Alegra, and to make matters even worse, had heard the real princess and knew she was in the castle.

Disaster, disaster, disaster. But the worst of all was that for some reason her magic wasn't working on him. It didn't make sense. Her magic didn't affect people when they were near their true love, but Larzen had been alone with her and it was as if her magic didn't even exist. Even Kiran was somewhat affected by her magic, but she got nothing with Larzen. Riadne was screwed. No, there had to be a way out. It was just a matter of finding it.

Right then, she heard muffled steps in the dungeon. The walls were rough and moldy, which made sounds quieter than they should be. She wondered if this was also meant to muffle screams. Not that she planned to yell for help. If anyone could hear her, she would have been silenced by now. To her relief, she didn't see anything resembling any type of torture device in the adjacent cells or in hers. What she did see was Prince Larzen approaching her cells with calm, slow steps.

He looked at her through the bars. "Is there anything you want to say? Any way you can explain yourself?" His eyes were pure blue fire, but there was a note of sadness in his voice.

Riadne was still sitting. "Haven't you heard it all?"

"Far from all, isn't it? I have no idea who you are and what you want, other than making me and my brothers... what? Kill ourselves? How is that supposed to even work? One kills another, then is killed by another, then what happens to the last one? Commits suicide?"

She raised a finger. "That's an idea right there."

He approached the bars. "It's not funny, Riadne, whoever you are. You planned this, you destroyed a family. Does it make you happy?"

"Does it make any difference?"

"Why? All I want to know is why. Why would you do that to Griffin? To Kiran? Whatever you were planning to do with me?"

Riadne shook her head. "You'll never understand. Now tell me what you want or what you're going to do with me."

"You are in no. Position. To make demands." He then spoke

in a soft voice, "You're in my power, and you're going to do as I tell you."

She shrugged. "I'm listening."

"Tell me why."

"Or what?" She wasn't denying him, she genuinely wanted to know what kind of threat she was against. There was a huge possibility that he'd kill her regardless, so there was no point in revealing her secrets.

Larzen sighed and shook his head. "You'll see. Now, maybe I do not care why, I do not care who you are or what you are or what you want. You can walk out of this with your life and your freedom, which is much, much more than you deserve. All I want from you is that you fix this mess. If you can use your magic or whatever to convince people, get Kiran to forget what happened, maybe even forget you. That's all."

Sure, so easy. "Kiran doesn't always respond to my magic." Larzen might not believe her, but she had to say it. "Not sure if you noticed it, but he has guards following me wherever I go. He doesn't trust me. I tried to make him more… malleable, but I can't."

"Try harder. Fix this mess. I don't want to see my brothers against each other. And for what? For *you*?"

He said it with the disgust he would have mentioned a rotten piece of meat. This was terrible, considering her original plan had been to seduce the three brothers. She had been doomed to failure from the start with Larzen.

He added, "You can obviously still do some convincing. I mean, Kiran is still engaged to you, while still wanting to kill Griffin, as if he could have done anything by himself. It doesn't make any sense, and now I understand it's your doing."

Partially. She could still command a small amount of adoration from Kiran, but not much more. But it didn't matter what she could or could not do, but the opportunity to get out of these bars, get her brother to safety, and perhaps even escape and forget that morbid plan. She nodded. "I guess I could convince your older brother. But it will take some time."

"How long?"

"A week, two. I don't know."

Larzen narrowed his eyes. "Griffin could be killed in a week."

"Why? You think he's dumb and can't hide?"

"Everyone knows what he looks like, Riadne. It's certainly not that easy for him to hide."

She waved a hand. "Nah. If he wears long sleeves, I doubt a single person will recognize him."

"So hilarious." He proceeded to unlock the door. "Come. I have something to show you." On one hand, he had a blindfold.

"How am I going to see anything with this?" she asked.

"We'll remove it when we get there."

She crossed her arms and let him cover her eyes. Now she'd need to pay attention to directions and try to understand where these dungeons were. Each and every detail could make a difference. Each and every detail could give her a chance to break free.

He then pulled her arms back and handcuffed them. She could perhaps fight back, try to run, but she had a feeling it was better to at least pretend to comply. Her chance for escape would come later.

Again they went up stairs, then walked back and forth, and she really did think it was back and forth and even in circles to get her lost.

When they stopped, Larzen stood behind her and put a hand around her waist. The gesture was so intimate and felt strange, but then, he knew she had been planning his and his brothers' deaths, so this was far from the worst that could happen.

She felt his face close to her shoulder as he whispered, "I'm sorry but I'll have to hold you back."

Then he pulled her blindfold. Riadne was in a dark hallway behind a window with a cloudy glass. Behind it, there was a room that looked like most rooms in the castle, with a table, chairs, some sofas, and a bed. Sitting at the table, her brother and Tris, the real Linaria princess. She tapped her fingers on the wood while Lukas observed her. No, not observed, admired her.

Larzen said, "I'm betting we both love our brothers, so I think it's a fair trade."

"What trade?" It was annoying to ask the question and not face him, but on the other hand she tried to look at the room, see if she recognized it or found anything that could help her.

His voice was still soft. "My brother walks out of this free, and so does your brother."

Riadne ignored the weird chill down her spine his voice gave her and tried to think. Of course, Lucas and Tris were in some kind of prison, even if not yet aware. The princess was anxious, looking around, while Lukas, poor Lukas, he wouldn't see a storm coming. And of course Larzen wasn't just going to ask please.

He added, "They are well taken care of. For now. I'd hate for it to change, you know?"

She felt hot where his hand touched her, which, again, was completely inappropriate and must have been some stress-induced thing. Riadne focused back on the issue at hand and asked him, "You are willing to imprison the Linaria princess?"

"Of course not. As far as everyone here knows, *you* are the princess. Unless everyone were to learn about these *mountain people* who kidnapped her. That's a threat to be taken seriously."

So he'd want Riadne to keep the charade. It made sense. At least until she managed to change Kiran's mind. And then... after that... who knows what would happen to her and even to her brother. Again she tried to find any detail in the room that could help her, but everything was so bare, so common. Still, she needed to keep talking.

"Look at that, my brother is an example of a man completely blinded by adoration. She manages it without any magic, and without even smiling."

"True, she is gloomy," Larzen agreed. "But you should never underestimate a guy's need to be a girl's hero. Perhaps he wants to be her sunshine."

"Night's about to fall in his case." Did she even guess they would never have much time? But then, perhaps adoring someone made him happy. And then she noticed the Linaria princess giving Lukas a small smile. Such a little thing, and yet a smile for him only, making his eyes brighten. Perhaps being locked in a room with the princess wasn't exactly a punishment for him. That was good because it gave Riadne time.

"Seen enough?" Larzen asked.

"Just barely. Let me spend the rest of the day here to make sure they will be all right."

He chuckled. "You've got things to do, *Riadne*." Again he used that mocking tone.

"I don't know why you say my name with such disgust. I like it very much."

"Of course, silly me. I forgot how proud of it you've been all these days."

"Just because I hide something it doesn't mean I'm ashamed of it or dislike it."

"Indeed." He put the blindfold back on her.

After more walking and turning, he untied the fabric from around her head in a bedroom apparently belonging to the royal residential area. Riadne had to learn about those passages. Then she would be able to free her brother and escape. Escape was all that was left for her, as she didn't see any feasible way to complete her plan. Her doomed plan.

Larzen crossed his arms in front of her. "Now that you know why I'm asking, I'm sure you realize why it's a good idea to tell me who you are and why you're doing this."

"Or what? You'll kidnap my brother? I'm afraid it's already been done."

"C'mon, you can't be that naïve. There are tons of things one can do or not do to them. Like give them food—or not. So tell me. Oh, and if something... let's say... something tragic happens to me." He shrugged. "I don't know, an accident, who knows? Then they'll be dead too. So don't get silly ideas."

The handcuffs and the position of her arms were hurting her. "Can you unlock these? Now that we've established I'm not going to murder you with my bare hands? Then I'll talk."

He did remove the manacles. She massaged her wrists as she tried to come up with an explanation. It wasn't great, but was what she had. "We're peasants and poor, and we hate the Royal family, since you're rich and never did anything for us."

Larzen rolled his eyes. "Really? That's the story you came up with? I expected better from you."

True. That had been beyond shitty. She tried again. "You won't understand. Now look at the bright side: maybe you were lucky, the real princess wants to start a war and kill her own family."

"As long as it's not my family, what do I care? Now tell me, what's this plan that requires me and my brothers to *destroy ourselves*?" He rolled his eyes as he said these last words with an overdramatic, exaggerated tone.

"It's a prophecy," she blurted. That was the closest she could get without revealing too much and while still being convincing. "It's said that once the Gravel Royal family destroys itself, we'll gain strength."

He frowned. "Please tell me you don't believe in prophecies. I thought you were intelligent."

Larzen would never understand and there was no point even trying. She feigned indifference. "I guess I'm not."

"Well, try to be, then, since you'll need to convince Kiran to leave my brother alone. Ideally you'll want him to forgive him and forget everything that happened. That's your task for now, and your brother's life and physical well-being depend on it."

Riadne shook her head. "If only you were powerful enough to guarantee someone's physical well-being..."

"While in my power, yes, of course I can guarantee that. Now, from now on, you'll go back to your routine. Do whatever you do with Kiran, and change his mind."

"Sure, and nobody will wonder where my brother went."

Larzen smiled. "Of course not. They left. They had come just for a quick *hello*." He pointed to the door. "You can go."

"I'm not supposed to go anywhere without my guards. I'm sure you understand how that would complicate my position with your lovely older brother. Put me back in my room."

"No. You just went out for a quick stroll and your guards were none the wiser. He can't think you're with Griffin, and you won't let him know you were with me, as you obviously love your brother very much."

Riadne shrugged. "Oh, well, I guess even if my brother

dies, it will be worth it to get you all to kill each other, then." Her idea was to scream for help, but it was too much of a crude idea. No, she needed time, she needed to think this over, or else risk her brother's life. "As you wish."

She crossed a small antechamber half fearing he'd come after her, put her back in that dungeon or something, but no. A door led her to a corridor near the royal quarters.

"Where are your guards?" Kiran's voice startled her.

"I..." She looked around. "They were following me just now." She tilted her head, trying to look coy. "I wanted to see you."

"Who's in that room?" His voice was harsh.

Great. She could get Kiran against his brother, which had been part of her original plan, but now, her brother... On the other hand, she had warned Larzen that she should have been escorted to her bedroom. Whatever happened, it wouldn't be her fault.

"You can look."

Kiran pushed her against a wall and held her chin. "I'm the king. Not a servant. Tell me."

"You're hurting me."

"No, I'm not. Hurting is different, and if you're curious I can show you. Who was with you?"

"Nobody. I wanted to see if I could get a room closer to yours, that's all. It's empty." She was counting on Larzen having escaped using one of his sneaky secret passages, or else things would get even worse than before.

ZORA UNDID the traveling hammock and erased any remaining traces of their camping site. Regret was little to explain what she felt. Her words towards Griffin had been as sharp as an enchanted sword, and yet she was the one who got hurt. Instead of explaining, apologizing, she'd told him the truth in the worst possible way. And mocked him. Now he really hated her, and it was awful to realize that she used to have a sliver of hope that he could have feelings for her. That had been stupid, of course he wouldn't, not in the way she wanted. Perhaps she had done that to squash those ludicrous ideas, to make him stop looking at her with misplaced admiration, to make him stop giving her false hope, but still, she shouldn't have hurt him. What she'd done to him was bad enough, there was no need to confess it in such a callous, almost cruel way. At least she'd never forget his look of disappointment. That would be like a knife in her chest over and over and over—which she deserved.

Still, he had to come back, he had to, for them to find that cup. Unless... Unbearable pain came to her chest, as she feared that he'd given up on everything and decided to end his life. But he said he wasn't going to use it. He wouldn't lie, would he? She wanted to call his name, yell for him to come back, then explain to him she'd do anything to reverse his curse, anything for him, but she didn't want to call attention to her position, not when there were guards searching for them. It was just... she felt so hopeless standing there, unable to fix anything.

Then she heard it; a twig snapping. Somehow it didn't sound like Griffin, but she had to be nuts to presume to know what his steps sounded like. She turned—and saw a guard, who advanced on her. Zora stepped back and unsheathed her sword, even if she wasn't sure she'd be able to slice a person the way she'd trained to do with human shadows.

"Easy there," the guard said.

Then another voice, from behind her. "I would drop that if I were you." She recognized it. Stavos! Wait, should she be happy it was someone she once considered an ally, or was she doomed, considering he worked for the kingdom? Three more guards approached. Zora was brave but not dumb, and it didn't take long for her to realize she was outnumbered. Putting Butterfly back in its scabbard, she kept her voice calm and steady, and asked, "Can I help you?"

"Very much." Stavos had a chilling smile. He then turned to the guards. "Take her weapons and detain her."

9

———

THE CASTLE

Zora almost wanted to make a run for it, as she didn't want anyone taking Butterfly from her, but again, she was outnumbered, so she couldn't get out of this using force. "Wait. I haven't done anything. We can talk."

Stavos didn't even seem to hear her, he just repeated, "Guards!"

Two hands pulled her sword, and someone put her hands in handcuffs. Zora tried to stay calm and feign innocence. "Is there a reason for this?"

The blond crown assistant approached her. "Where's the disgraced prince?"

"I don't know."

His hand moved faster than she had time to dodge, landing a blow in her face. "Where is he?"

"I don't know." She tried her sweetest, most innocent voice. It was so sweet it made her almost sick. "All I wanted was for him to get me out of the Dark Valley. He did. I was going to Gravel City to speak to his Majesty. He'd offered me a position in the castle. I'd like to take it."

The blond man laughed. "Oh, you think he'll accept you?"

Zora shrugged. "I wanted to ask. He seemed interested before. But I assume you'll be taking me to the castle, and I understand the precautions with..." She shook her handcuffed hands and hated herself for pretending that she still wanted any kind of deal with Kiran.

This time she saw when Stavos's hand moved, but figured it would be better for her not to try to do anything. The slap hurt and she had to hold back tears of anger. How dare he hit her?

Stavos's lips formed a thin line in a weird grimace-smile, then he said, "We're not going anywhere without Griffin. So you'd better yell for him or else I'll make you."

"Oh, you found her." A female voice.

Zora turned to see a woman with short cropped hair and deep brown skin. She had a uniform similar to what she'd seen in Gravel City, but her rims had some extra gold embroidery. The woman continued, "King Kiran has ordered that she be brought to the castle immediately once found. I'm sure you don't want to disobey him."

Stavos narrowed his eyes, clearly irritated at the interruption. "No. I want to please my king and collect the reward by bringing the disgraced prince."

The woman shook her head, her tone calm. "Those are not our orders, Stavos"

The blond man laughed. "Irene, Irene... Who do you even think you are? Your little regiment won't last long without the brat prince to allow this insanity."

"At least I'm following orders."

Stavos smirked. "Oh, really, while alone and outnumbered?"

She put two fingers on her lips and whistled. Three more female guards approached her.

Irene then said, "I'm not outnumbered, and I can take her to the castle. *Unharmed.*"

"I found her first." He sounded like a bratty kid now.

"We'll both accompany her, then." Irene sounded calm but firm.

Stavos puffed. "Very well."

Irene... The name was familiar, but not quite. Zora wasn't sure who the woman was, but even though the end result would be the same, she felt much safer with female guards among her entourage. They put her in a carriage similar to the one they had used to bring her to the castle before. Zora was left alone in it, but handcuffed. Mounted guards rode beside the cariage. It turned out to be a good thing Griffin had left, so that at least he hadn't been caught. But then, what good would it do, when he needed her for the cup? Zora would have to find a way to escape. Unless Kiran still wanted to kill her—or worse. She didn't want to think about it and felt as if a part of her was missing with the lightness on her back and no Butterfly.

THE TWO GUARDS who usually followed Riadne came running, perhaps having heard her voice.

Kiran stared at them. "Dismissed. Both of you."

Their eyes widened, astonished, perhaps not under-standing how she had left her room.

"Dismissed!" the king bellowed.

The two guards ran. Kiran then grabbed Riadne's elbow

and pushed her into the room. There was nobody there. So there was indeed another secret passage here, from where Larzen had escaped. The issue was finding where.

Kiran laughed. "Alone, you say? Let's check."

He turned the bed over. It fell over the wall and its wooden structure cracked. He then overturned a wardrobe and threw a vase on a mirror. Riadne was getting scared, and tried singing for confusion, to make him forget what was happening.

He just stared at her. "What's that?"

"Singing... calms me."

He pushed her against the wall. "And why are you nervous?"

Because he was acting crazed, but if she told him that, he'd get even worse. Another reason was that her song for confusion apparently hadn't worked. She wondered if there was something wrong with her magic, then tried using a song for attraction.

His look changed from hatred to admiration and he ran a hand over her face. "Alegra." It was weird to go back to her fake name after being caught by his brother. He smiled. "Do you realize what's happening?"

"No." Indeed. She had no clue what was going on with him.

"We're alone. In a room. You know what that means, right?"

Riadne swallowed. "You broke the bed."

"Let's break it some more," he whispered. Perhaps he'd meant it to be seductive, but the result sounded rather creepy and scary.

"The wedding. You know I want to wait." She was glad these people had this weird custom, as it had been her excuse to avoid him. Funny because when she'd first come to Gravel, she feared falling for Kiran, and now she wanted nothing to do with him.

He bit her ear, which was quite disgusting. "I don't. See? I'm trusting you, trusting that nothing was your fault. But you need to help me."

Riadne pushed him. "You know I need to wait."

"For the wedding?"

She nodded.

"Five days, then. I'll tell the constable."

She gasped. "That's... that's too early. I need to call my parents, we need to plan the party, I need a dress..."

"That's why I'm giving you five days. No more. Unless you decide you don't have to wait, then we'll have all the time in the world to plan all these nonsensical details. Your choice."

He walked out and left her there, perhaps forgetting to get new guards, forgetting she was, for the first time, unattended. Riadne would run if she could, but she had to consider Lukas.

Damn it, Larzen, how could he expect her to convince Kiran to do anything for Griffin when she was barely escaping alive. She should have run away after her feat in the arena. That moment had told her everything she needed to know about her ability to stick to her plan and get the brothers to kill each other. She should have run, but she didn't, and now she was paying the price.

No, no, she had to think. The silver lining was that she had been left alone, this room had a secret passage, and she would have time to look for it. Perhaps there was still a way out. The issue was saving both herself and her brother.

After much pleading and begging, the group taking Zora stopped for her to get some time for "girl stuff". Irene and a female guard escorted her away from the road to some bushes. Irene... Zora finally remembered where she'd heard that name. Could she maybe help her?

"You're the commander who assigned Isabelle and Natasha to protect me, right?"

"Yes," the woman replied. Then she whispered, "You have friends here, but please don't try to escape on the road. Anything can happen away from prying eyes."

"I wasn't going to escape. What am I even going to do while handcuffed?"

"Hum. I thought that was why you wanted some time to yourself."

Zora crouched behind a bush. "No." Doing this with her hands bound would be tough, but at least they were in front of her. She could perhaps punch someone if she wanted—which would be quite dumb, considering the amount of guards around her. But that was not the reason she was here.

Zora blurted the truth, "I gotta change my pad. And pee." She had to throw the old one since there was no place to wash it. Yuck. Good thing they finally stopped, or the tissue would take no more, and Zora would get to the castle all bloody and disgusting. Thank the Light she had another in her pocket. Her bag had been confiscated too, which sucked because she had potions, clothes... All her things.

Zora considered what the woman had told her. "But why do you say..." She lowered her voice. "I have friends?"

Irene crouched so that she could whisper. "You saved our prince. Many people are still loyal to him, including my whole regiment."

Griffin had told her about it more than once, and it made sense. "Because before him, you weren't allowed…"

She nodded. "Menial jobs, yes, or healing, some things considered non-essential, but not part of the Royal Guard, like now. We remember."

"Well, leave me and help him, then. I mean, he's the one they want killed."

"We are helping our prince by making sure you are safe."

Zora shook her head. "You could go out there and prevent them from finding him or something. I'll be fine."

"You will. And I'm a commander and I know what I'm doing." She patted Zora's shoulder.

Hopefully that was the case. She walked back to the carriage feeling calmer and much, much cleaner. But she still had a tight feeling in her chest fearing that Griffin could be caught, fearing what could happen to him. Perhaps he'd been lucky that he had walked away. But then what if she got killed or imprisoned, what if he gave up on her, gave up on the chance that the cup could revert his curse? Those troublesome thoughts kept her company all the way back to Gravel City.

Upon arriving, two guards grabbed her arms and pushed her into the castle. The castle. They weren't taking her to the prisons or dungeons. Ugh. She was probably going to see the king and her insides curled, partly fearing he'd order her killed, partly fearing what else he'd want. Irene was following the men and was the only reason fear hadn't completely taken over Zora. But then, there was little a commander could do against a king.

They entered a room with many chairs and a pulpit, Zora being held all the while. She could feel her heart beating, and now more and more her thoughts turned back to Griffin. It was worry tainted with regret. Regret for her unnecessary, harsh words that morning, regret for her actions that made her "win" the Blood Cup and now made him depend on her.

After many minutes, Stavos stepped in with Kiran, who smiled when he saw her. "You wanted to speak with me?"

Zora wanted to punch him and tell him he was the most disgusting man in the world, but that was not what she said. "Yes. I would like to be your potion master, if the position is still available." The words sounded wrong and awful. Should she have apologized instead?

He tilted his head and had a smile that chilled her to her bones. "Yes, of course. I'd love it very much. Stavos, put her in the *special* guest room." There was an odd emphasis in that word and Zora tried not to wonder too much what it meant. "Then come back here."

Irene had been ignored throughout this interaction. As the two guards escorted Zora to whatever room she was going, she noticed that the woman was no longer with them. This couldn't be good. Zora dug her nails in her palms as guards climbed many sets of stairs, then unbarred a heavy metal door that would stop the strongest human shadows. Inside, she found a room with a mattress on the floor, a metal bathtub in one corner, with pink bedsheets and curtains. The dungeons would have made her feel much calmer than this.

Then two female servants came in with buckets of hot water. They were preparing a bath? The door opened, and Kiran came in.

"I hope this is comfortable."

Zora shook her hands with the handcuffs. "Yeah, great."

The king laughed. "I'm glad you think so. For now, you said you wanted to be my potion master and I'm sure you under-stand the scope of the position. The first rule is dressing accordingly, so please obey your attendants. And don't forget you'll always have at least three guards outside your door." He smirked. "To ensure your safety. If you wish to see me before I come to visit you, just let them know."

When Kiran left, even the air got lighter. To her relief, a guard removed her manacles. For a brief second, she wondered if she should make a run for it. A run where? She was high up in an area of the castle she didn't know, without her sword, and there were two armed guards in her room and who knows how many more outside. She wished she would have been more attentive in the morning, she would have been smarter, she wouldn't have been caught unaware.

The guards left her alone with the two women. One of them was middle-aged and had her silver hair in a bun. She said, "Take your clothes off and get in the bath."

The other woman was young and had long blond hair. The issue was that they were both staring at her.

"Can you... wait outside?" Zora asked.

The older woman shook her head.

"Can you turn around, then?" Hopefully they would understand her need for privacy.

"Silly girl, we're not going to pay attention to you. All we're going to do is make sure you're ready," the older woman said.

This was terrible. "You know, I changed my mind," Zora said. "Can you ask the guards to take me to a prison or the dungeon?"

The woman frowned. "Get in the bath or we'll call them to help us put you in there."

"No, no. I gave up. I don't want no potion master position, I..." She didn't even know what to say, wasn't even sure what she feared.

The older woman sighed and got up. "That's it. I'm asking the guards to strip you naked."

"What? You can't do that."

The woman ignored her and walked to the door.

"It's just a bath," the younger girl whispered. "Please cooperate."

"Fine!" Zora yelled.

And that was how she got in the bath, which was quite pleasant. And it wasn't that she was afraid of water or any of that, just that she wondered what nefarious plans the king had that required two women to "prepare" her. She tried to ask them their names, make conversation, but the older woman just shut her down, while the younger one had apologetic looks, but never talked either.

The older woman got up and left Zora alone with the blond girl, and Zora whispered, "Do you know what's going to happen to me?"

The girl had a faint smile. "You're worrying too much. You have friends here." She then looked away as the older woman approached.

When Zora came out of the water, her clothes were nowhere to be found. "I need my clothes back!"

The woman shook her head. "Trash. Those ugly things are trash." She showed her a short nightgown in a thin fabric. "You'll wear this for now, as you need to rest."

"But it's day! How am I going to go anywhere—"

"You're not leaving this room, so why worry?"

"I want my clothes back, my things." She did. Her top had been sewed by her mother and Zora had had it for a long time. Then she looked at the shortness of the gown. "And this is indecent."

The woman shrugged. "You can be naked instead."

"It's barely any difference!" Then she spoke at a lower volume. "And I need pads."

"Go fetch some," the older woman said to the younger, who left. Then she turned to Zora. "When the king comes, tell him you want to go to the dungeon and you want your rags back. I'm sure he'll comply. Don't mess up my job."

"Sorry." She hadn't considered that the woman was just following orders, but then... "But it's humiliating to be forced to be dressed like that, don't you think?"

She rolled her eyes. "It's comfortable. Far from a torture device. And if being pampered and taken care of is not something you want, I'm pretty sure your majesty won't insist."

"Oh, yeah, I had my clothes thrown away. If that's not pampering, I don't know what it is."

"You got a comfortable room for yourself and a warm bath. You don't know what suffering is."

"I do."

"Then shut up and let me do my job."

The blond girl came back and Zora put on that stupid nightgown, which was so sheer it made her feel naked. She didn't even have shoes, and understood that this was another way to ensure she wouldn't escape. Where could she even go like that? But on the other hand, perhaps it was better to comply for now. She had to escape and had to help Griffin fix his curse. She also had to figure out how the cup could help her valley. These things were bigger and more important than being annoyed at the way she was dressed.

When the women left, Zora proceeded to search the room for anything that could be used as a weapon, but, other than the mattress, there was no furniture. The pails had been taken out of the room, and the tub was bolted on the floor. A curtain rail? Not even that. They were attached to the wall above the window. Perhaps she should take the curtains and strangle someone? She had no idea how to do that.

What she did do was take a sheet and improvise a more decent-looking dress. No way she'd let Kiran or anyone see her in that semi-transparent gown. She tied it on one shoulder, then wrapped the rest and tied it again on her waist. No apparent nipples, so that was much, much better. The thought that he'd made her dress like that on purpose and was probably planning on coming into the room to see her made her flinch with anger. But this was not the time for anger, but for careful thought.

As she tried to come up with a plan, the woman came back with a loaf of bread and a water skin. Really? Not even a glass? Did they think she was that dangerous? Perhaps she should be flattered, but she was just annoyed. There went her hope for at least a fork or even better, a knife. Perhaps she should not eat the bread, but instead hide it, then wait until it got hard, then perhaps hit someone with it. Right, against swords, how far would she go with a hard loaf of bread? And how many days would it take? Zora was trapped. Even her thoughts were trapped in a continuous, endless circle leading nowhere. But she had to escape. For Griffin. For her valley. She'd find a way.

WAITING WAS THE WORST. Griffin had never been patient, and doing nothing until nightfall got him on edge. He hid in a cupboard in the castle hallway. As fewer and fewer people walked by, the more he could hear his heart thrumming in his chest. This morning had been a blow. Zora, in his mind, had been many things, short-tempered for sure, but not ambitious, not someone who could lie that easily and without any remorse. One lie could always lead to the other, and then he'd be caught in a web of falsities. One lie and then another and she would be no different from Alegra: false, cynical, manipulative. Griffin should have learned, but no. He had truly thought Zora was different, that she had a pure and honorable heart, that she was a ray of light casting away shadows of deceit. Well, no. She was casting her own lies. Without any remorse. Was everything that surrounded him false?

But seeing Zora caught had been a bigger blow. It had taken all his self-mastery not to challenge the guards surrounding her. He'd snuck past them and hidden under the carriage. That had been a faster way to get to the castle, for sure, but a tortuous way too, as he had to hold himself with both arms and keep silent. Well, he could have whispered something to Zora, but he had no clue what he was going to do or when he was going to act. And then he wasn't completely sure he trusted her. There was this thin suspicion that perhaps she would seek help from his brother, and perhaps he wanted to see how it would all play out. But now it was anguish, as she was Kiran's prisoner. If it had been a few days before, Griffin wouldn't have been as worried. Now he had no clue what his brother was capable of. But he needed to be patient if he wanted to escape with Zora. Regardless if he could trust her or not, he needed her. He needed her for the cup.

Perhaps what hurt was realizing that the anguish he'd felt from her wasn't from fear of seeing him dying; it was guilt. Guilt, not... whatever he'd thought. At least now it made more sense that she had pushed him away. He was done with liars anyway and it didn't matter, if the cup didn't reverse his curse, he was done with everything. Of course it had been mostly

Kiran's fault, but still, the thought that someone he trusted, someone he'd done everything he could to protect, would stab him on the back like that... For what? For a prize that meant nothing to her. And then maybe he should have rigged the games for him to win instead of trying to stick to some pointless honor that could get him dead or worse.

But now his heart was beating for a different reason: all that mattered was to see her safe. This morning he'd been so immersed in his own anger he'd neglected their security. If something happened to her, he wouldn't forgive himself. And that was the whole confusion; he didn't even have a clue how he felt. He was in equal parts upset at Zora and worried about her. No, he was more worried than upset, and perhaps reminding himself what she'd done to him was just a way to ease the pain.

One knock followed by a pause and two knocks snapped him out of his thoughts. He opened the door and saw a blonde girl who gave him a key.

"Guards?" he whispered.

"Asleep."

This was the time. It would have been faster if he hurt or killed the guards, but he couldn't bring himself to do it. He had used help from commander Irene and a couple more loyal guards, who had told him where Zora was, gotten him the key, and given a sedative to the guards. Most of the work, really.

After the girl's steps quieted, he waited a couple minutes and proceeded to the door. The guards were fallen beside it. Three guards. Some exaggeration. Griffin inserted the key in the hole and opened the door as silently as he could. The room was lit only by a small lamp and he imagined it was something that wouldn't make Zora comfortable. The bed was empty and there was no wardrobe, nothing where she could hide. Griffin trembled, wondering if he'd been tricked, wondering if he'd been too late. The only other piece of furniture was a metal bathtub. When he approached it, a figure with a weird white robe came out of the tub and ran to the door. The flicker of the lamp illuminated brown hair with blond tips.

"Zora!" he whispered.

She turned. Instead of clothes she was wearing some kind of fabric tied around her. Her eyes widened in surprise, then before he could say anything, she had her arms around his neck and her face beside his.

"I'm so sorry. I truly am. I..." It sounded like she choked a sob.

"It's fine." He stepped back to look at her. "Are you all right?"

She nodded, and those beautiful calm golden eyes were misty. All the anger he had felt was gone. She could trick him and lie to him a thousand times; he'd probably still forgive her. That was a scary thought.

He dried one of her tears with his finger and tried to lighten up the mood. "I wasn't expecting the warmest welcome, but I'm not sure seeing me is so bad that you need to cry."

Zora laughed. "I'm happy, silly. I was worried about you."

That was it. He wrapped his arms around her and pulled her close, their hearts beating together, feeling the rise and fall of her chest against his. If only he could always hold her this close. If only he were sure that the curse would be reversed, that he would survive. Still, in that moment, none of that mattered, as a calming warm feeling took him over. He could stay like that forever, but it wouldn't be wise, as they'd better escape soon.

Begrudgingly, he broke the hug. "We'd better get going."

She nodded and smiled. "Thank you for coming."

As she turned to the door, it opened, and a bunch of guards swarmed in. One of them grabbed a hold of Zora and pressed a sword against her neck.

10

BROTHERS

Griffin had a sword, but there were too many soldiers. He'd need to calculate this right to make sure they would escape.

Kiran walked in the room. "So touching. And I can't believe that after being betrayed by women over and over you're still that gullible. Sad, really."

There were six guards with swords drawn, pointed at him, but it was Zora he was worried about, as she was being threatened by one guard and held and gagged by another, so he raised his arms. These men were not from the Royal Guard, but perhaps recently promoted. Griffin didn't know them— and they didn't know him.

As much as he wanted to ask them to let her go, he figured it would be worse if his brother thought he cared, so he just asked, "What do you want?"

Kiran laughed. "Me? Want? I don't want anything, and you know why? Because I already have it all. You, on the other hand, tsk, tsk, tsk. So gullible. Then people use you."

Griffin had no idea what Kiran was talking about and tried

to find a way to escape, a way at least to get Zora out of that mess where she shouldn't be.

He listened in silence.

His brother pointed at her. "Now see? You think she's your friend, don't you? You think she's on your side. Do you want to guess who poisoned you? Do you want to guess what she did to convince me to help her?" He chuckled. "Do you want to know why she's undressed?"

Griffin peaked again at Zora's clothes and realized her weird dress was actually a bedsheet wrapped around her body. Blood started to rise to his head and the only reason he didn't lose control was because he feared she'd get hurt. He truly hoped his brother hadn't done anything inappropriate, or else he'd have to kill him even if he died in the process.

Burying all his emotions, he shrugged. "If you two are so close, why is she being held?"

Kiran had a smirk. "For her security." He stared at her. "But she's smart, and that will keep her alive." He stared at her as he said it, and it sounded like a threat. "Guards, release her."

Griffin mentally begged for Zora to take the chance and run, while he pulled his sword from his back. But she didn't go anywhere. Instead, her right hand's fist landed on Kiran's chin. His brother staggered back and leaned on the wall for support, then screamed, "Kill them! Kill them both!"

Griffin jumped in front of Zora, sword in hand, and yelled, "Let us go and we'll spare you."

He backed against a corner of the room, so she would be behind him. Skilled or not, she was unarmed. Three guards approached him. They had their swords extended before them, and the arms too, as if afraid of getting hit. This was too easy. In a swift stroke, he hit their swords, which fell to the ground. They had to crouch and pick them up again. Four other guards stood at a distance. At this point, he noticed that Zora had picked up a sword and stood by him, just slightly behind, giving him room to maneuver. There was a chance. The issue was getting out of that corner, through the door, and outside—then escaping. Three other guards tried to swarm him at once but all they managed was to get in each other's way. Griffin disarmed them and they retreated. These people looked as if they had been recruited on the street. And yet, as terrible as they were, they were many.

Kiran stood at a distance and yelled, "Kill them! A thousand crowns to the one who draws blood first. Aim for the girl!"

Griffin pushed Zora behind him. No way the guards would get past him. But then, eventually they had to get out of there. If he kept disarming them and giving them time to go back and pick up their swords, he'd probably get tired eventually. Zora could fight too, but not against that many. Kiran observed the scene with a smirk. Perhaps he could appeal to his pride.

"Challenge me!" Griffin yelled as he blocked a blow, then disarmed one, then two more guards. "One-to-one. Let's see who's better."

Kiran laughed. "Oh, silly little brother. You might have the delusion that being skilled in battle means anything. It doesn't. I'll never sully my hands with the likes of you. You only. I had no problems sullying my hands with the girl you're defending."

"Asshole," Zora yelled from behind Griffin. "You're king and yet you have to harass women to go to your bed. Had you been so good, they'd come willingly."

"Oh, don't distort facts. You were quite willing when you came asking me to help you defeat Griffin. Now the stupid kid is here thinking he's saving you."

"Liar!" she roared.

"I know," Griffin whispered, afraid she'd lose her temper. His brother was trying to get him and Zora on edge and he hoped she didn't think he believed in any of that nonsense. Regardless, if they found some peace, they'd need to talk. If they ever escaped that corner. There was no way to get an opening.

He wondered if he should suggest to Kiran to take him and let Zora go, but based on what he'd seen so far she wouldn't be safe. Time was ticking. He was getting tired. And if he didn't find a solution soon, he and Zora would be caught. Unless… His one chance would be if he went for the kill. He could kill guards, and he assumed so could Zora. Eight lives in exchange for theirs. Fair or not, this had been their choice, and this was his only shot. He wouldn't last long disarming and waiting for them to attack again.

"Stop. I don't want to hurt you," he warned as he disarmed three guards.

Kiran let out a light chuckle. Of course. He wasn't the one risking his life.

When two guards advanced, he disarmed them, then swung his sword by their abdomens. The men fell back, crouching and bleeding. He didn't have time to see how much he'd hurt them, as another guard advanced. This time he disarmed him at the same time as he swung his sword lightly over the man's right hand, not enough to cut it off, but enough to cause a deep cut and prevent him from attacking. Two guards came from the other side and he tripped one and stabbed the other. The three other guards kept a distance.

"Kill them!" Kiran yelled.

Griffin was moving towards the door, Zora right beside him. When two guards advanced, he disarmed them both, then stabbed one while Zora hurt the other. There was no time to consider if what he was doing was right or wrong, and in any case, nobody had been killed yet. By the door, Griffin disarmed and punched the last guard. He and Zora were in the hallway.

Kiran didn't try to attack them or do anything.

"This way," Griffin said, planning to go to his room. But steps from both directions made him stop. They were surrounded, with guards on both sides. Griffin couldn't possibly block them all; five on each side. Zora was skilled with a sword, but not good enough to fight that many at a time. They had to find a way to escape. He'd need to do his best to cover his side and some of hers. Kiran stood at the door, smirking.

"Stop it!" A voice made the guards freeze. "Brother, or rather, *brothers*, what's going on?"

It was Larzen, staring at the scene in shock.

"None of your business," Kiran said between gritted teeth. "If you interfere, you'll be the next to fall."

"I'm just asking!" Larzen protested.

His oldest brother smiled. "And now you'll see them be killed."

"Even the girl? Surely she hasn't done anything," Larzen insisted.

Griffin was wondering if there could be an opening for them while his two brothers had this conversation, a way to get past the guards blocking their exit.

"She helped him." Kiran shrugged. "For me it's enough."

Griffin needed an idea, fast.

"Attack!" Kiran bellowed.

The only exit would be to fight like he'd never done before and hope that Zora could do the same. It was as if time stretched. Larzen said something as the guards got closer and closer. Then a sound made him stop. An amazing, familiar sound. No. Something was wrong. He realized who was singing even before her red appeared behind Larzen.

"Let's run," Zora said.

She pulled his hand, and then they were dashing through hallways while everyone was immobile back there, ensorcelled by that strange singing. Zora was leading him in the wrong direction, but in a way it was good, as it wouldn't raise suspicions to where he really meant to go. They descended a few sets of stairs then he pulled up his hood to cover his hair and part of his face, and asked her to walk. They were in a hallway in the workers' area, by the kitchen and pantries, and the few servants they crossed were obviously aware that they didn't belong there, especially Zora, with that weird bedsheet she was wearing, but it was better not to run and call even more attention.

She was now following him but no longer holding his hand. He looked back at her face, seeing some fear in those eyes.

"We'll be safe soon," he said.

Her answer was a thin smile that didn't hide her worry and even fear.

They crossed the castle using the servants' passages until they were right below the hallway leading to his room. It wasn't by accident that it was in a fairly isolated wing. They climbed a set of stairs, then he saw his door ajar. What had once been his office had its furniture turned over. He opened the secret door to his bedroom. It had been ransacked too, and none of his belongings were there anymore. But where he was going was still a secret, and so far, nobody had found its entrance.

It felt strange to bring someone to this place that had always been only his, like a secret part of himself, something he had hidden from the world. But then, Zora knew about it, so she belonged there. It was still strange; opening up like that made him feel vulnerable. It was like lying down weaponless before an enemy. But then, she wasn't an enemy.

Larzen watched as Griffin and Zora ran away. Riadne sang as if she were having a good time, while the guards watched as if frozen in place. His older brother also watched her, but his eyes had a glint of something dangerous. She stepped back as the guards stared at each other in confusion.

"Get her, get her!" Kiran yelled.

Riadne raised her hands. "I'm already here. What do you want?"

Kiran pushed her against a wall. "You. Helped them. Escape."

"I didn't," she grunted.

That was when Larzen realized his brother had a hand around her throat. If he were to tell him to stop, it would only make things worse. Instead, he said, "Kiran, focus on Griffin. He's going to escape."

His brother turned to him. "He's in the castle. We'll find him." He then glanced back at Riadne. "As long as our enemies are dealt with."

A strange sound came from her mouth like an anguished scream, and Kiran's stance changed. Riadne pushed him then addressed the guards. "Get him!" She then turned around and ran away, while the guards restrained Kiran. She was dangerous and Larzen shouldn't let her escape, but then, she had acted in self-defense and he couldn't fault her for that. Meanwhile, Kiran restrained and surrounded was a more pressing matter.

"Stop it, stop it. Let him go!" Larzen yelled.

The guards stopped and had a confused look, then Larzen said, "Run after her!"

In reality he thought she was too far away, but didn't want his older brother saying they would be killed for assaulting him. If the guards took two seconds to think, they would realize they could overpower and kill Kiran and Larzen, and things wouldn't be pretty. Now they were running away, hopefully never to come back and face his brother's ire.

"What have you done?" Kiran yelled.

"Saved you! Now if you want to find Griffin, let's do it together."

Kiran had a crazed look. "He was here, about to be killed, until you arrived. Until she arrived. Are you working together? Are you with her?"

Larzen shook his head. "No. She ran, didn't you see? They all ran away and the guards, they behaved strangely."

"She ensorcelled them. I knew it. She's a... a witch."

"She's the Linaria princess." He couldn't believe he was lying to his brother like that. "I'm not sure what happened just now."

"Unless these men are traitors. Traitors, all of them."

Another guard came from the room and Larzen took a look inside it. Five men lay hurt, while the others were treating them.

"Incompetent idiots." Kiran shook his head as he watched the scene.

"I can help you find Griffin." Larzen tried to sound helpful.

"You'll do no such thing," his brother said. "If you intervene again, you'll face the death penalty like him."

Larzen nodded. "Very well. I'll stay away." He walked back to his room. Perhaps Riadne's plan to have the brothers against each other was working after all.

11

———

THE SECRET ROOM

There was even another room hidden inside Griffin's room. Zora recalled the night she had brought him here, how he'd opened his eyes and said her name as if he had been happy she was there. She still recalled the feel of his hair in her hands.

"Here." Griffin's voice snapped her out. "It's safe. Nobody knows about it."

A part of the wall opened to reveal the thinnest stone stairs she had ever seen. He gestured for her to go first and she passed him, arms crossed covering herself, since the sheet had fallen somewhere along her run. She felt almost naked with that nightgown, and so angry that she'd been forced to wear that, that her clothes had been thrown away, that her sword had been lost. But she was glad to be here, on these rough stone stairs that were so thin she had to descend them sideways.

The room was not really a room but some sort of private dungeon with stone walls and ceiling. It was as big as the office and room together. On one side, it had chains attached to a

145

wall and a mattress. On the other side, a table with some strange objects, then a divider and what she assumed was some kind of private area with buckets. The place felt gloomy and eerie. There were lit lamps in two corners, so someone had been there recently, hopefully Griffin himself. His steps echoed as he descended behind her.

"How are you?" He had that concerned look.

"Better than an hour ago." She smiled.

He glanced at her crossed arms over her chest. "Are you cold?"

"No. It's just..." How was she going to explain that her gown was see-through? For some bizarre reason she felt ashamed of the way she was dressed, even if it wasn't her fault. "I had a sheet around me and it fell at some point, and..." Zora trailed off.

Griffin stared at her for long seconds, until eventually his eyes widened. "Oh." He took off his cloak and handed it to her.

Zora tried not to notice that he had no shirt on as she turned around, put the cloak on, then secured it with a knot so that it would be closed in the front. It smelled like Griffin, a pleasant, soothing smell, and she wondered how come she knew what he smelled like. She turned back around and he was staring at her, no shirt on. He had a nice chest and a flat, not overly muscular stomach, and it was awkward that he wasn't looking for a shirt or rather, a vest.

"Zora." His tone was serious. "Did he touch you?"

She shook her head. "He sent two women to bathe me. They took my clothes and gave me this, but he never came into the room." She'd been fearing that, fearing he'd see her, fearing so many things that had made her stay in that room a nightmare.

He exhaled and nodded. "I was watching the hallway. I just wanted to make sure."

"I guess it was a trap for you."

"It was." He smiled. "But we got away."

They were still within the castle walls, though. That said, it was good to be far from Kiran and his guards. She looked at Griffin, who still wore nothing other than his pants. "Aren't you going to put on a vest, a shirt? Something?"

"I don't have it." He shrugged. "And I'm fine. I often train shirtless."

Of course. Men's nipples were not something they had to hide. Zora wasn't sure if she wished hers could be free like that.

She felt awkward being in a room with him only half dressed, but on the other hand, she was glad the cloak covered her. "I see."

Yeah, she was seeing a lot.

He looked away, then back at her. "I wanted to apologize."

That came out of nowhere. "For?"

He smiled and shook his head. "This morning. I... it was my fault."

"Well, no. You're right to be upset I almost got you killed. You're right to be upset I took away your chance to get the Blood Cup and now you're not sure—"

"I know. It's fine to be angry at how things turned out. But none of it was your fault. Yes, your motivation for winning the cut was frivolous. But you're also right that almost everyone's motivations were. People go on and on after frivolous, stupid goals, telling themselves it means more than it does. Do people stop to think about what matters?"

She looked down. "For me, my family and my valley

matter. I thought... I thought it would mean something if I won."

"But it did. The issue is that you didn't arrive the right way, but the kids I saw were happy to hear you had won the games. You gave them a sense of pride. I mean, had things been different, had you arrived carrying a prize, maybe your valley would have some festivity..."

That image warmed her heart, but how much would that really mean? "It wouldn't change the shadow creatures in our valley or the walls surrounding it."

"It would give people hope. Aren't you the one saying it's important?"

"Hope that eventually one of us can go out and bring a prize, as if to prove our value? As if we didn't have any value before?"

He looked down, thinking, then back at her. "I don't know, Zora. You're the one who was willing to cheat to win that thing, and I'm trying to look at things from your point of view. Plus, if it weren't you, Kiran would still have found a way to get me killed, but then you wouldn't save me."

"I'd still try."

"Maybe you wouldn't know." He looked at her. "How did you do it? Did you really conspire with my brother?"

She didn't want to hide things anymore. Didn't want to hide her shame. "Yes. He suggested I make a potion for you. And I did."

Griffin crossed his arms, which only accentuated his pectorals. "And he didn't ask anything in exchange for his help?"

"He wanted me to be his *potion girl*." She rolled her eyes and had some revulsion in her stomach recalling him telling her that there would be *some riding* required. "I know what he wanted, but I was planning on winning the competition and leaving."

Zora usually liked his eyes, but sometimes, like now, there was a dark glint that made them scary. "You put yourself in danger, Zora. After I warned you."

"I thought I had it all under control." She swallowed. Then another thought came to her mind, and she was glad to change the subject. "She saved us again. The princess."

"I noticed it this time. It was strange, wasn't it?"

"Perhaps she still likes you." Zora was curious to see his reaction.

Griffin shrugged. "I have no clue. What about Larzen? He invited you to that picnic. Did you and him..." He put his fingers together.

Zora felt nauseous wondering what he could be thinking. "What are you suggesting?"

"Conspire together or something?"

"Oh." She exhaled in relief. "Conspire. Yes."

He was aghast. "Yes?"

"Larzen helped me with the first tasks. I mean, he just told me what the challenges would be."

He exhaled. "Ah. Well, lots of competitors found ways to learn about the challenges in advance." His eyes narrowed. "But did he ask you to do anything?"

"Yes. He asked me to flirt with Kiran. Not flirt. Apparently rebuffing his advances worked just fine, but he set me up to meet him in a garden one day."

His eyes widened. "Wow. And you didn't find anything suspicious about it?"

"Yeah, but it wasn't my problem. He said I wouldn't need to do anything with Kiran, but I had to make him think he had a chance or something. In his words, he wanted me as his pawn in his games."

He stared at her. "And you were fine with that. Being someone's pawn."

"Why not? I was getting the information I needed. He also got me the dresses I wore at the balls. It sounds stupid, but I wouldn't even know where to find those."

"That was his job, though." He frowned. "So he chose your dresses?"

"Him or someone else. I don't know."

Griffin was thoughtful. "So that was why you were the most beautiful—" He paused.

"Sure. Had it not been for his help I would obviously look hideous." Zora wasn't sure if she was flattered or offended. But then it was probably true. Wait a minute, had Griffin said *most beautiful*?

Griffin laughed, then was thoughtful again. "He wanted Kiran to notice you. And he did. But why?"

"No idea. Maybe he wanted Kiran to forget Alegra? But that would make no sense."

"No. It makes a lot of sense."

"It doesn't. Kiran would want both of us at most."

Griffin was thoughtful. "But he would get distracted and not pay as much attention to her. Or she would be jealous? I don't know."

That made some sense. "He said he wanted me to support him in his flirting games, to create a distraction. You think he was protecting you?"

Griffin grimaced. "I don't think he had a clue about me and her, and if I were to guess, even now he wouldn't believe I caught any girl's eye."

"That would be incredibly dumb of him."

He shrugged. "My brothers for you. They think if you don't brag you don't... But I don't want to talk about it. I think Larzen wanted Alegra for himself."

Could it be? "I don't know, but if that's the case, I'm sure you can empathize."

Griffin grimaced. "I didn't play games and I had no ulterior motives. With him... Maybe he wants Linaria's gold or something."

"Maybe he's in love. If it's true he wanted her."

Griffin let out a low, soft, laugh. There was something intimate about him laughing while not wearing anything from the waist up. "Larzen and love? Nope. Hopefully he's realized now that going after Alegra is too risky, though. Kiran is understandably jealous and upset, but he's being quite possessive, don't you think?"

"The part I don't get is that it looks like he's forgiven her, but not you. Why?"

Griffin shrugged. "No idea. Maybe she lied to him, who knows?"

"Has Kiran always been like that?"

"Like what? Aggressive? I wouldn't think so. We as brothers had some rivalry, of course. For him it was worse. I'm not sure you know that his mother is not the same as mine and Larzen."

That was odd. "No."

"She died giving birth. My father married my mother after that, and she raised him as if he were her own son. But it didn't keep him from thinking she preferred me and Larzen. Maybe she did. Well, not me, I could always eventually be taken by the curse, so... But Larzen, for sure."

"Siblings always think their parents favor the others. It doesn't mean it's true."

"Maybe. The thing is, for me this cup was always a possibility, not a guarantee, so I was told that I should enjoy my time, knowing that maybe I would never make it past my twenties."

That was a hard way to live. But she tried to cheer him up. "We'll find the cup and it's going to work. Can we start? You said we could use some books and tools..."

"I thought maybe you wanted to rest."

"I'll rest when you're free of your curse and my valley needs no more walls."

He closed his eyes and looked down, then sat on the bed.

Zora had an awful feeling. "What?"

He took a deep breath and looked at her. "Will you forgive me?"

"It depends."

Griffin fiddled with his wristbands. "I saw you there, with your family, your life, in your home, in your valley you love so much. I know you say it's bad, but all I saw was a loving family..."

Zora felt as if someone had punched her in the stomach. "You lied. The cup can't save the Dark Valley, can it?"

He sighed. "I mean, I don't know. It's not impossible. There's so little I even know about this cup that sometimes I think it doesn't exist."

Her insides were turning cold. "Griffin, you made me hope. Why? Why light up that hope in me if you knew it wasn't true? Do you have any idea how I'm feeling now?"

"It was shitty and vile. I'm sorry. I'm not a great person, Zora. Faced with the possibility that I might have to drink poison or become something monstrous forever I might have resorted to cheating and lying. You, out of all people, should understand that."

She should, of course she should, it was just that it hurt to realize that someone she trusted had played with her hope, and plus it showed his real opinion of her. "You thought you had to lie to me so I'd help you? You don't believe I'll do everything I can for you to get rid of your curse?"

"I wasn't sure."

"You don't get me. At all. You think I'll quit if it gets hard, don't you?"

He got up. "I don't know. Can we stop? Yes, I made a mistake. But so did you. Neither of us is perfect. Let's call it even and move on."

"I guess... we are even. On that." But then there were all the past things nagging on her. "But what about everything you did during the games... Lock me in the library?"

He paused and took a deep breath. "Let me get everything straight. The only thing I did was try to make the challenges work against you. That was all, as offensive as you may think that is."

"Who locked me in the library, then?"

He thought for a moment. "Alegra, probably. She was there with me."

"Oh, what were you reading?"

"We weren't reading."

There was something about the way he said it... Zora couldn't believe it. "Oh, gross. In a library?"

"It's not gross. Anyway, that's beside the point. But the reason we went there was that she wanted to see the foreign section, see books in different languages."

Zora rolled her eyes, annoyed to hear about Alegra and her talents. "So the princess is multilingual?"

He stroked his chin. "No. That was the odd part. She

wanted to see what kinds of different writings we had, but she can't read Continental."

Zora frowned. "Don't they also use it in Linaria?"

"They do. But she can't read. At all. She was curious about different writing symbols."

"Shouldn't princesses know how to read?"

"I thought so. But what do I know? The thing is, she left after me, so she was the one who locked you in, Zora. I'm sorry. It's not like I asked her to close that door and I have no idea why she'd do that."

It made no sense. At that point, Zora hadn't even met Kiran, so it couldn't be jealousy. Unless... and that was a thought that had occurred to her only recently, unless she'd been jealous of Griffin. But their interactions had been pretty antagonistic until then.

He added, "I know she probably cursed your horse or something."

"You think she also sent the assassin to kill me and used dark magic on your dogs?"

"It had to be her."

"But she saved you."

He shrugged. "Well, there's a difference between you and me."

There was. And she felt cold all over thinking that the princess maybe still wanted Griffin and fearing that perhaps he could want her back.

"Zora." She looked. He continued, his voice soft. "You do know she used her magic on me, right? She manipulated me."

Zora looked down, unsure what he meant to say with that. "Yes." She had no idea why Alegra had helped him and perhaps it was better not to keep thinking about it. "But let's start moving. I want to get that cup as much as you do. Even now."

"We have to wait to leave the castle. If they're after us, they must be on high alert right now. Let's give them some hours to start to slack. And there are a few things we can do right now. But before that, I thought you'd like to eat." He walked to a counter and took a cloth that was covering some bread and cheese. "I know this isn't great, but..."

Zora rushed to it. "I am starving. All I ate was what we had this morning, then a loaf of bread."

He chuckled. "Well, more bread for you."

The bread was fresh. "At least it isn't dry."

"I'm so sorry I let them catch you. You have no idea how bad I feel."

Zora shook her head. "I was dumb and careless. But it's over." She took a piece of bread and some cheese.

Making sure she had something to eat was sweet and attentive of Griffin. The fish that morning too. But this was someone who was desperate to get rid of his curse, who maybe would do anything for her to help him. Zora could understand it and why he'd lied to her, even if it hurt that he didn't trust her. And it hurt so much to lose that thin spark of hope that she had carried for her valley. But maybe even she had known that it sounded too good to be true. As to Griffin, Zora had better not get any ideas in her head or feelings in her heart, even if he stared at her with that attentive, concerned look.

Everything was falling apart. Crumbling. And Larzen had no way to fix any of that. He opened the door to his quarters feeling exhausted. A flame on a lamp flickered in a corner.

Odd. His office had been dark when he left. His eyes moved to the other corner, where, in an armchair, Riadne was sitting. Instinctively, Larzen touched the hilt of his dagger. That was beyond dumb. Since when he'd been scared of one single lady? And then, maybe there were good reasons for him to fear Riadne, but a dagger wouldn't solve anything. What was he going to do? Cut magic?

"What do you want?" His voice didn't sound half as harsh as he wished.

She showed the palms of her hands. "Peace. I'm conceding defeat. I want a truce. Whatever you people call it."

"Are you going to fix Kiran? Not sure you noticed but I have a problem here."

"That's not my fault. I didn't do that. Not sure you noticed but he's been threatening me too."

Larzen did recall the way his older brother had held her throat, her slight look of panic, and how she'd run. But still. "I don't know. You might be trying to get my sympathy."

"I am. I saved your brother, in case you didn't notice that either. Wasn't that what you wanted? I did my part. Now let *my* brother go and I'll leave never to bother any of you again."

Larzen crossed his arms. "Oooh. Tempting." He looked up, as if he were thinking. "Let me see... You drove my older brother mad, you're about to have us tearing ourselves apart, and now I let you go. What do I get with it?" He scratched his chin. "Hum... let me see... Nothing." He glared at her. "You think I'm stupid?"

"I saved your brother. I didn't have to. It was a gesture of goodwill. Ideally, I should have been smart and asked you to release Lukas before saving Griffin. Silly, stupid me."

"Your gesture is appreciated, Riadne. But now you need to fix Kiran."

Riadne got up. "There's no fixing, don't you see? I can't do that and I'm starting to fear for my life."

"One reason to be motivated to solve this mess."

She chuckled bitterly. "You don't understand. Eventually I might have to use my magic to save my life. Eventually other people could get hurt. Would you like that?"

That was likely true. The guards had blocked Kiran from going after her. Could she ask them to kill him? Maybe. But Larzen still had a bargaining chip and planned to use it. "Sure. Except for the part where you're supposed to get us all to kill each other. And that other part where I have your brother."

"I don't want to get you all to kill each other. I stopped Kiran from killing Griffin! These things, these prophecies... I don't know. Some of us believe that it's all written, that life is not a straight line but a circle, and that you can find the end in the beginning. It's all there. I wanted to challenge that. I wanted to change things. But I don't even know how much of it is true. I do hate your kind for what was done to us. I hate you all, from the bottom of my heart. But I gave up. I just want to leave and enjoy the rest of my days in peace. The way Kiran's acting, that's not my doing. Yes, I got him jealous, but there's something else going on there. I don't want to deal with this. I'm done. I just want to leave."

Compelling. All she wanted was to walk away. Except that he knew she was a manipulative liar, and this could be part of her plan. "I need to trust you, then. Trust you that you won't try to hurt us anymore. And I still need to find a solution for Kiran, so maybe you can help me. How about you tell me who you are and why you're doing this. Let's start with some trust."

Riadne snorted. "Right. I'll give you something without anything in return. I have no idea how I always thought you were the smart one."

"You're very observant. Now ask for something else. Not your brother's freedom, that won't do. Not yet."

Glaring at him, she raised her hands. "Whatever. If your older brother dies on his wedding night, don't say I didn't warn you."

She was about to walk past him to the door when he grabbed her arm. "Resorting to threats now?"

"It's a fact. He wants to get married in five days. Unless he changes his mind and decides to put me back in the dungeon or kill me. I'm never sure these days and don't know which is worse."

There was a hint of fear in those eyes, but then again, Larzen could never be sure with Riadne. He shook his head. "Five days? How rude of you not to invite me."

She shook her arm. "Let me go."

"I can give you something you want. And you'll give me information, how's that?"

"What do you want to know?"

"Who you are and why you're doing what you're doing. Maybe then I'll trust you more. Maybe you'll convince me to let you walk away." No way, but he had to use her wishes.

"And you think you have something I could want other than setting my brother free?"

Larzen smiled. "Time. I'll give you time."

12

———

SEEING THE TRUTH

Eating while being watched was awkward, and it was ten times more awkward if it was Griffin with his overly-concerned look, compounded with his shirtlessness. But Zora was hungry.

He looked at her and chuckled as if seeing something funny.

"What?" she asked.

"When we met. You attacked me. You said it was because you were hungry?"

That was an embarrassing memory. "Part of it."

He had his heart-stopping smile. "Well, then you've come a long way."

Zora caught a breath, then looked down. "I didn't have my sword tonight."

"You had a sword." He pointed to the weapon she had grabbed in the room.

"True. Do you want me to threaten you?"

He chuckled. "Maybe." He then got serious and stared at her. "I'm sorry for lying. Really."

"You have nothing to be sorry for." Of course she understood people's need to lie. She just had to remember not to trust him. "Can we get started?"

"Yes." He moved to one of the counters in the room and took a leather book. He opened it and showed a page where an older, partly ripped piece of paper had been glued.

It read:

In each generation one son is open to the darkness.

The darkness has been contained within the royal family. Held back until they come of age.

To be undone, a champion must wield the Blood Cup.

Not anyone, but the winner of an open contest for strength, courage, skills, and smarts. Sealed with a blood sacrifice.

The champion will find the cup and undo the magic embracing the darkness.

It was so vague... "There's more, right?"

Griffin paused, as if surprised. "No. This is it. Apparently it has been copied and preserved for hundreds of years."

Zora's stomach lurched. Hundreds of years. And yet nobody had ever reversed this curse. "Do you know who wrote it? And how long ago?"

"Apparently it was about four hundred years ago."

"Like the Dark Valley."

He nodded. "Yes. Something happened then. And that's why... Maybe I thought... But it wasn't honest."

She was trying to understand how this little piece of writing was going to help her find the cup and hoping this wasn't all they had. "I assume people who won the games and tried to get the cup have written more information, right?"

"They all died in the last challenge, or before, due to

illnesses or something. There was once a winner who was not a prince. He died after the competition."

"Murdered."

He shrugged. "I suppose."

"And..." Zora sighed. She understood that he'd clung to that piece of paper as his only hope. By the Light, she understood the need for hope, even pointless hope. But the idea that his hope could be pointless brought her another pang in the chest. And yet, she had to ask, "How are we going to find the cup?"

"*You* will find it." He got up. "I actually have something."

She was thinking maybe he had some map, something, but he pointed to a basin with some water. "This is a truth basin. It's quite rare. You can use it. Peer into it while asking where the cup is, and it will show you the answer, or at least a clue. But you need to be calm and clear your mind, or it could interfere with the answer. You might want to try it tomorrow, when you're more rested."

"I'll just be anxious, Griffin. I know you think I obviously don't care about this cup, since it's only meant to reverse your curse, but I do care, and I want to find it."

"I never said you didn't care."

She rolled her eyes. "Sure. That's why you had to tell me it would free my valley."

"I'm not proud of it and I apologized."

"I just meant to say I'm not gonna be able to sleep without any hint whatsoever to where this cup is."

He kept staring at her. "Eventually sleep catches you. I know it from experience."

"Let's do it. If we can do it now, I want to see it now."

Griffin took a bottle with a silvery liquid and turned to prepare the basin, his bare back to her. And it was silly that she felt awkward or felt something just because he wasn't wearing a shirt. It wasn't that much different from his usual bare arms. She'd better stop thinking about that and focus on the cup. But that *was* something she wanted. Seeing Griffin finally free from his curse, his fear, his lingering, subtle sorrow would be worth anything. And maybe it meant she cared about him more than she should, but there could never be anything wrong in wanting someone to stop suffering, even if their paths were to part eventually. She wanted that cup, and this time there was nothing selfish or superficial in her want.

"Think you're ready?" There was some plea and urgency in those beautiful, dark eyes.

"I am. What do I have to do?"

"Stare at the basin while thinking about your question. In most cases, the black liquid will form some kind of figure which will give you the answer."

Yikes. Zora didn't like the vagueness in that.

He continued, "In some cases, you can have a vision. It's some form of truth and relates to what you're thinking."

Zora took a deep breath, while repeating mentally, "Where's the cup?"

The dark liquid was thicker than the clear one, which was probably water. She tried to squelch her fear that it would only give her a vague clue. No, she was going to get her answer about the location of the cup and the right way to find it. As the black liquid moved in the water, she thought that it looked like a squid, at least the ones she'd seen in pictures. No, she had to relax instead of trying to force images out of that basin. She just looked, while thinking about finding the cup, looked at the black liquid swirling in the basin without trying to make anything happen.

She felt herself lying down, soft grass beneath her back.

Griffin was on top of her, and it felt good to feel his chest against hers, his skin against hers, the way they moved in unison. His eyes were unfocused, his breath ragged, and... Their hips were moving. Together. No fabric between them. Completely united. He was... She could feel... Zora trembled and fell backwards. She hadn't been expecting that. Hadn't been prepared for that.

"What's wrong?" Griffin was kneeling by her. Shirtless.

"Nothing." She was breathless as if it had been real.

"You're staring at me as if I were a monster. No, worse than that. What's wrong, Zora?"

She didn't know what to say and had no intention of ever telling him what she'd seen. "The vision... it felt real and... it was overwhelming. That was all."

He got up and put his hands on his head. "It's not gonna work. Is that it? Was that what you saw? That I'd be transformed forever?"

"No. No. It was just me. Lying down. And it felt strange."

He shook his head and crouched. "Zora, please don't lie to me. You said it yourself that it hurt to have hope awakened then taken away from you. Don't do this to me, don't make me wonder what's going on. I might go insane."

"It was nothing. Nothing. Had nothing to do with the curse. Nothing even to do with the cup, if you want to know."

"You're trembling."

"I was taken aback. But it was personal. I assure you, it had absolutely nothing to do with your curse or the cup. Nothing. But it bothered me and I'm not going to say what it was."

He crossed his arms. "Zora. This is important for me."

"It's not about you. At all. So it doesn't matter." Except that it had definitely been him lying over her, his skin bare against hers, his...

His voice snapped her out of those thoughts. Kind of. "Weren't you thinking about the cup?"

"I was." At least she thought so. Now all she felt was that the room was getting terribly hot and stuffy. She had to focus back on the cup. "Maybe I can try again?"

He shook his head. "You're never supposed to ask the same question twice, and you should wait at least a few days before asking something else."

"I'm sorry. I swear I was thinking about getting the cup, I swear."

He rolled his eyes. "Clearly."

"We'll figure out something."

"Yeah."

His voice was dry and he was visibly annoyed. But it wasn't Zora's fault. For sure she hadn't chosen to go to that basin and experience something she wasn't ready for.

He added, "We'd better rest." He then sat on the bed. "Do you mind if we share? It's big enough."

Right. After the hammock, they were in co-sleeping arrangements. The vision came back to her and she trembled, imagining what could happen this time.

Before she replied, he said, "Nevermind. I'll get a corner on the floor."

"No. No, it's fine." He didn't want him to know what she'd been thinking. "It's not like it means anything. It's not as if we'd... And not as if, as if..." She had no clue what she wanted to say, and shrugged. "It doesn't mean anything."

He had a half smile. "Of course. Nothing at all. But I can still sleep on the floor."

"Don't be silly. You'll need to be well-rested tomorrow."

"As long as you don't mind..."

"I don't. It's a big bed and it's not like we even need to touch or anything. There's enough room."

Zora lay down but she could feel the mattress move when he lay beside her and her heart sped up. Sleeping together was something she hadn't even done with Seth, and with Griffin, the previous night was in a hammock, which was technically worse, since it had less space, but... being on a bed... after her vision... Still, it wasn't right to make him sleep on the floor. It wasn't as if he'd try anything.

She was still trying to figure out what that vision had been about. Basin of truth? Was that her future? But shouldn't it have more to do with the cup? Perhaps it had been his fault, being half naked and all. Perhaps a part of her was considering that doing the one thing a prince would want with her could be worthwhile. He was good looking. Gorgeous, in fact, and had the best kisses ever. Still. She was certain that the biggest part of her found the idea terrifying. And like that, with no warning, no foreplay, it was disgusting. Not that he was disgusting.

"Zora?" Griffin asked, almost as if he guessed she'd been thinking about him.

"Yes?" She kept staring at the rough stone ceiling, her cheeks burning.

"I was rude just now. I know that the basin can be strange, and I knew there was a chance it wouldn't work."

She moved her gaze and saw him leaning on his elbow, staring at her, his look apologetic. His ability to say he was sorry was something she admired and liked a lot, but he shouldn't be apologizing. "Well, considering you fear you might die soon, I think you've been taking it all pretty well."

"It's my life. Perhaps you'll understand. You dealt well with maybe being attacked by a shadow creature your whole life, haven't you?"

"Not always. I didn't like it when other people got hurt or killed. I wish things were different."

He sighed. "I wish I had done more when I could."

"Are you afraid? That we won't find it?" Zora was wondering if that cup was real, and maybe even that had been the basin's answer: there was no cup.

He plucked some lint from the sheet. "Does fear change anything?" He looked at her. "I'll keep going."

"Do you have any clue who caused the curse?"

"It's vague, but maybe yes. Let's leave it for tomorrow, Zora. It's late."

She wanted to reach out and hold his hand, or maybe reach out and hug him, comfort him, but on the other hand was really afraid of doing that while on a bed with him. Plus, she had no idea if he felt anything for her and didn't want to express more than he could reciprocate. What did she even want to express? She caught a breath. What was it? No, no, no. Zora couldn't be falling in love. Not yet. Not when there was so much to do. Not for a prince.

The Secret Room

There was something heavy on Griffin's arm and it felt numb. He opened his eyes and was surprised. Zora's head was in it. His arm was fine. More than fine.

With eyes closed, she looked so peaceful. He ran his finger through her hair, from her brown roots to the blond tips. He recalled then her horrified expression after peering into the basin of truth. It didn't bode well. At all. He really wished she could trust him and tell him what she'd seen. Meanwhile, he had important things to do.

ZORA WOKE up to the sight of Griffin by the bed, staring at her. At least he was wearing a beige cotton shirt. With long sleeves, a miracle.

"You had something to wear?"

He chuckled. "Last night? I do hate sleeves but it's not like I'm gonna lie just to remain shirtless. All I had was the cloak. But I got a few things this morning." He had a cheeky smile. "There's something I think you may like."

"Food again?"

He grimaced. "Old cheese and bread. But I have something better. Come and look."

She got up, making sure the cloak was well tied in the front, then, over a cabinet, she saw an object she had missed dearly; Butterfly. "You got my sword back! How?"

He had a satisfied smirk. "I've got some talents. And you haven't seen it all."

Zora felt her face heat, thinking about her vision, wondering what talents he was talking about, when she noticed her old clothes beside her sword. "You got those too! It was Irene, wasn't it?"

He nodded. "Yes. A couple of her guards, to be honest."

Everything was there. Her pants, boots, scabbard. She examined Butterfly to see if it had been damaged, but it looked fine, just slightly less enchanted than it should be. "I was afraid I'd never see my sword or my clothes again."

"I thought so."

She turned to him. "I'd go to the end of the world to

reverse your curse regardless, just so you know. You didn't have to do that. But this is nice." Way more than nice. It had been incredibly thoughtful of him.

He smiled. "I know." That smile that had always made her heart stop.

Her heart was stopping even more thinking that he knew exactly what would make her happy. Zora felt twice as guilty that she had no clue how to find the cup. She even wondered if her winning didn't count. But then, this whole thing was so incredibly illogical. Of course there was a big chance that there was no cup. Had the basin told her to stop worrying about the cup and spend her time doing better stuff? But it wasn't better. As long as he was cursed, nothing would be better.

An idea came to her. "Can't you look into your basin of truth? Find out where the cup is?"

He nodded. "I might. But I can't ask the same question. You're not supposed to, with this basin."

"I see." At least now she wasn't seeing as much. But then, his shirt had a large opening, and she could see some of his collarbone, which caught her eye. Well, last night she'd seen much more than that. Not as much as Alegra. For some reason the princess's voice came to her mind, saying, "You know what your problem is? You wish it were you."

Zora trembled. She recalled her vision and the feeling of grass behind her. "Griffin, I know where we need to go."

He raised his eyebrows in surprise.

"The temple," she blurted. "I mean, I don't know if we'll find the cup there, but we'll find something."

He grimaced. "Those ruins?"

"Yes." She had an odd certainty. "Yes, we have to go there."

"We'll go in a couple hours then, when there's a lot more

movement of servants in and out the castle. It will be easier to sneak out among them. Meanwhile, I have some books that I need to show you."

"It's weird that we're safe here, right under your brother's nose."

"This place is soundproof. Neat, right? And has a passage outside. But we'll need to prepare well. Coming back in would be quite dangerous."

"You did it this morning." She feared he had taken unnecessary risks for her.

He shook his head. "The package with your things was left right beside my exit. I barely went anywhere. And it was worth it."

Of course he had his heart-stopping smile. Griffin was definitely out to get her heart. She'd better focus. "You had some books to show me?"

He nodded and took a book with a green leather cover from a corner. "This is meant to be a legend, and it's very unclear, but it's about what happened right before we got cursed, in the year three hundred something."

"That's... when the dark valley was created."

He sighed and nodded. "I know."

These two things had to be related somehow, and yet she feared it was her stupid hope creeping up again, wondering if there was an easy solution for her valley, for her people's freedom. She opened the book and the first thing she saw was an illustration of a woman with dark wings. It reminded her of some of the tales she had read as a child, and how the Flying Witches were always the evil to be defeated. If only evil were as simple as that... She stared at Griffin. "But they don't exist."

"Don't they?" He raised his eyebrows. "That's what it says,

that they cursed the royal line. They also created the Dark Valley."

"Wasn't it my great, great, great, grandparents who created the magic of the dark valley?"

"It's what every book says, except for a few."

"Hum, creepy flying winged women. I can totally see how they'd blame them. We should have these stories in the valley. It would sure make us feel better."

He ran his hands through his hair. "Apparently they were all killed. For what they did to us."

"That's really dumb. Wouldn't they be the ones who could fix this?"

Griffin pointed at the book. "It says that they created the curse but also created the cup."

"Why would they create something to revert their own doing?"

"Perhaps some sick way to torture us? I don't know."

Zora glanced at the book. "I'm not gonna read it all now."

"It's pretty boring. It's mostly on how to kill them."

"Is there a special technique or something?"

He shook his head. "No. They can be killed like most people, you know? Heart, head, enough injury. But they hide in the mountains, dislike light, usually move in groups. I mean... It's basically about where they could be found, things like that."

There was something that came to her mind. "Can't they enchant people? By singing?"

"It's unclear. They had magical powers for sure. If they existed."

"Alegra."

He paused for a moment, then laughed. "Well, I mean, for one, she doesn't have wings."

Zora gritted her teeth. "I guess you would have noticed."

"Most likely."

It was like a knife in her gut thinking about the two of them together. Still, perhaps that princess could be one of those witches. "But she can sing and bewitch people."

"There are other magical traditions in the continent. My parents sent a master who had some of these books. The basin too." He pointed to it. "He was from Rock Island. Have you heard of it?"

Zora shook her head. It was weird because she thought she knew all the regions and kingdoms in the Continent.

"Few do. But this master, he was from there."

"Was? So he's dead."

His eyes were hard and glassy. "Executed. He killed my parents."

"Oh. I'm so sorry."

"It hurts because they brought him for me, to try to help me. Try to find some other solution." He sighed. "Apparently he got caught in some nonsense prophecy."

"And you kept it secret."

"Well, of course. I mean, you don't tell your subjects that you had a Dark Magic master. It's not that, he was a scholar, but still. And we didn't want to let people know the queen and king were murdered. If anything, people would start asking questions, you know?"

There was something she wanted to bring up. "Once, when I brought you to your room. Because you were sick," she added quickly. "There was a weird book about turning someone into some kind of animal."

"I know. I don't really understand it. It's what's called dark magic, meaning using the magic of darkness. But... I don't know, you lived in the Dark Valley and had none of that."

"None."

He shook his head. "It's all confusing." He then changed his tone. "We'd better start getting ready to leave."

"Can I redo the enchantments on my sword? It's quick. Give me yours too."

"I thought you needed a special place or something."

"I have some ingredients in my bag. All I need is a flat surface."

"Like here?" He pointed to the empty part of the table beside the basin.

It would be better if it were completely empty, but this could do. Zora laid down Butterfly, then took some sage, pepper, and lavender, spreading it over it, feeling their energy being absorbed by the sword. She was glad to see it shining with a powerful enchantment when she finished.

Griffin was frowning. "Did you just... make the herbs disappear?"

"The sword absorbed them."

He raised his eyebrows. "That's some screwed up magic."

"Everyone can do it."

"If you learn it when you're young, maybe. That's transmutational magic."

"That's an enchantment, and even six-year-olds can do it. I can teach you when we have some more time."

Griffin nodded, then passed her his sword. That was a long sword with a thick blade, very unlike the quicker, faster swords they used in the Dark Valley. When she took it, it weighed her hand down. "Wow, is this made of lead or something?"

"Iron."

"Why so heavy, though? You know the point of the sword is to cut your enemies, not hit them in the head and kill them with its weight?"

Griffin grinned. "It doesn't hurt to be multifunctional."

"Seriously, now I get why you have arms like that."

"Like what?"

She rolled her eyes. "Thin and weak, obviously. You do know you can lift weights and practice sword fighting, you don't need to do both at once?"

He shrugged. "Multitasking is fun."

Putting the sword on the table took some effort. It was wild that it could weigh so much. She thought that she should enchant it to hit true and for speed. No idea how she'd make that thing have speed, but it was worth a try. It was just that she wanted to do something nice for Griffin, but wasn't even sure if he cared about enchanted objects.

He then added, "I got it when I was twelve. I thought... I don't know, I thought it would make me strong, or mean I was stronger. I named it Thunder."

Zora remembered his dogs. "You like meteorological events."

"It's this magnificent power of the skies. And yes, I was obsessed with watching storms at that age."

"Well, my sword is Butterfly and I named it when I was five. Because it was cute."

"It's a neat name. Fast and light. And I bet it was heavy for you back then."

"I guess."

She focused back on his sword, then decided to use just pepper and sage. She'd heard feathers could make swords lighter but he probably wouldn't want it to have a different balance. As the ingredients were absorbed, she thought about protecting him, making sure he was safe. Slowly, the sword started to shimmer. It got more brilliant than she had expected.

"It's ready."

He took it and looked at it. "Why is it blue?"

"I don't know. The metal underneath, the size. The color varies."

"It's... flashy."

Perhaps he didn't like it that maybe it would shine and draw attention at night. She tried to explain why it wasn't so bad. "Dark creatures find us because of our smell, so it makes no difference if our swords glow or not. If you want to move stealthily you can use a dagger or something, not walk with a sword in hand."

He raised an eyebrow. "I'm not complaining. I find it unique." He took it and put it aside, together with some of his things. "Let's start preparing, then. I got your bag back, so I think you have most of the supplies you need. I'll bring the bread with me. I also have a wig and an over-jacket for you."

"That's how we're going to sneak out in plain daylight." She had been thinking how they would do that. His plan sounded decent, or at least decentish.

He nodded. "I got a wig too.

She smiled, wondering what he'd look like with different hair. "That's gonna be interesting."

"I just gotta do one thing before we leave: I'll peer into the basin."

It made sense. "Yes, maybe it will give us another clue or better instructions on how to find the cup."

"Maybe. But I'll ask a different question."

13

ZILILEMONIA

Larzen observed as Kiran spoke to the healer.

"Zililemonia?" His brother made a disgusted face.

The healer nodded. "Unfortunately, yes. But she would like to see you. As long as you're careful and don't get close..."

Kiran waved a hand and snorted. "No, thanks. How long until she's good again?"

"Ten, fifteen days."

"Let me know."

Larzen approached his brother with an innocent and curious expression. "Something wrong?"

Kiran grimaced. "Are you here to ruin my life? To protect Griffin?"

"I just want to know what's happening."

"The golden snake is sick. We'll have to postpone the wedding."

Larzen was taken aback. "Snake?"

His brother snorted. "C'mon, we all know what she is."

"Yet you still want to marry her."

Kiran stared at his nails. "Not sure. It depends on what her face looks like after this zili thing. She could get all blotched."

"Isn't it wiser to cancel the wedding?"

He waved a finger. "No, no. Linaria is a good ally. She might be a snake, but it's still a golden snake."

"Why would her face make a difference, then?"

Kiran grimaced. "I'm not getting an ugly wife. Now you, shoo. You're annoying me."

"Kiran, you have to realize that if she's a liar, it's possible our younger brother is inno—"

"Don't you dare defend him. Don't you dare defend him." His finger was one inch from Larzen's face.

"I just want to see you happy."

Kiran smirked. "Liar. But nice try." He turned around and walked away.

Larzen clenched his fist. He didn't appreciate being threatened and his patience was waning. His brother had no idea who he was dealing with. The upside was that Kiran had bought the lie about the disease and, as predicted, wasn't even going to see his betrothed.

He walked to the small room adjoined to his, from the time the royal family kept a servant with them at all times. Riadne was sitting on the small bed, arms crossed.

Larzen was surprised she was still there. "You didn't run?"

Riadne rolled her eyes. She was dressed in simple servant's clothes and somehow still managed to look breathtaking. "Don't be ridiculous. You know you've got me tied with invisible chains. Happy?"

He glared at her. "Opposite of happy and you know it. But your wedding was postponed. That will give you some time to come up with a solution for Kiran. And to tell me who you are."

"I didn't lie. My people live in the mountains between Gravel and other kingdoms. You know, Linaria, Kentosa, and Saral, but mostly on the Gravel side. Very few of us remain. We are dwindling."

"And what does it have to do with me and my brothers?"

There was a hardness in her eyes. "Your ancestors killed us."

"I'm sorry. Really. But why do we have to destroy each other? What's the point? Is it gonna turn back time or something?"

She looked away. "It's a prophecy. It will end our suffering."

"What suffering?"

"You want too much information at once." She was testing his patience.

"Riadne, this is not a game."

She got up. "Why don't we do something nicer? Your family also burned our temples and libraries. We lost all our knowledge. But I believe some of it was kept. Help me find books written by my kind."

Larzen looked up, as if thinking. "I think I'll ask the librarian tomorrow to find books by some mysterious people. It surely won't be hard."

She laughed, then shook her head. "You probably know about these books. We don't write in words. It's triangles and circles. It would look like some nonsensical drawings to you. There's nothing in the foreign section in your library; I already looked. But I doubt you don't have anything more."

Chills ran down his spine. He had heard about books like that, with lines and drawings. Griffin had once sneaked into a locked section in the library and told him about it. They were locked away for a reason, as they were considered powerful magical artifacts, and extremely dangerous. Riadne could be playing a much more dangerous game than he'd given her credit for. But he wanted to know more about her, so he pretended not to know the horrific type of book she was referring to. He only asked, "Why should I do that?"

"Didn't you want to know more about my people? Well, so do I. Help me, then." Her brown eyes were wide and pleading. She was great at looking innocent.

Larzen sighed and shook his head. "I don't mean your past. I mean now. If I understand your motivation, and if I understand why you might change your mind, maybe I'll let you go."

Riadne snorted. "Maybe. Now listen, the past and the present are a circle. They're two sides of the same thing, feeding on each other. In this case, the past is the key." She looked down. "Perhaps there's another way for us to stop suffering."

"You mean a way not to have us destroying each other."

"Yes."

He was trying to get information from her, and he thought it would look better if he seemed interested. "Would that book teach you how to fix Kiran?"

"I don't know. Perhaps it could help me find a way to enchant him and calm him down? Maybe."

He narrowed his eyes. "Or maybe you're going to do some dark magic and kill us all."

"Nope. You have your answer to that. My brother's still in the castle."

"I mean after you leave."

Riadne exhaled in annoyance. "You heard me. I wanted to make you destroy each other. It might be mathematically impossible, and I might not have considered that. It also might be impossible because I can't get through to Kiran or you. Not even Griffin, recently. I can't do it."

"So you'll quit and everything's fine?"

"Nothing is fine. But maybe there was a reason I came here, and maybe it was not destruction, but answers."

Convincing, compelling, but she could be playing him. "You need to make me trust you first. Then, maybe."

Riadne glared at him. "Don't make me angry, Larzen. At some point I'll give up on negotiating." Lovely. Showing her true colors.

He smirked. "And risk your brother's life?"

"You need to show me some goodwill. So far all you've been doing is asking, and asking, and asking."

He shook his finger. "Not true. I kept your secret. You're an impostor, Riadne. How quickly you forgot that. You could be facing a trial now. I could send you to Linaria to be judged for kidnapping the princess. I've done none of that. Yet. I also gave you time away from Kiran. You know why? Because revenge doesn't suit me. It won't solve my problems. But any other person in my place would want to see you dead."

She sighed. "So grateful. Touching, really. I saved your brother."

"From a handful of guards? You think he couldn't escape?"

"I don't *think*. I'm sure. The girl is an above-average fighter at most." She narrowed her eyes. "He'd die trying to protect her— and you know it."

"You think he's in love?"

"I think he's a fool. Very different."

This conversation wasn't going anywhere he wanted, and he had an idea. "Riadne, I'll consider finding these books of yours. But again, I need to trust you. Let's calm down. I'll bring a meal, a bottle of wine, and we'll talk."

"I never talk while chewing." She was definitely determined to test the limits of his patience.

"After eating."

She stared at him for a moment, then smiled. "Oooh, exciting. Do you always invite your prisoners to creepy dates?"

Insufferable. If he could describe Riadne in one word, that would be it. But Larzen kept his calm and smiled. "You're not my prisoner. And I don't see what's creepy about it. And it's most definitely not a date."

She raised her arms close together, as if they were bound. "Invisible chains are still chains. It's creepy because I'm not in a position to say no. And a man and a woman eating and drinking wine is always a date."

His patience was running thin. He raised an eyebrow. "Would you rather I use torture to interrogate you?"

"Instead of what? Charm?"

She was exasperating. Larzen sighed. "Friendship. Communication. Openness. Tell me more about the suffering of your people. Maybe I can help you."

"Get me the book."

"First explain why you need it. And for the record, a date is when both the man and woman look their best and you expect eventually there will be some... kissing. Which we both know is not the case here."

She chuckled. "Are you kidding me? I look magnificent. I doubt you'd refuse to kiss me."

"Considering everything you've done, considering you're engaged to one of my brothers and slept with the other, it's obviously a no, Riadne."

Her brown eyes locked on his and she smiled. "Oooh, so it was a yes before. How cute."

"In your dreams, maybe. I've got taste."

"And is it sweet or sour? Maybe bitter?"

Some nerve she had to act playful towards him. But it was

better to make her think he was falling into her trap. He just smirked. "It's something you'll never find out. And you know what? I won't get you any book. Just find a way to fix Kiran. If you're thinking I'm not capable of ordering people killed, you got me all wrong." He turned to leave.

"I never said no," she said.

He stopped. "To what?"

"Your creepy date."

Larzen turned back to face her. "What's creepy about it?"

She stared directly at him, posing a challenge. "Let's find out, shall we?"

As Griffin poured the dark liquid into the basin, Zora shuddered remembering her vision. She wasn't even sure if it had been right. Was that what it felt like? At least he was fully dressed now, not that it changed much. He looked good all covered up, like in the first ball when he'd felt sick.

She could feel her heart beating, eager for an answer, for something to give them a direction, or maybe dreading the kind of answer he could get. Then again, perhaps they shouldn't trust a magical object that much. He was asking if the cup could reverse his curse. Zora wouldn't know what to do if the answer wasn't *yes*, and even her bones chilled with the small possibility that it could be the case.

He stared at the liquid as she looked at him in expectation. It felt as if he stood there for an eternity. An agonizing eternity. Eventually, he peered closer, fists clenched. Zora caught a breath. It couldn't be, it couldn't be. Perhaps she could still convince him to ignore whatever this crazy, perverted basin told him. Then, after a few seconds, his posture relaxed. That had to be good. Then he turned to her, and there was something different in his face. His eyes were not his usual concerned eyes, but there was a certain calm, confidence, and maybe he was seeing something else because it was as if he'd been looking at something wondrous.

"Griffin?" She didn't know if he was alert or still having some kind of vision.

"Zora." He chuckled as if in relief.

His eyes were brilliant, that was what was different, and he managed to look even better than ever, as if it were possible. Still, that stare was slightly uncomfortable. "You saw something funny?"

He was still staring at her as if noticing something amazing for the first time, then smiled. "Something good."

That made sense. It was not that he was seeing anything in her. He was relieved and happy that he'd get rid of his curse. "So the cup will work?"

He chuckled and nodded.

"What was it? The vision?" Zora was dying to know it.

He stared at her for a few seconds, then said, "I'll tell you when you tell me yours."

"I guess I'll never know, then."

"One day you will." He stared directly at her.

Oh, no. There was something... Could it be that his vision had been similar to hers? "Why? Does it have anything to do with me?" It felt presumptuous to ask that, but she had to know.

He smiled. "Why would you think that?"

Zora was an idiot. Of course she wouldn't be in his vision. She shrugged and spoke fast, "No reason. But you're saying one day I'll know, and... you're staring at me, and—"

"Hey, it's a fair question. I'm just wondering where you got the idea."

"It was stupid, nevermind. And I don't want to know what you saw. If you're saying the cup will work, that's all that matters." It was true.

His eyes were intent on hers. "Lots of things matter. But we can start by getting the cup."

She'd better stop trying to guess what he had seen and focus on what they had to do. "Let's go, then."

CREEPY DATE. It was not creepy. And most definitely not a date. Riadne was perhaps out to seduce Larzen, but the question was why she thought being obnoxious and rude would accomplish anything. In fact, considering he had her brother, she should be a lot nicer and more compliant. Well, it was true she had saved Griffin and perhaps he should give her the benefit of the doubt. Right, doubt. As if he hadn't heard with his own ears that she wanted to get him and his brothers to kill each other. As if he hadn't seen the damage she'd done to Kiran and Griffin.

But there was a method to his actions. Killing or punishing her would be useless without getting to the bottom of who she was, how much danger she presented, and how to counter what she'd done. The answer was easy. Just a few drops of serianty. Although bitter, it could be imperceptible in the right wine. It wasn't like a potion that could force people to say the truth, but it gave the drinker a feeling of trust, calm, a feeling that in most cases would make a person open up and speak. This was his bet to crack Riadne's secret. He doubted she'd confess anything if he threatened her brother or with any other harsh method. She would just make up lies. But serianty, wine, and some charm, that could work.

He knocked a few times on her door but there was no answer. Great. He pushed the door open and saw Riadne sitting at the small table in her servant's quarters.

"You didn't hear me?" he asked as he turned to pick up a tray with food, which he put on the table.

"I did. Why?"

"You could have answered." He went back to the small corridor and picked up the wine.

She twirled a lock of hair. "I thought men liked to be the ones to open doors."

"Riadne." He closed his eyes. "You do realize there's nothing romantic in this, right? It's two people with mutual interests trying to reach an understanding and help each other. And you've been involved with my brother. It would be quite awkward."

"So you gave it some thought."

Larzen exhaled and tried to keep his cool. She wanted to play, he'd better play. He smirked. "What if I did?"

He placed the bottle on the table and made sure to give her the cup with the serianty on the bottom.

She smiled. "Perhaps you're still wondering."

"I think *you're* the one who's wondering."

Riadne got up and whispered in his ear. "Of course I am."

Her voice sent shivers down his body, and this was so, so, wrong. She had ruined his brothers, wanted to destroy his family, and yet he was wondering. It could be nothing, just a onetime thing. Why not? Sure, she'd been with his brother, but why not? Well, duh, because he'd be falling into her trap. Larzen stepped away from her. "You do realize we're alone here and you don't need to whisper, right?"

"Can I scream here too?"

"Don't worry. If I decide to torture you, it will be in the dungeon."

She sat down again and crossed her arms. "You're so boring."

"Boring or not, I have your brother and your book."

She glared at him. "Yes, start by threatening me. That will make this dinner pleasant."

"I'm not threatening anyone, just reminding you why it's in your interest to be my friend."

He poured the wine and uncovered a platter with several thin slices of different meats and some cheese. He'd picked it because it was easy to bring and also because he'd noticed she liked those platters. Her smile confirmed it had been the right choice. They ate in silence. She was beautiful to watch eating, if he ignored the fact that she was probably evil and out to get him. And had ruined Griffin's life. Well, some of it had been his brother's own doing. Larzen wasn't sure he could blame him.

"So, where did you grow up?" Larzen asked when he noticed she had finished.

"We have houses in the mountains, but I went to Linaria when I was twelve. I worked in the castle. It's a fairly isolated kingdom, with few visitors. It's a good place for my kind."

"And what's your kind exactly?"

She smirked. "We're the insanely good-looking people of the mountains."

"No doubt you'd call yourselves that, but what do other people call you?"

Riadne looked down. "If they don't know we exist, they don't call us anything, do they? We are the people who live in the mountains, that's it."

"But how could we have killed you if we didn't know you existed?"

"The past is buried in mystery, isn't it? Sometimes we think we know it all, but all we get are bits and pieces. We see only ruins, never the whole building, and then try to make up a story with it. What I mean is… I need more pieces. That's why I asked for your help."

It looked like the drink was starting to work on her.

"You seemed very certain we had to kill each other. For a specific goal."

"You must have misunderstood me." Her eyes were calm and her tone sweet. "I was never certain of anything. I just thought it was worth a try, but I didn't realize how hard it would be. Have you ever seen anyone you love dying?"

"My parents." He felt a bitter taste in his mouth.

She sighed. "With us, most of us, at some point in our lives, and it can be when we're eighteen, twenty, but more often than not at twenty-four or later… We get sick. It's not… a peaceful sickness, but a horrible, horrible disease, a horrible way to die."

He wasn't sure if he believed her. "Have you sought healers?"

Riadne shook her head. "It's a curse. It's the darkness. The royal family here, your ancestors, they had dealings with the darkness, they cursed us. And it's said that the curse will end when the family destroys each other." She sighed. "Maybe it was foolish. I thought I could make it work. This thing… it causes so much suffering and pain, there's only one way out. I gave it to my older sister. I killed her, a dagger in her heart. A quick way to end unbearable pain. Can you imagine that?"

In a way, yes, and it was strange how much he understood

her. "I can. I really can, Riadne. I mean, perhaps not the pain, but the killing. I'm truly sorry you had to go through that."

She looked down. "It's over." Then she took a deep breath and looked in his eyes. "I see that whatever happens still hurts you." Her voice, her tone, her expression were full of compassion, understanding.

Larzen took a deep breath. "It follows me like a shadow. I never told this to anyone, and it has been gnawing at me, it's suffocating." Perhaps he shouldn't tell her, but if anyone could understand it, it was her. And he couldn't take this anymore, he had to tell someone. "I killed my parents."

Riadne didn't flinch or look at him with accusatory eyes. If anything, her eyes were still full of compassion.

He continued, "The worst part is... I'm not sure I regret it."

"You must have had a good reason." Her voice was soft, calming.

"Maybe. I was a curious child and found secret passages in the castle. There was one right to my parents' quarters. Not the bedroom, thankfully. This was recently, about two years ago. I was no longer a child, but... strange that I don't remember why I was there now. It had to do with a trip or something. I guess they had a surprise I wanted to find out. Well, it was a surprise for me. They were planning on poisoning Kiran and Griffin."

Riadne frowned in confusion.

He continued. "I know. Strange, right? Who would kill their own children? But it was because of some prophecy, for the greater good, and words I didn't even catch. There was a "magic master" in the castle, and apparently he had poisoned their minds, or at least my father's mind, who insisted that one son was enough to carry the line. But it was a horrible thing. What would you do in my place?"

"It must have been a hard choice."

He snorted. "It actually wasn't. I couldn't go to my brothers and ask them to hide or anything. I mean, how can you do that? 'Hey, brothers, mom and dad are planning on killing you.' Would they even believe me? And how would they feel? And I couldn't confront my parents. I kept thinking they'd just decide to get rid of Larzen, the troublemaker, and leave another one of us alive. Well, perhaps I *could* have confronted them, tried to talk to them, at least my mother. But... Again, so many things could happen. It was easy to do it. They had the vials with poison on one table, and their pitcher of water nearby. I knew they always drank at night and in the morning. From their conversation, I knew that the poison was clear and tasteless. I don't even know what it was. I just... I took the vials, emptied them in the pitcher, and filled them with water. I told myself I wasn't doing anything, just giving them what they meant to give my brothers."

Riadne was listening attentively. Perhaps it had been a good choice to tell her that. She understood. Larzen chuckled. "To be fair, there are some rare times when I regret it. But it makes it all so much worse. My first thought is not that maybe I shouldn't have killed my parents. You know what I think?"

"That you ruined your chance to be king?"

Larzen nodded. "Exactly. Then I think: well, not really. My parents would still be alive now. But then, sometimes, when I see Kiran, and I swear, he wasn't like that, when I see him over-reacting, treating the kingdom as his playground, I think, 'What have I done?' It's double the guilt. It means not only I have no remorse for my parents, sometimes I wish my brothers were dead instead of them. And I loved my parents. My mother, especially. We spent a lot of time learning about the world, other kingdoms. She always said I would need to connect Gravel with the rest of the world, represent us. I thought she meant that I should take that responsibility, you know? Now I understand what she meant. Perhaps she never wanted Kiran to be king. I just don't get why Griffin, though. He was her son. I don't get it, and I don't regret what I did. I don't regret it. That's the worst of all. When a tinge of regret crosses my mind, it's because I wish I could be king."

She tilted her head. "It's normal. Who wouldn't sometimes wonder what it could have been like? Who wouldn't sometimes covet more power? What you did is incredibly selfless, Larzen. You were guided by love for your brothers, not ambition."

He scoffed. "But I *am* ambitious, that's the worst part. I am. But I guess I thought about my brothers. And maybe I wanted some freedom from my parents. As sad as their passing was, since they died, even me and Griffin have been doing a lot more for the kingdom, have had the freedom to do things our way. Maybe I wanted that freedom. But can you understand now why it kills me to see my brothers fighting? Why it kills me to see Griffin almost killed? Why I hate you for wanting us to destroy each other?"

She stared at him for some time, then said. "You should hate me. Except you don't."

That was true. And it made no sense. He wiggled his fingers. "It's your magic thingy. How do you do it?"

"My magic doesn't work on you and you know it."

He snorted. "Right. You want me to believe that?"

"You saw it yourself." She shrugged and stared at her hand as she circled the rim of her cup with her finger. "But you can believe whatever you want."

"How did you do it? Why? Why would you pick Griffin?"

Riadne stopped and stared at him. "I didn't pick anyone. Perhaps *he* picked me. Have you considered that?"

"He's clueless with women, Riadne. It's all your doing. What I don't understand is why."

"No, no, listen. I was set on my plan, you know? Get you three against each other. And then we got involved and it got all messy."

"Do you like him?"

"I don't *dislike* him. I mean, in the end he was pretty rude, and I don't appreciate rudeness, but he was all right in the beginning."

"But you didn't love him."

"Loving is not something I'm capable of, Larzen. My heart is too shattered for that. But there are tons of reasons to get with a guy that don't involve love."

He leaned forward. "Did it feel good? To fool around with someone you wanted to see dead?"

Riadne leaned back and put her hands behind her head, as if stretching. "Felt great, actually. But that part was easy. Seeing him dead wasn't. He's an idiot who doesn't deserve a second with me, but he doesn't deserve to die either. Not like that, at least."

"How compassionate."

"Too much. What about you? You say I'm manipulative, which might be true, but what was your point in throwing the Dark Valley girl at Kiran? I saw you whispering, and you weren't interested in her. What was your goal?"

Opening up was scary, and yet it was what he wanted to do; tell her everything. For some reason he was starting to trust her, feel confident and calm in her presence, serene. Serene. Damn it. He then realized he had just told her his most private, darkest secret. He knew why it had happened, and should keep his mouth shut, but he couldn't. "You switched the cups."

14

THE TEMPLE

Riadne blinked. "Did I? But what difference does it make, if the cups have just wine?" Her smile contradicted her innocent tone.

Larzen's previous sense of trust and comfort was gone, now that he understood why he was feeling that way. How could he have been so dumb? But now he wasn't going to tell her anything anymore. Larzen shrugged. "No difference. It was just that I noticed it."

"Wonder how you realized it." She got up and walked to him. "What would you have done in my place?"

"So you're confessing?"

"That I switched two innocuous cups of wine? Maybe. An enemy invites you for dinner, what am I supposed to think?"

"I'm not your enemy."

"Right. You're my friend. Locking up my brother is sooo friendly. But I'll confess I sincerely hope there wasn't any poison in the cup, Larzen."

"What do you take me for? And of course I'm your friend. I

haven't told anyone about you. You know what would have happened if Kiran had found out your little secret?"

"No idea. I'm sure you haven't noticed it, but he's nuts."

"Because of you."

She waved a finger. "No, no. Not my doing." She then smiled. "But perhaps now we can be friends. After all, friends keep each other's secrets, don't they?"

"Absolutely. I mean, what can you do with a secret without any proof to support it? It can only serve to cement a friendship."

She took her cup "So cheers then. To friendship. And if there was nothing in the wine, I'm sure you can drink some more."

He stared at her. Like that, she'd ripped out his most guarded secret. So far he had gotten nothing from her. Riadne had this weird ability to play him like a fool. Which he was. And it seemed so effortless. As he tried to measure his next steps, he heard a knock on his door, which was close enough for him to still hear it. He almost feared leaving and letting her poison his cup or something, but he wasn't going to drink anymore. He walked to his room, opened the door, and saw Tania, who gave him an envelope.

There was a note inside, telling him that Griffin had been sighted. No idea how he'd escaped and why he was still so close to the castle, but Larzen had better get to him before Kiran did. At this point he was starting to think that there was no solution for his older brother, and the best he could do was help Griffin escape Gravel. At least for now. That would give him time to try to sway Kiran. But he had to do something and he didn't trust his younger brother's self-preserving abilities. He'd likely get himself killed.

Larzen closed his eyes. What about Riadne? Yes, there was

little she could do with the information she had, but he could never be sure. It was as if she was always one step ahead of him. He returned to his room, then went to the servant's quarters that he had given her.

She was sitting down, arms crossed. "I thought you had forgotten me."

Ha. As if she were upset or something. She was nuts. Larzen smiled. "Don't count your luck just yet. We're going somewhere."

"Out? Do you want to share Griffin's fate or something? Kiran will be furious if he sees us."

"He won't."

She rolled her eyes. "Planning on murdering me and dumping my body?"

Larzen chuckled. "You think I'd resort to something so violent, bloody, and complicated?"

Riadne shrugged. "One can never know."

"I don't want you to die."

"Then we need a serious conversation about you getting me that book. Maybe there's something there, a solution for our curse. Otherwise I might have a painful, horrible death in a few years."

"How dramatic." He didn't believe in her story.

"Larzen." There was something about the way she said his name that tugged on him. She stared at him. "It's true. I could start dying at any moment."

She sounded sincere, but he shouldn't trust her, he knew he shouldn't. "We'll discuss it later."

GRIFFIN with short brown hair and a long-sleeved shirt was an interesting sight. He still looked good, but he wasn't as easily recognizable. His room led to an area by the servants' entrance, from where they left the castle. Zora felt chills as she crossed guards, but it seemed to be true that they didn't look at them. The hard part was not having Butterfly with her. Griffin was carrying the swords in what looked like a sack of fruit or something, again not to draw attention.

Soon they were away from the city, and then they got their swords back.

"Let's keep our ears sharp," he said. "But we'd better be ready to defend ourselves."

Zora hoped it didn't come to that. They walked in silence, taking a path she didn't know. Griffin was different, there was a hint of a smile when he looked at her, there was a new lightness and confidence in him. She appreciated his light mood, but on the other hand, more and more she started to believe that his vision must have been similar to hers. When he stared at her with a glint in his eyes, all she could think was that he was imagining the two of them doing it, and it was unsettling.

After an hour, Rooster Peak appeared in the distance, as well as some of the top of the temple. Her hunch had better be right, or she would make a fool of herself. Worse, they'd have no clue what to do and where to go.

As they approached the temple, she felt a bitter taste in her mouth. It still hurt to remember seeing Griffin and Alegra's clothes, and it hurt even more to remember the way he'd acted towards her in the picnic.

His voice broke her thoughts. "You never told me what I said to you that day, that made you upset."

"You really don't remember?"

"I think Alegra did something to me."

Zora rolled her eyes. "She did a lot of things to you, didn't she?"

"I guess." He shrugged, then said, "I just never meant to hurt you, and I'm sorry if I did. And maybe I'd like to know what happened."

"Nothing much. You said I shouldn't be at the picnic because I wasn't part of the family, then you asked if I was sleeping with Larzen."

He grimaced. "Ouch. I swear I didn't think it was the case. You two weren't flirting or anything, and he didn't seem interested. But I was wondering what he was trying to do by bringing you. Perhaps part of me wanted to understand what was going on."

"I'm sure there are better ways to ask that."

"No doubt. I don't think I was myself. You might not believe it, but you've seen what Alegra can do. I'm sure she did something."

The mention of the princess annoyed her. Zora rolled her eyes. "Yeah, you're never rude. That's got to be some bewitching."

"I'm not rude." His frown then turned into a smile. "And you know it."

"Most of the time."

They were close to the ruins now. Zora tried to think, tried to understand what she needed to do, but perhaps she'd only recognize what she was looking for once she found it.

Griffin pointed at the door leading to the dungeon-looking part of the temple. "In there?"

"I think so." Zora had a cold feeling in her stomach and didn't know if it was fear of finding nothing or dread for whatever was to come.

They descended a set of decrepit stone stairs. Last time

she'd been here had been with Kiran, when she still had no idea what kind of person he was. All their previous interactions made her nauseous, especially the way he'd held her hand in the arena, when he was about to have his younger brother killed. But then, Griffin was alive, was here with her, and for that she was quite thankful. There was still a lot to do, but she'd face a thousand lions if that was what it took to save him, to make up for her mistakes.

They were in that room with cells with rotting metal bars and strange triangles on the wall. But there was nothing there. It was strange because she remembered these drawings as if they had some meaning, but they were just some nonsensical triangles carved in the stone. Circles too, now that she looked carefully. These were not carved, but had a different, rougher texture, as if they had been scraped with something.

As she tried to focus, she felt eyes on her, and a familiar chill in her stomach. Griffin was staring at her, not looking the least impatient or skeptical, more as if he was finding something fascinating to look at.

"What?" she asked.

He chuckled. "Nothing."

"Give me some time. I'll figure it out."

"I have no doubt of that."

He was still staring at her in that weird, unsettling way. It wasn't predatory, flirty, or sexual, but it looked as if he was happy and satisfied about something to do with her, and that was why she thought his vision might have been similar to hers. And it was a terrible idea to recall it then, as she remembered vividly his chest against hers. That was not what she was supposed to be thinking about; she had to find a clue to the cup, not think what it would feel like to...

Zora took a deep breath and looked at the wall again. Only

triangles and circles. If only there had been a door, something. Had her idea been foolish? She pressed her hand against the stone wall, feeling silly. A glance told her Griffin was not skeptical. If anything, it looked as if he trusted that she was about to find the cup or the way to it. She'd hate for his trust to be misplaced.

Zora closed her eyes. Should she feel something? Then she heard a feminine voice; *It's a puzzle, but there's a door.*

"Where?"

Just look. Look and you'll find it, that voice replied.

It had all been in her head, and yet, it felt real. She stepped back and looked at the triangles and circles, just looked. There were bigger circles in a line getting smaller and smaller, then getting big again. Zora moved to the small circle in the middle and saw that there was a groove around it. She pressed it—and fell down a trapdoor.

15

FINDING THE WAY

She fell on soft sand. At first she couldn't see anything, just darkness.

"Zora!" came Griffin's yell from above her, then a loud thud told her that he'd jumped down the trapdoor. "Are you all right?"

"Are you nuts? You didn't know how deep this was, and you could have fallen over me."

"I looked," he said. "I know what I'm doing."

There were tons of good reasons for him to have remained on the upper floor, including the possibility that there was no easy exit from here, but she was kind of glad he had jumped after her without barely thinking. It gave her a feeling of comfort and warmth in her heart. As bad as this fall had been, it was nothing compared to the way she'd been falling for him. Now that she thought about it, it was scary to be that vulnerable again. She'd better focus.

Thin rays of light illuminated parts of that secret room and her eyes started to distinguish more forms. The walls were also stone, and the ground was covered with dark forms. Oh, yuck.

Human bones and skulls. Zora turned around in disgust and Griffin wrapped his arms around her.

"Don't look," he said.

"But I have to."

The truth is that she'd love to spend a couple hours in that hug, but that was not why they had come to this place. She moved back, then turned around and tried to see what was in there other than the piles of human skeletons in the corners. Despite being much bigger than the room above, this chamber had no furniture or cells with bars. All that was in there were the bones of the past, of what would have been at least fifty people.

Beside her, Griffin sucked in a breath. "This... is horrible."

"Any idea who they were or what happened?"

"I don't even know what this place was."

Zora looked around. "It's as if this was a shelter of some kind, but they ended up trapped."

"A shelter should have two doors, though."

"Perhaps it does."

Zora had no clue what this all had to do with the Blood Cup, until she noticed that the far wall on the other side had more drawings. She overcame her disgust and unease and walked across that place where even the air smelled of tragedy and decay, even if any flesh had been long gone from the bodies.

That other wall had vertical lines and sets of drawings. Under one of them, there was a text in Continental: *The red chalice lies where the mountains bleed, from where life springs, where the hero will find.*

There was something foreign about that sentence, with some words missing. But then, *red chalice...*

Griffin was beside her and she said, "It's about the Blood

Cup. It's like a different name or something." She felt an odd certainty about that and wondered if their entire quest would be based on hunches that could turn out to be wrong. She tried to guess the meaning of the sentence. The only mountain chain in Gravel was in the west, near its border, so it had to be there. But where exactly?

"Any idea where the mountains bleed?" she asked.

He narrowed his eyes. "It could refer to many different things. The mountain range is huge. But maybe you'll figure it out?"

Sure. Zora, who had never seen a mountain up close, would definitely be the one to know the answer. But then, she had studied the geography of Gravel. Looking back, she didn't understand why they learned about it, why they learned about the Royal family and the kingdom. In a way, it helped them realize that there was a bigger world that they weren't part of, but it also made them yearn for more. It didn't matter now. She tried to recall the names of the peaks.

Not a peak, no, something else... She wasn't sure. To be fair, she hadn't studied the mountains that well, which made sense considering she'd never thought she'd step foot anywhere near them. "It's a place with a big hole, like an abyss." An image came to her mind. "It's like... a womb."

"The Void," Griffin whispered. "It's the largest chasm in the Gravel Mountains."

"You think we can go there?"

"Yes, yes. I mean, it's not an easy place to reach, but we're both good climbers."

"Are you going to be upset if I'm wrong?"

He shook his head. "We'll keep trying. These things... Something I learned about magic is that it's never precise, logical. So if this cup was made and stored using magic, we won't find a straightforward map leading to it. This way seems right."

Zora glanced at the bodies again. "I'm still wondering how they died."

"Protecting this secret, maybe?"

"Or maybe just hiding? Or maybe there are many secrets here. Have you seen signs like this before?"

He bit his lip. "There are a couple books safely stored away in the castle. But even I didn't have access to them. They said they contained dangerous magic."

"Right. That one book you were reading sounded so safe."

"True." He chuckled. "And we can never know if something's truly dangerous if we don't understand it. Anyway, it's not like we can return to the castle and check more books. We need to get to the mountains." His voice was soft now. "This won't be an easy journey."

"You think I'll quit or something?"

He shook his head. "I'm just... I'm sorry you got involved in this... In all of this."

"You'd rather I weren't here." The realization hurt.

"I would rather you were safe, and yet, that's a lie, right? I mean, I took you out of your valley. I wish I could find a solution without you, that's all. I wish you didn't have to do this for me. But I'm thankful you're here. I really am."

Zora forced a smile, then looked away. It felt as if he were poking at her with something sharp. She liked to be around him, and that was obviously not how he felt. At least he was being honest.

She tried to change the subject. "You should have stayed up there. Then you could have reached down a hand for me."

"I know what I'm doing, Zora."

As they reached the sandy part where they'd fallen and

she looked up, her stomach lurched. "It's closed."

"Obviously. Perhaps... Perhaps they were trapped here." His voice had no hint of fear or worry.

"Is there a reason you are so calm about it?"

Zora's heart was racing. Yes, to be very honest, she would love to spend the rest of her life with Griffin, but this wasn't exactly what she had in mind.

"I can open it." He sounded so calm.

"Right. I guess all these people died because they missed a trick or something."

"They were killed," he said. "They were not just closed in here. If there was someone up there, they could trap them, or maybe they set fire down here or something."

"The bones are not charred."

"They could have been asphyxiated, not burned."

"You know many ways to kill people."

"I do." He then smiled. "I also know many ways to open doors."

Griffin climbed on the wall as if the grooves were deep enough to put a hand, then punched the stone where the trapdoor had been. It opened just a little, but he pushed it away, and pulled himself up. Then he reached down a hand for her. "Jump and grab it."

Zora did as he had told her, and was lifted out of the chamber.

Griffin had a half smile. "You should have more faith in me."

"That was impressive."

"Nah." He shook his head, as if disagreeing, but the spark in his eyes told a different story.

She had a feeling he enjoyed showing off. It reminded her of the first time she'd seen him when she thought he was saying "look at me, I'm a man, and so strong, and oh, so much better than you". There was some truth in that, just maybe not in the second part. Zora no longer thought he underestimated her, maybe just a little, but then perhaps she sometimes underestimated him too.

"What?" he asked.

"You like to show off, don't you?"

He paused for a moment. "Who doesn't?"

"I don't."

"Weird, because that was the first thing you ever did when we met. You pulled your sword on me, Zora."

She felt silly. "I already apologized, and I feel bad for that."

"I was never angry."

"Why? And how did you even let me defeat you? I mean, I'm thinking that you shouldn't be caught so off guard, right?"

"I'm a calm, reasonable person, in case you haven't noticed, and it takes a lot to make me angry. And I was distracted, yes." He then put a finger over his lips and pointed outside.

Zora heard faint voices from outside the temple. It didn't necessarily mean that they were after them, but it could be. She pointed to the trapdoor and whispered, "Should we hide there?"

"We need to run."

There was a hole in the ceiling, and Griffin jumped there, then reached down his hand for her. They were on top of the ruins now, and lay down so as not to be seen from afar.

Soon a clear voice came from below them. "They came this way." It sounded like Stavos. She'd have to ask Griffin later if that was really him and why the man was acting like that.

"Looks like they already left," another voice said.

"Let's search the area and the ruins," Stavos said.

At this point, Zora was sure the voice belonged to the

blond man. Annoying. He'd seemed so nice. But then, even Kiran hadn't seemed that bad at first. She wondered if they should try to run and looked at Griffin. He made a gesture with his hand as if he were pressing something down, which meant that they should remain there. Then he made a circle in the air with a finger. Right, they were surrounded and their best bet was to hope that they didn't see them lying on the roof. How many people were even there? Some twenty, if they were all around the ruins, considering she could still hear steps and voices around them.

Griffin was serious, focused. He unsheathed his sword slowly, silently. Zora followed his lead, her heart racing. She didn't like to fight real people and also knew she wasn't great at it. In a swift movement, Griffin got up, and Zora did the same. A guard advanced on his side.

Zora turned around, to watch the other side, and heard the clanking of swords and a grunt that wasn't Griffin's behind her. Soon she heard more steps and saw a guard advancing in her direction. As he lunged for her, she stepped aside and tripped him, then kicked him between his legs. It was mean, but it would assure he'd remain fallen for a while.

Two more guards advanced towards her. She didn't even have to glance back to see if Griffin was busy. First, based on the sounds, he was. Second, he'd probably come help her if he could. The guards hesitated.

"Two against one. That's unfair," she teased.

One guard attacked her, and she managed to disarm him. He still tried to hit her with his fist, but she moved her sword swiftly against his arm, causing a deep cut. She then crouched to avoid a blow coming from the other guard, who was then disarmed by Griffin. Zora stabbed his foot, then got up.

"Let's run," Griffin whispered.

The guards on the roof were hurt and fallen. Griffin led her to the edge of the temple and they climbed down, then ran to where some of the guards' horses were. They had three guards coming after them. It was better to turn and face them. Zora stopped and Griffin followed her lead. Two guards came at her at the same time, and she stepped back. One of them clashed his sword against Butterfly.

Griffin stabbed him in the stomach and the guard dropped his sword. The prince then took a horse and pulled her in front of him.

She asked as loudly as she could while still sounding natural, "How long until Sapphire Bay?"

That was not where they were going, but she wanted to throw off the guards.

"Less than a day," Griffin replied, keeping up the charade.

Would the guards fall for such a crude trick? Still, Griffin and Zora were clearly galloping in the direction opposite of the mountains, and that should also confuse the men who saw them running away.

She wanted to look back, but couldn't see much with him behind her.

"They're not following us yet," he whispered.

Zora was trembling. The sight of blood usually made her nauseous, and she felt guilty that she had hurt those guards who were probably just following orders. But she couldn't let them take Griffin or take her, or else they'd never get the cup.

"You fought well," he added.

"You were much better."

"Well, of course."

So conceited. Zora wished she could take back her words.

"But you're better than me against shadow creatures," he added.

That was true. And when they had confronted them in the Dark Valley, he had followed her lead and supported her. She took back her mental comment about him being conceited.

They kept galloping, going east, the opposite of where they had to go, until they reached a shallow river. He crossed it, then they dismounted, let the horse go, and turned north. The sun was setting on their left. They walked fast for about half an hour, then turned back to the west. That was a lot of extra walking just to lose the guards, but it was important.

When the sun was almost disappearing, he said, "Let's get that hammock up and rest."

Zora climbed a tree and set it up as fast as possible, so glad that Griffin had gotten it back. They ate some of that hard bread in silence, their ears peeled for any sound. Griffin then lay down and stretched out an arm, as if asking her to use it as a pillow. The vision came to her mind, then the memory of their kiss, but she was too tired, in too much shock, and plus, it didn't mean anything. Well, actually, now that she was that close and felt his warmth and his scent, it meant a lot. But it wasn't as if they were kissing. Perhaps she shouldn't have thought that, because he moved his head and nuzzled her face with his nose, his lips almost touching hers. This was a question, an invitation, just like her first kiss.

Zora wanted to kiss him back desperately, but she also didn't want to get hurt, and wanted to wait at least until his curse was reversed to make sure he wasn't doing it just so she wouldn't stop helping him. Perhaps she also needed to figure out what that vision had been, and maybe it was the vision and where this could lead that scared her. Zora moved her face down, between his neck and chest. She thought he'd get annoyed and push her away, or grunt in frustration, but he kissed her forehead and hugged her tight, as if she hadn't just rejected him. Perhaps it was a trick because now she really, truly wanted to kiss him. But there was so much they had to do, so much to figure out, she'd better not get even more distracted than she already was. And by the Light, Griffin was distracting.

LARZEN SMUDGED some soot on Riadne's cheek. The touch felt... good. He should have considered how intimate it would feel to touch her face, and he should have asked her to do it herself. She was probably getting a kick out of his reaction considering she liked to tease him, and perhaps she hadn't given up on seducing the three brothers. Larzen had to remind himself that she wanted him dead more often than necessary.

He stepped back and looked at her worn pants and jacket. "There. Now you look like a male servant. Sorry. I know it must feel bad to look ugly."

She rolled her eyes. "I still look magnificent."

Larzen chuckled. Yes, Riadne was beautiful—just not right now. "I guess it's a matter of taste."

They left through a secondary entrance and Larzen addressed a carriage driver. "I'll take this by myself."

She frowned and whispered, "They'll really think you'll be taking a servant around?"

"Of course not. You'll be the one guiding the carriage." He smiled. "I'll go inside."

"I might take you somewhere else."

He smirked. "You won't."

After stepping inside the carriage, he looked out the window to make sure they were really heading to the Mystic Ruins. With her, one could never be sure. Perhaps it was mean to dress her as a coach driver, but he figured it would draw the least suspicion.

When they approached the ruins, he signaled for her to stop and got out of the carriage. There was a cart from the royal guard with wounded guards on it. Coldness crept up on him. With so many guards and a confrontation, he doubted his brother had escaped. He approached a healer. "What happened here?"

"The fallen prince, your highness."

"Where is he?" Larzen feared the worst.

"Escaped. He's headed to Sapphire Bay."

"That will be enough," a cold voice interrupted the healer. Stavos. Larzen had told Griffin to sack the man the moment his parents were no longer there, but his younger brother hadn't listened to him. The blond man smirked at Larzen. "Your help won't be necessary."

"Forgetting to address me properly?"

Stavos shook his head. "No. I didn't *forget* it."

If Larzen didn't have more important things to do, he'd thrown that excuse of a human being in the dungeon. But he wanted some information, so he tried to make small conversation. "I guess you know where he's headed, then."

"Exactly. None of your concern."

Larzen took a look at the wounded. At least some six guards. Quite plausible that Griffin had defeated them all, perhaps with the help of the Dark Valley girl. She might have scratched a couple.

He took another look at Stavos. "I'll give you a piece of advice. My brother, his Majesty, tends to be quite moody. I'd bring Griffin alive if I were you. You don't want Kiran chopping off your head in case he changes his mind and no longer wants him dead."

"Quite moody." Stavos smirked. "I'd be careful too. What if he changes his mind about which brother he wants killed?"

Larzen had no idea how the man had gotten so bold, but just smiled. "Exactly. One more reason to bring Griffin alive."

As he got to the carriage, Riadne was still there, staring at her nails as if bored.

"Let's go back," he said. It was annoying that Larzen had missed his brother, but at least he had a clear direction as to where he had *not* gone.

"We should check the ruins," she whispered. "They came here for a reason, right?"

Could she be right? At first Larzen thought it had been a coincidence that his brother had been found there, and that maybe he'd chosen it as a place to rest and spend the night, but it wasn't a fast escape route from the castle, regardless of the direction he was going. Perhaps his brother wasn't escaping aimlessly, but looking for something.

"Right. Let's just wait for them to leave. Thank you. For the suggestion."

"We're friends, aren't we?" she said between gritted teeth.

Larzen laughed.

ONCE THE GUARDS WERE GONE, Riadne and Larzen stepped into the ruins. She had told herself many times that these ruins were unimportant and had nothing to do with her people, but her heart was beating fast, afraid of what she could find.

"Do you have any idea what he's looking for?" she asked.

"No, not really."

Riadne tried to remember what Griffin had been focused

on before everything happened. "What about the Blood Cup? Does he have it?"

"I... I don't know. I don't even know where we keep it, to be honest. I'd assume he didn't have time to get it, but it should be in the castle, shouldn't it?"

She chuckled. "You're asking *me*?"

"I'm thinking out loud. I'm not that dense."

"Huh, you guys host a competition for a prize and you have no idea where it is, forgive me if I have my questions."

As they stepped inside a chamber in the ruins, her legs trembled. The walls had their sacred writing. Nothing much, just a message that this was a temple of knowledge, with a secret door to a hidden chamber. She didn't want to show the chamber to Larzen, unless she had to, but having this writing here could be helpful. "See these marks on the wall?"

"I'm not blind, Riadne."

"Tell me what they are, then."

Larzen raised an eyebrow. "Triangles. Where are you going with this?"

"Look better. There's more."

He rolled his eyes. "Circles too, so?"

"It's my people's sacred writing. If you want to know where he's going, and I think you do, I can help you, but you know what I need."

"The book."

Riadne nodded. "If you want to find him, of course."

"It could be a coincidence they came here."

"Sure. But then, maybe not."

"You can read these signs?"

"Read is not the proper term, but yes, I understand them."

"What do they say?"

Nothing much. "I need more context, that's why I need—"

"The book, yeah," he finished her sentence.

She'd have to do more to convince him, especially because she thought that the answer was below them. Without much choice, Riadne pushed the button that should open a trapdoor, and it did. Larzen looked at her in astonishment.

"I'll go down and check," she said. "Stay here and push this circle when I call you."

"Are you sure?" He sounded worried for some bizarre reason.

"Oh, no. I think I'll fall down never to return again."

She narrowed her eyes, expecting a retort, but he shrugged. "Go on."

Perhaps it was risky to go down into a chamber and depend on Larzen to get her out, but he was clearly interested in keeping her alive.

Upon looking at the chamber, she felt as if her heart stopped. It wasn't that the bones surprised her, it was just that it hurt to think that people could be so cruel, that people had to die for no reason, just because they were different. So much pain, so much needless violence, so much injustice. She swallowed back her tears and they brought a bitter taste to her mouth. The taste of anger, a reminder as to why she'd tried to save her people. An unfortunate reminder that so far she'd been failing.

This had probably been another place where her ancestors had been massacred. Massacred. So unfair. At least it had some information. Riadne crossed the chamber and, on the opposite wall, saw texts with locations of other temples and an interesting part about a *red chalice*. She knew exactly where it was and where Griffin was headed. But she would only tell Larzen once she got her hands in one of her people's ancient texts.

16

THE ANCIENT BOOK

Larzen couldn't believe himself as he opened the safe in one of the most secure sections in their library. If he hadn't seen the signs in the ruins and hadn't guessed that maybe that writing could mean something for Griffin, he certainly wouldn't be doing this. He took the three books that were in the safe. They all had dark covers and no writing, just those strange symbols. He knew that there was a chance that Riadne could want these books to learn some dangerous magic and perhaps curse them all. But there was also a chance that she could help him find Griffin, and he still had her brother, Lukas. It was in her interest to help. Or perhaps Larzen was a fool. He'd been wondering about this more often than usual lately.

Riadne waited for him in the servant's room, still wearing those drab clothes. When she saw the books, her eyes widened like a child seeing a dessert. He almost changed his mind, but then, he'd known she was eager to get her hands on those texts. And then perhaps he also wanted to know what was in the books, wanted to know what she was, and wanted to be certain about what she wanted to do. Curiosity had always been his greatest weakness, and he truly hoped he wasn't dooming the kingdom with it.

Her lips parted when she opened the first page.

"What's it about?" He didn't hide his curiosity.

Her hand moved over a page. "History."

"And the others?"

She frowned. "A cookbook," she said as she held another book. Then she took the third one. "Poems."

Odd. "You can write poems with triangles?"

"I guess *poems* is not the right word. Inspirational messages or sort of."

"And... You think it will help you know where Griffin is going?"

She looked at the book. "This? No." She smiled. "But I already knew it in the ruins."

"And you didn't tell me."

Riadne shook her head. "Well, you had to give me something, right? If you let me keep them, I'll tell you."

"If I don't find him, I'm not releasing your brother, Riadne."

"Can I keep these books? Please?" It sounded like a sincere plea, with none of her usual bite. "I'm not sure what this Blood Cup is, but maybe the explanation is here. Maybe we could help Griffin."

He knew it could be a trick, but again, Larzen was curious. "Sure. And where is he?"

"Headed to the Gorge."

"I have no idea where it is."

"Wait." She put a hand on her head. The gesture was cute. No, nothing was cute about Riadne, who was an impostor and a potential murderer. She looked at him. "You have a different name. It's a hole in the mountains."

"A cave? There are many."

"A vertical cave."

"The Void." He frowned. "Why would we put the cup there?"

She raised an eyebrow. "You think your people are the ones who put it there?"

The question was a challenge, but he had no clue what the answer could be. "Who did it, then?"

"Perhaps my people."

That made no sense. "Why?"

She waved the book. "Perhaps the answer's here."

Larzen nodded. "Get ready, then. We leave when the sun rises."

"I have to go with you?" She blinked as if puzzled.

"Of course. I'm not letting you out of my sight."

"Well, as far as I know I won't be around you for the entire night."

He also could tease and play. "Why, you'd rather come to my room?"

She smiled. "What an interesting question."

Oh, no, he'd thought she would shut him down, and now he'd better not think about whatever she was implying. He tried to imagine her and Griffin to see if his thoughts would go away, but he could never imagine the two of them together. Still, thoughts or not, she didn't have to know about them.

He gave her a cold, controlled smile. "For you, maybe. I sleep with my eyes closed, so you'd be out of my sight regardless."

Riadne had a cheeky smile. "So I could spend the night anywhere?"

"As long as you don't escape or get in trouble, I don't care."

She extended both hands. "You still got your invisible chains around me, Larzen. So don't be paranoid."

Sure, as if it were easy.

Zora and Griffin woke up, had more hard bread, then walked towards the mountains. Her stomach was starting to protest and demand something more sustainable, but she just told it to shut up.

Griffin led them to the Border Forest, which was slightly north of where they wanted to go, but away from roads and rivers. The trees were tall here, and sunlight came in rays from between the foliage above. The ground had roots, rocks, and small vegetation, which made it hard to walk, but that was the point; horses wouldn't come here.

"Do you want to rest a little?" Griffin asked, that concerned tone and look.

"We rest at night," Zora whispered.

She was no longer in her difficult days of pain and blood and wasn't sure what it took to convince him that she didn't need more rest than he did. Plus, she didn't want to waste time. As much as she wanted to believe that the guards had been led astray and would pursue them in the opposite direction, she still felt uneasy, with the strange sensation that they were being followed, that someone would catch them, perhaps try to kill Griffin. At this point she started to believe that there was something incredibly wrong with Kiran that went beyond simple jealousy, but she wasn't going to say that to his youngest brother.

He then said, "I was thinking of climbing a tree and looking at the road. Just to make sure."

"Sure. I'll climb too."

They found an old tree with a thick trunk and rough bark. There were no branches near the ground, but there were some vines allowing them to move up. From a high branch, they could see parts of the road far below.

Zora turned to him. "You also think we're being followed?"

He nodded while staring down. "The thing is how many, and where they are headed."

"There are some villages by the road, right?"

"We'll avoid them."

They spent some ten minutes there, as if waiting for something. It didn't make that much sense because someone could have come in that direction when they were walking, but if they were sending large numbers, they'd see them. It didn't seem to be the case.

Griffin sighed. "Nothing so far. Let's continue."

Zora was about to descend when she thought maybe they could wait just a couple more minutes. Perhaps it was just some laziness after all that walking. "Not yet."

"You see something?'

She shook her head.

He looked down at the road, then. "Someone's coming."

Zora felt her heart beating.

Griffin continued, "It looks like just regular travelers. Two horses."

"It's nothing, then."

He stared at the road attentively, then caught a breath, as if surprised. "That's... that's Larzen. With..."

Zora looked and had no clue how Griffin knew it was the other prince. But then, had it been her sister walking on the road, would she recognize her from that distance? Maybe.

Griffin shook his head and bit his lip. "You see his companion?"

"Not very well..."

"Anything familiar about that rider?"

"No."

He still stared attentively, his brows furrowed. He shook his head. "Impossible. It makes no sense."

"What?"

"That's... That's Alegra."

Zora squinted, trying to see better. "It looks like a man to me. Poorly dressed, in fact."

He shook his head. "It's something about the way she rides. It's her, Zora."

There was that familiar pang in her chest reminding her that he knew Alegra so well. Could even identify her by the way she rode. She tried to get her thoughts back on track. "Are you sure it's Larzen, then?"

"That I'm absolutely positive."

Zora wasn't as positive. She could see the wavy brown hair, but the rider was wearing shabby clothing, and Larzen had always been the most princely of the three brothers. But Griffin knew him and had to be right. But it didn't make sense. "What are they doing together? If it's really her."

"It is her." Griffin insisted. "Well, it's not that mysterious, right? You saw her magic. She must have ensorcelled him."

The question was why. Then a thought hit her "She must want the cup."

He was thoughtful. "She never showed any interest... But she could be pretending. But it's as if... they know where we're going."

"Unless she wants to stop us from getting it. But she saved us. Twice."

"I know she did, but who knows what her motivations were. Larzen would need to be completely insane to be out there, alone with her. He knows what happened to me, and traveling with Kiran's betrothed could be a disaster to him too."

"She's disguised, though. Perhaps Kiran won't learn about it." Zora was trying to think, trying to understand what was happening. "Maybe..." It was a bit crazy. "Hear me out: what if she's one of those flying witches? Perhaps the stories are wrong and they don't have wings. If they were the ones who cursed you, maybe... I don't know."

Griffin was silent for some time, then said, "She's dangerous, for sure. I'm worried about Larzen. You have a point there. But I'm not sure about her being a flying witch. Still, we'll have to slow them down and get to the cup first."

"They're on horses and we're on foot. How are we going to slow them down?"

He smiled. "Have some faith in me."

THEY'D BEEN RIDING for a couple of hours. Larzen still sometimes feared Riadne could do some creepy magic and get him killed or worse.

She approached his horse. "You can't expect me to decrypt a book if we're riding the whole time."

"We'll rest soon and have plenty of time for that."

"I don't understand the hurry. If they go up the mountain, they gotta come back, right? We can just wait."

Larzen wasn't sure if she really thought so or wanted to learn more about his plans, or if by any chance she wanted to get to Griffin. He had a weird fear that she could still be attracted to his brother. Despite everything, he decided to be honest. "You think he'll come down the same way he came?"

"Hum, not sure. You think he'll decide to take permanent residence in the mountains?" She arched an eyebrow, not hiding her sarcasm.

Larzen laughed but then shook his head. "He'll continue, cross the border, escape without a plan or means. It's not that he isn't smart, but he doesn't have as many contacts as I do, and he's impulsive. How far do you think he'll go? That's why I need to stop him, then get him to take a boat and escape properly. You said you didn't want to see him dying, maybe you'll help me."

"I am trying to help, Larzen. What do you think I'm doing?" She thought for a moment. "Once he's safe on a boat, away from Gravel, will you free my brother and let me go?"

"If you promise not to try to harm us again, sure."

"Oooh, what an improvement. So now you value my word? I can make a bunch of promises, you know?"

"I don't trust you. Or your word."

"Yet you still want a promise."

"What's your problem? You want to stick around or something? *My* word is not worthless, and if I'm telling you I'll set you and your brother free once Griffin is safe, that's what's going to happen. Even if it's more than you deserve. Way more."

"Do you believe it, then? That I can't change Kiran back to whatever he was? That I would if I could? That I regret some of my actions?"

Larzen shrugged. "A little, maybe. Either you can't or you don't want to fix Kiran, and I guess there's nothing I can do about it. We'll be safer with you far away, Riadne, so I guess that's the best I can do."

"And yet you are keeping me close now." She tilted her head. "Why is that?"

He shook his arms in frustration. "I don't trust you, that's why."

"And you'll let me go while not trusting me."

"You definitely want to stick around. Is that it?"

"I want to know, Larzen, I need to know what I'm getting into. I want to know if you won't change the terms once Griffin is safe and far away, if you won't decide to imprison me."

"For the last time. If I'm saying I'll free you, it means I'll free you. Is that understood?"

She looked down. "Yes. Forgiveness is a rare quality."

"But I didn't forgive you. Perhaps it's true you can't do anything about Kiran now, but it was your actions that made him act like that. You know why it's like a knife in my gut."

"Right. It's all my fault." She rolled her eyes. "Poor, innocent Griffin."

Larzen stared at her. "Whatever he did, it wasn't part of a scheme to get anyone to kill anyone, so yes, there's a huge difference, Riadne."

She looked away. Great, when she had no answer, she gave him the cold shoulder. It didn't matter. The sooner they got to their destination, the better. Talking on the way would only slow them down.

After a couple of hours, he saw the edge of the lake and, far on the other side, the cabin where he was headed.

As they got close, Riadne asked, "Don't tell me we're going to spend the night in a house."

"Why, would you expect me to *camp*?" He didn't hide the derision in the last word.

"No idea. Thought we should be more discreet, that's all."

"This place is discreet. It's empty."

That was one of the houses his family had around the kingdom for when they traveled. They had also spent some summer days here, fishing at the lake, playing on its sandy beaches. Larzen still recalled his mother holding him in the water, one of his earliest memories. So poisoned now.

They dismounted and headed to the stable, but there were two horses already there.

"I guess it's not empty," she remarked.

Two men came running in, swords drawn.

"Who are you?" one of them asked.

They wore the royal uniform, so they were just guards. It made sense someone would be taking care of the house.

Larzen put his hands on his hips. "Who I am? Don't you recognize me?"

The guard lowered his sword. "Not in the dark, with those clothes. Apologies, your highness. We weren't expecting you."

"Who exactly were you expecting?"

"The youngest prince. We were ordered to arrest him if he came by."

"Right. Do you believe the two of you could handle him?"

The guard lowered his head slightly. "It's our orders, your highness."

"Great. Now I have better orders for you. Go back to wherever you came from, as I want to relax in *my* house."

"Our orders are to stay put in case Prince Griffin comes by." He glanced at Riadne, who was still wearing men's clothes and had her hair hidden in a cap. "Who's your companion?"

"None of your business." Larzen was losing his patience.

Riadne stepped forward, and a strange sound came from her mouth. Right, her freaky magic that by some miraculous luck didn't affect Larzen. The downside was that he wasn't stunned or whatever and had to hear that dreadful singing. He also had no idea what she was planning on doing.

"Who ordered you here?" she asked.

Both men's eyes were glassy and distant. The oldest one replied, "King Kiran."

"And who do you think I am?"

"Prince Larzen's lover."

Riadne glanced at him with a grimace, then turned back to the men. "Why are you here, when Griffin is on his way to Gold Port? You want to go there. And forget you saw us. You want to go to Gold Port. Now get your things and leave."

The two men rushed inside, and before Larzen could even come up with what to say to Riadne, they were back out, bags in hand, saddling the horses.

"You could have ordered them to cook us dinner, take care of our horses, you know, since you were going to do that."

She rolled her eyes, then whispered, "I thought you wanted privacy. And the less time they spend with us, the more likely they are to forget they ever saw us. That guard there obviously noticed I'm not a man, for example."

"Not necessarily."

She widened her eyes. "You like men too." There was surprise in her tone, but no judgement.

"I like a lot of people."

She didn't ask anything else about it, and they entered the house once the guards were gone.

"We can rest here," Larzen said. "And we're still on horses while Griffin is on foot. We'll catch him."

"What about your older brother? Won't he wonder where you are?" There was a hint of apprehension in her tone.

Larzen snorted. "He'll be more than glad I'm not meddling,

and it's not like he'll miss me." Strange to realize how they had grown apart.

"I guess." She walked to the kitchen and he followed. There was a pan on the stove, and Riadne lifted the lid and revealed some hot soup. She smiled. "Well, we do have food."

"And beds. And a fireplace."

She raised an eyebrow. "It's not even cold."

"But it's charming."

PERHAPS LARZEN SHOULD FEEL guilty that the men had been sent away without eating, but he didn't want news getting back to Kiran about where he was. Yes, his older brother would likely be glad not to see Larzen, but he could also assume he was helping Griffin and send people over there. If Riadne's singing really could make the men forget what they'd seen, it would be a wonderful help. That said, her magic gave him the creeps. Imagine if she had told the men to kill Larzen. But he still had her brother, so she wouldn't kill him. At least not yet.

Larzen fed the fire just because he thought it would make the evening cozy. Perhaps he could get the false princess to open up, perhaps he could understand more of what was going on.

Riadne took that dreadful book that Larzen still wasn't sure didn't contain some insanely dangerous magic. A couple sheets fell down, and he caught them before she did. These were not circles and triangles, but words in Continental.

"Give me that," she said.

"No." Larzen pulled the papers. *The Late History of Solanas in Continental*, the first page said. He smiled. "Guess who has a translation?"

"Our ideas are not easy to translate. I bet this thing is all wrong."

"Well, perhaps we can read and compare."

She glared at him, then went back to her book as if she didn't care about his paper. "Perhaps. Let me know if you find anything interesting."

He sat down. His pages were old and handwritten, not always legible. It appeared that it was some kind of history of those people, Solanas, whatever they were. At least he'd gotten a name.

The text wasn't a translation, but more as if someone had read the book and taken notes, trying to get the gist of it. A summary; even better. So far it was all right. Nothing discussed techniques on how to kill from a distance or how to compel brothers to kill each other. There wasn't anything about weird singing, though. It seemed that these Solanas had been advisors and protectors of knowledge. At least if these papers were really about the book, then it was harmless in Riane's hands.

Then a part caught his attention. *They created the darkness in the Royal line. One son cursed at every generation. Only sons born, no daughters.* That was true, the kings of Gravel never had girls, for some reason. He'd always thought it was a coincidence. But it was magic? And what was this thing about a cursed son? He continued reading. *Solanas refused to undo the curse. Each generation, one son is consumed when he comes of age. Or he'll consume the kingdom.* Larzen wondered what exactly the word "consumed" meant here. *The only answer is a magical object; the red chalice. Solanas won't reveal its location. They say fate will reveal the one who can wield it and undo the curse. Fate manifests in a competition with sacrifice and blood. Only to its winner the location of the chalice will be revealed. The red chalice is the solution for the Royal stain and its cursed sons.*

Larzen's hand was trembling. Could this be true?

17

IN THE DEAD OF NIGHT

Trying to undo his curse. It was the only explanation for Griffin's behavior. For going after that cup.

Larzen snatched the book from Riadne's hand. "I have a few questions for you, and you'd better answer them."

Her eyes were wide, as if she could even get scared. "Or what?"

"Let's not find out, shall we?"

"Well, ask, and stop looking at me like that." She cowered on the sofa, as if afraid he'd hurt her or something, which was ridiculous.

"Like I hate you? Why? You don't like that? You should get used to it."

Her lips trembled. "You're scaring me."

He laughed. "You're kidding, right? You have weird magic that could convince me to dive in the lake and never come up. You know you could. And you dare pretend you're afraid of *me*?"

"My magic doesn't work on you."

"But if it did, you could get me killed, couldn't you? Perhaps you could get me cursed."

"Killed, yes, cursed, no. But it doesn't work on you."

Larzen took a deep breath. "Fine, then, great, I'm free from your evil. Lucky me, right? Griffin is not as lucky now, is he? And you know exactly why he needs the cup."

"I don't. I really don't. Talk to me like a normal person, Larzen."

He decided to pretend she was stupid. "Your people cursed the royal line. Are you going to deny that?"

Her eyes widened. "We didn't."

"Great. You don't know anything about one cursed son every generation? A Blood Cup to undo the curse? Or do you prefer a *red chalice,* Riadne?"

"I don't. Didn't I tell you our knowledge was lost? Why would I need this book if I knew what was in it?"

"Yet you've been reading it and you didn't get to this part?"

She pointed at the book. "It's thick. You don't think this whole thing fits in your meager pages, do you? So far the book is just about some random King of Shadows. But if you tell me what you're talking about, maybe I can help you. Maybe I can find a longer explanation here. But you need to stop accusing me of knowing things I don't."

There was a small possibility that she was saying the truth. With Riadne, one could never know. Larzen took a long, deep breath. "It says here that your people cursed the royal line. In each generation, one son is cursed, and the way to undo it is by finding the Blood Cup. Considering how much Griffin wanted this cup, I'm sure you can assume the rest."

"You think he's *cursed*?" She grimaced. "Cursed with what? He seemed normal to me."

"I'm asking you. And I'm trying to understand why he's the first to be on his way to the Blood Cup."

"Maybe he isn't the first. Who knows what happened? Larzen, let me get something straight; we don't have any kind of magic that could act throughout generations, we don't."

"Well, didn't you say you lost your knowledge? Make up your mind."

"Losing knowledge is different from doing things that don't make sense, that are not in our tradition. But maybe we had knowledge like that before. I doubt it, but maybe. Even if it was my people, you do realize it wasn't me, right? Your ancestors killed my people, and I don't hate you."

He snorted and waved a hand. "Oh, no, no hate at all. You were simply trying to kill us, or rather, get us to kill each other."

"It wasn't out of hate. I thought it would fix our curse."

"Your curse which you still haven't told me about."

"I have. We get sick and die painfully. I told you. Tell me what's written in your thing."

He passed her the paper. "Read it yourself."

She looked down, then back at him, as if she were embarrassed. "I... can't. I can't read your writing. A little, yes, but..."

"No, it's fine." He took the paper and read it to her.

She listened attentively, her brows furrowed, as if it were indeed new information for her. Then she shook her head, looking puzzled—or pretending. "I still don't see why we would have cursed the royal line. It doesn't make any sense."

"I don't see why my great, great, great, great grandparents would kill your people. It doesn't mean it's not true. It doesn't mean it's true either, I don't know."

Riadne nodded. "The Blood Cup, which, I mean, you can see it's a crude translation, it looks like something we would create, yes. When we create some powerful magic, there's usually a failsafe, a way to undo it."

"Why? Is it some sadistic pleasure? Is going after the cup some trick?"

"I can't speak for what was done hundreds of years ago, but even when a spell is done with good intentions, things can change, at one point there could be a need to undo it, and rather than requiring more magic to fight it, there's a simple way to reverse it."

"Give me an example," he asked.

"Of what?"

"A nice spell and a way to undo it. I'm just trying to understand it."

She thought for a moment. "My hair."

He blinked in confusion.

She continued, "It's not red. I changed it. The key to unchanging it is in a rock that I left it in the mountains."

"What color is your hair?"

"Light brown."

"But why then just a rock and not a dramatic competition or something?"

"Because it affects just me. If it's something bigger, fate has to play a hand."

"But it's just one family line, Riadne."

"Well, I didn't do it and I don't understand how they could have done it or why. It's not the kind of thing we do. But I can read and find out. If you let me, and if you trust me."

Larzen stared at her and gave her back the book. "So, according to what you know, if Griffin is cursed, this cup will cure him?"

"That's what it looks like, isn't it?"

"Is there a chance that finding it could be a trap?"

"Not a trap, but maybe dangerous. When fate plays a hand, it can't be anyone who can do it. But defeating the lion was dangerous already, so... I don't know."

Larzen covered his face with his hand. "He didn't even defeat the lion. Can it be someone else?"

"I don't know. It seems so, but what you have is obviously a crappy translation from an opinionated person. I'll have to read this carefully." She shook the book.

"You're sure you have no idea what Griffin has?"

"No," she insisted. "He never said anything, I never noticed anything. But maybe he's on his way to fixing his problem, so there's no reason to be angry. And you'll help him escape the kingdom after that. Boom. Happy ending."

"Yeah, his ending is wonderful, exiled from his kingdom."

She paused, looked away, then back at him. "Kiran has other problems, Larzen. How many times do I have to tell you? If he's overreacting, he would eventually overreact for other reasons. And aren't you his brother? Why can't *you* fix him?"

"He doesn't..." Larzen closed his eyes. He was going to say that Kiran had been shutting him out, that he couldn't find a way to get through and reach his older brother, that it was as if he was another person. What if Riadne faced the same thing? No, that was stupid, she was the reason he was acting like that. It was the only logical explanation. "You know you did something, Riadne, and if you're not a horrible person, you'll try to make up for that."

"Sure. You're all so nice. Kidnapping my brother and all."

"Maybe I won't let your brother free while Kiran is acting all crazed."

She laughed. "Great. Going back on your word. That was quick, Larzen. I knew it. I knew you had no plans of letting me go."

"That's not what I meant. I'm asking. Please. Please get Kiran back to normal."

"And I'm telling you I can't. I can't, Larzen. If I could, I would already have turned him back to whatever state of absolute goodness he was in before evil me arrived. Of course I would, or do you think I like to know that my brother is locked up? You know I'm scared and I want to leave. You asked one thing of me. Of course I would have done it! But I can't."

Larzen crossed his arms. "Maybe. Find what you can about this cup, then, and this curse. I'm not gonna hold you accountable for what your ancestors did. But let me help my brother. He has a kind heart."

"I know."

"Yet you hurt it."

She rolled her eyes. "Doubtful. I never even got close to that heart of his. But yes, from a distance, I noticed it was kind. As I told you before, I saved him, and I think you should thank me."

He snorted. "Saved him from what? Ten guards?"

She paused and stared at him as if about to say something, then smirked. "Saving is saving, it doesn't matter against how many, does it? Now let me read this thing so we get to the truth and stop speculating based on poorly written notes."

She removed her hat and let her locks flow down on her shoulder. So her hair was fake. He had seen girls using potions and herbs to change their hair color. Men too. It shouldn't surprise him or upset him. It was just that nothing about the girl he once thought was Alegra was real. And perhaps her laughter, her humor, and her lightness had meant something to him one day. All he had was an impostor full of lies who had ruined his family. And yet, fake or not, by the Kingdom she was beautiful. And it was true that even with those ugly men's clothes she still managed to be magnificent. The worst was that she knew it.

"Isn't it too obvious to stop by at a house belonging to the crown?" Zora asked, still unsure about Griffin's plan, and tired from walking so much.

"He's not the one being chased, and I frankly doubt he can even set up a tent."

"What if there are guards around there, waiting for us?"

"We'll be discreet."

A small crescent moon illuminated the waters of a large lake, a cute stone house on its edge. There weren't lakes that big in the Dark Valley, and Zora wished she could spend time there and appreciate the view, perhaps even swim in its waters. But it wasn't what they had come to do. She hoped Griffin was right and this wasn't some kind of trap.

The stables had only two horses, so Larzen and Alegra were probably alone there. That was good.

Zora and Griffin looked at a window from a distance. Alegra was on a sofa, reading, and Larzen was apparently sleeping on the other sofa.

"No," Griffin said in disbelief.

"What?"

"She's got one of the forbidden books. That's some dangerous dark magic."

"Do you want to... talk to your brother? See if he's well?"

He took a deep breath and shook his head. "I don't trust her. We could put ourselves at risk."

"You're worried about Larzen."

He closed his eyes. "Of course. But let's get the cup first."

They went back to the stables, then Griffin took the horses by the reins and they walked away in silence. When they were far enough from the house, he put Zora on one horse and mounted the other. She was afraid of riding at night and unsure about controlling that horse, so Griffin sent it away, and they both mounted one single horse, trotting away in the direction of the mountain, Zora behind him, clinging to his waist, afraid that sleep would take her and make her fall. They stopped after a few hours and set camp.

Zora's eyes were almost closing as she tied the hammock. Griffin lay down and she didn't even have any strength to refuse his embrace. And it felt so good.

RIADNE HEARD the sounds of steps. She heard the horses being taken from them. Had Larzen not acted like an oaf a few hours before, she would have woken him up. As it was, it was well deserved for him. He slept quite peacefully for someone who claimed to be so afraid of her. With eyes closed, he looked innocent. She perhaps preferred him like that, without the blue fire of his eyes, the blue fire that had turned against her with hatred not long before. Without those eyes drawing her to them, she could notice more of his face, his jaw, his lips. Some weird thoughts came to her mind and she shut them down. Sure, Larzen was good-looking, but what difference did it make?

She had tried to read the book. Solanas didn't write words per se but represented ideas, and from what she had gathered, the stupid translated summary was right, as much as it upset her. What she didn't understand was why they would curse a family line. It was so absurd that she had trouble accepting that they'd done something like that. But then, perhaps that was what ancestors did; senseless, horrible things.

Her thoughts turned to her brother. Was he being treated right? Was he suffering? Larzen sometimes almost convinced her that he wanted to be her friend, that he meant well, but he still had locked up Lukas. He still could go back on his word. The worst was that her magic didn't work on him at all. He didn't seem attracted by her most of the time either, which was only proof of his poor taste.

Trusting him was quite foolish. Trusting anyone of that family. Perhaps there was no way they could overcome whatever kerfuffle had happened centuries ago. She had to be smart. As silently as she could, Riadne stepped outside and walked many minutes, until she was far from earshot, then snapped her fingers. It was probably useless, as Griffin or the Dark Valley girl probably had her, but it didn't hurt to try calling her mare. Riadne snapped, snapped, snapped her fingers.

It was like a vision, a mirage, an apparition when the animal came galloping towards her. Riadne was free and she had a plan. Yes, her magic didn't work on Larzen and worked poorly on Kiran, but it still worked on everyone else. She'd find whoever was keeping Lukas and get them to release him. Simple, so simple. By the time Larzen got back, she'd be long gone. As to him and his brother, well, they'd find a way to meet, he'd find a way to help Griffin, and they would be happy. Happiness was never perfect, that was one thing Larzen didn't understand, with his comfortable, problem-free life. Happiness was in the small moments, in freedom. Everyone would leave this world one day, so every single life ended in death. And it didn't mean it wasn't happy. Perhaps she didn't have much longer to live, but that was what she was going to chase: happiness.

The words he had read to her and the images from the book kept circling in her mind, though. That "Why, why, why?" ringing in her ears. The obvious answer was that people had been incredibly stupid in the past, but there had to be more... Well, if the king was killing her people, perhaps it made sense that the Solanas would retaliate. It did. And it didn't. Why curse generations? Whoever had the skill for such a powerful spell should obviously have the skill for something more immediate. Why not kill the royal line and get rid of them? It would make more sense. It was just... illogical. Senseless. Pointless. Why couldn't she just accept that people in the past did things that made no sense?

But then the pieces suddenly snapped together in her mind. Riadne stopped. Her brother could wait a day or two more. She turned around and galloped toward the lake house.

BEING LOCKED in a windowless room for three days could drive anyone insane, but somehow, Tris had been coping well. There were many ways to lock up someone, and they didn't all have walls or bars. Lukas had been her captor once, now they were allies. He wanted more. She saw it in his eyes, his voice, his smile. She wasn't sure she'd ever be able to reciprocate, but her conscience was clear that she had never given him hope for anything romantic.

On the first day, she convinced him to stay put, but now he was too worried about his sister. They placed their plates of food through a revolving compartment. There was another, lower revolving door where servants changed their buckets and gave them clean water. When he heard the sound of the metal turning, he asked, in a desperate voice, "Help, help, she's sick."

Tris tried to make her best imitation of a yell of pain. Lukas' reasoning was that if they were getting such good food, clean water, and comfort, their captors wouldn't want them to get sick. He probably knew what he was talking about, having kidnapped her once.

"Help us, please," he pleaded again.

Even she felt moved by his desperation, and had to hold back her laughter. He looked at her and smirked. Their eyes connected for a moment, before she looked away. Tris had promised herself she'd never give him hope.

The compartment stopped turning, and whoever was there stepped away. Lukas gestured for her to continue, and she screamed again.

After some minutes, a door opened revealing a woman. "What's..."

She didn't even finish speaking when Lukas knocked her unconscious. He picked up the key in her hand and opened the other door, which led to a dark hallway. After trying for some time, he found another door, and then they were in a corridor in the castle. Their plan was to escape, as they did not yet know who their enemies were in that place. They had barely walked two steps when Lukas grunted.

Tris looked around to see if there had been an archer or someone who'd thrown something at him, but the hallway was still empty. "What's wrong?"

His scream of pain almost deafened her, as he sat, then lay down, still screaming. There was no blood, no visible wounds, but she feared for him, watching his face contort in pain.

She stood and it was as if they had switched places, but

this time the anguish and desperation were real. "Help!" she yelled. "Somebody, please! Help!"

GONE. The horses, Riadne, Larzen's dignity. He put his hands on his head. Brilliant, just brilliant. For all his thoughts on how he didn't trust the impostor princess, he'd fallen asleep leaving her with what could possibly be a nefarious book. Having her brother wouldn't do much if she decided to get back to the castle and use all her power.

The worst was that Larzen still wanted to find Griffin before his brother made some terrible life decisions, but he doubted he'd reach him before he crossed the mountains, and he wasn't sure if he wanted to chase him beyond the border. He'd counted on outrunning him on horseback. Yay to walking. So tiring. Humiliating. He sighed. Perhaps he should just leave his brother to his own decisions and to the consequences of his own actions. After all, Griffin probably had enjoyed his time with Riadne, even if he thought she was princess Alegra. He must have done something right for her to choose him. Larzen had better chase away these thoughts because he'd go nuts if he tried to understand what had driven these two together.

He didn't even want to go back to the castle and face Kiran and his weirdness. And if Riadne escaped, he didn't want to know how his older brother would react. Perhaps Larzen should take a boat for himself and start a new life somewhere else. He wondered if being a former-prince was a qualification for anything. So many nonsensical thoughts. Too many. Head spinning, thoughts whirling, keeping him busy and not hurting. As if there was something to be hurt about.

The murderous, conniving, backstabbing, liar, fake princess impersonator had betrayed him. How shocking. What had been unpredictable was Larzen acting like a gullible child. Why? Now he had to choose between two horrible options: a shameful walk to the castle or a shameful walk towards his younger brother—who he wasn't going to reach any time soon.

As Larzen contemplated the lake, wondering if perhaps he should just stay put and start a new life right where he was, he saw a horse in the distance. Riadne on a horse. She was coming back? Now, that was freaking him out more than her leaving, considering all her evil plans.

He stood there by the door and didn't even bother to greet her in the stable.

When she approached, he smiled. "Had a nice morning ride?"

"You know what I was doing. I was going to get back to the castle, free my brother, and run."

"And you took my horse."

She shook her finger. "That wasn't me. I think your brother paid a visit. Larzen, I need you to listen to me." Her usual sarcastic tone was gone, as if she were saying something serious, but he could never be sure. "Listen to me as if I had never planned to have you three killing each other, as if I had never lied, as if I had never pretended to be the princess I'll never be."

He decided to be honest to her. "I'll listen, but it's not like I can forget who you are or what you planned to do. It doesn't go away."

"Fine, fine. Don't forget it. Just ... listen to me as if I weren't the most evil creature you've ever met, as if I were capable of good intention sometimes. As if I were a normal human being, someone who makes mistakes sometimes, gets taken by anger, jealousy, hatred, but who can also love and have compassion. I'm not a bad person, Larzen."

"Never said you were."

"You're thinking it. Your eyes last night told me all I had to know about you. But I think you can still care. You might hate me, and that's fine, but deep down in your heart, you're a good person."

"I'm not that sure."

"Please, just listen to me."

He crossed his arms. "You say it as if I hadn't been listening all this time. But don't blame me if I don't believe you."

Riadne sighed. "I saved your brother."

"Oh, that again... There weren't that many guards and you know it."

She shook her head. "I don't mean then. I mean before. Do you know how Griffin and Zora escaped the arena? Have you ever wondered how they slipped past all the guards? Don't tell me you didn't wonder about that, Larzen."

"They... ran away?"

She snorted. "Your little brother was unconscious, fallen on the ground. The pitiful Dark Valley girl was weeping over him, knowing it was their end. Kiran threatened his guards, that if they didn't kill him, they would be killed. So just try to picture your little brother fallen, unconscious, while one girl decided to take one last stand against dozens of guards, not to count archers on the top of the stands."

"Nobody said that."

"Because they don't remember. I stopped them, I don't even know how I did it, but I stopped the guards and everyone, so that your ungrateful younger brother could escape. So that *they* could escape. I swear, as much as I didn't like that girl, in her moment of bravery, pain, and desperation I felt for her."

The accounts about Griffin's escape were somewhat confusing and contradictory, so there was a possibility she was saying the truth. "Why didn't you tell me that before?"

She rolled her eyes, back into normal Riadne fashion. "Think, Larzen, just think. Why wouldn't I want this feat to be advertised to the four corners of the kingdom? Why?"

"You don't want people to know your power."

"Well, no. I can't even guarantee I can repeat that, but get that information in the wrong hands, and they could try to use me. Normal people don't understand that magic is fickle and moody, they don't understand how it works. And I wouldn't want to be used for anything. But I'm telling you so you know. If you value your brother's life so much, thank me. I'm the reason he's still alive and about to climb that mountain. I don't want your eternal gratitude or your forgiveness. All I'm asking is that you listen to me, that's all."

"I am listening. What is it you want?"

Her voice was soft, almost pleading. "We have to stop Griffin."

THE MOUNTAIN

The sky was getting lighter as the sun was coming up, and yet Griffin still heard the buzz of crickets and more night insects. Zora, still asleep, had her head against his shoulder. They had barely rested and hadn't eaten properly, and yet she had never complained, pushing them forward. He ran his fingers through her hair, from the brown roots to the blond tips, and then was greeted by hazel eyes and a thin smile.

"Rest," he said. "I'll water and feed the horse, and we'll leave."

"So early," she mumbled.

"I know."

He kissed her forehead, and she closed her eyes, as if she liked it. He then kissed her cheek, almost at the corner of mouth. Zora turned her head away, but it only made her bury her face between his shoulder and neck. She wanted him close, that was clear, but she didn't want to kiss him just yet. Griffin sighed then held her even closer. That felt good too. The rest was just a matter of time.

IT HAD TAKEN a few hours for Griffin and Zora to get to the foot of the mountain range, riding through the forest, far enough from the road that they wouldn't be spotted or heard by travelers. The lower part of the mountain was much like the hill in the Dark Valley, with trees, but then it had walls of stone.

He pointed to a trail through the lower hills, then to a rock wall. "We can walk around it. Or we can climb those rocks."

With Alegra after them, the earlier they got this cup, the better. "Which is faster?" She had a hunch she already knew the answer, but it didn't hurt to ask.

"The trails are long." He pointed to the rocks. "But this is not easy either."

"If it's faster, let's climb."

He nodded. Just nodded, didn't warn her again that it was difficult or anything like that.

Zora could feel the wind as she dug her fingers in the first groove she found and pushed her body over a steep rock. It turned out that their way wasn't as steep as it looked at first, it was more like large stairs with giant stone steps, which they had to climb. Their rhythm was brisk and she felt her heart beating fast from the effort. There was also the anticipation of finding the cup—and the fear of perhaps not finding it, or that it wouldn't work. So much uncertainty, and yet, as they moved up, it was as if there was no doubt that they were on their way to reaching a goal.

She paused as a memory came to her mind. No, a dream. Dressed all in gold, a woman led her to a chamber in a cave. The Sun Goddess?

"Are you all right?" Griffin's soft voice interrupted her.

"Do you know how we go in? Into this abyss?"

He bit his lip. "I've never been there. But we'll figure it out."

"Wait. I'm thinking."

Clouds were gathering overhead, darkening the sky. Zora remembered when these clouds could mean danger for the Dark Valley, an unexpected night when they were not ready. Here, it would only mean they'd get wet. And the floor could get slippery. She tried to recall her dream, vision, whatever. "I think there should be a lower entrance."

He nodded. "Maybe."

Zora closed her eyes, trying to think, trying to remember something that as far as she knew wasn't real, some information she never had. And yet, if all this was based on vague magic, perhaps that was the way to do it. The wind howled on the mountain above them and down below shook the trees. This wasn't going to be an easy climb if there was a storm.

Then, along with the wind, she thought she heard something. It was as if the wind was calling Griffin's name. She looked at him.

"You also heard it?" he asked.

"Yes."

He approached the edge and looked down.

Zora heard it clearly this time, a yell, calling, "Griffin!"

He turned to her, frowning. "That's my brother. Larzen."

"They reached the foot of the mountains," Zora thought out loud.

Griffin grimaced and sighed.

"Stop!" Larzen's voice sounded small against the wind and the enormity of the mountain.

"Do you want to talk to him?" Zora asked.

Griffin stared down for a few seconds. The yells came again, "Griffin," and then, "Stop."

The youngest prince closed his eyes and shook his head. "I can't see well, but Alegra is with him. I mean…"

"You think she's behind it."

He nodded, his jaw set in a pained expression.

Zora still had her suspicions that perhaps the princess had something to do with the people who had cursed Griffin and created the cup, it was just that it didn't quite fit the fact that she was the Linaria princess. Still, Alegra could have some kind of sinister goal.

"We'd better hurry before they reach us," she said.

"It should be fine. I'm not betting on them rushing up the mountain. He wouldn't be down there yelling if he could come and get me."

Zora still felt anxious. "Maybe." Then she tried to focus. "I'll see if I can figure where that entrance is."

Griffin put his hand on her shoulder. "We'll find it." He cocked his head as if pointing to the forest below the mountains. "Let's pay them no mind."

His smile set her heart at ease, or rather, perhaps made it speed up a bit. But they were far ahead of Larzen and the princess, so there was no point in thinking about them.

"THERE'S no point yelling any more, Larzen. They heard it." Riadne's voice was cold, and she sounded resigned.

He was about to say that she couldn't be sure, but his yells had been loud enough, as he used a large leaf as an amplifying cone.

The rocks were steep and he wished there were a way to get to Griffin and Zora that didn't involve so much physical effort with the added risk of not reaching them in time.

"This way," Riadne got his attention. "There are trails around the mountain, no need to climb these rocks. The trails are much easier. Even you will have no trouble with them."

Trails, right. Larzen followed her as she walked towards a path among bushes. That made more sense. Wait. Something she had said did not make any sense. "What do you mean *even I* will have no trouble?"

She was still walking, and said, "I mean... you're not as physically—"

He was right beside her, as the path was still wide enough. "No, no, no. You're getting me all wrong, dear. For the record, I can climb. And let me set it straight that even if I don't usually show off my arms, chest, or stomach, it's all extremely defined."

She rolled her eyes. "Wonderful."

Larzen wasn't sure she was being sarcastic, and asked, "You don't think Griffin is stronger than I am, do you?"

"Is that even a question?"

"I just asked, didn't I?"

"There are millions of different types of strength, Larzen. But if we're talking about physical strength, well..."

"Well what? It's not like you compared us, is it?"

"No. But for example, can you even fight properly with a sword?"

"Why would I?" He showed a dagger on his belt. "When this is much more elegant, quicker and deadlier? A sword is clumsy and attracts unnecessary attention."

"Whatever you say." A smile crept up on the corner of her mouth. "The skill is what matters, right?"

Shit. Larzen wished he could disappear as he realized what he had just said and the meaning she must have gleaned from it. "I'm so incredibly skilled you have no idea, Riadne. And it has no correlation with my physique. And you know I'm bigger, I mean, taller than my brother, right? And I'm ripped. Absolutely ripped. I can show you."

Riadne closed her eyes, as if annoyed, even if she was the one who was irritating him. "I'll be delighted to check every single marvelous muscle of yours. Meanwhile, let's keep walking."

Larzen gritted his teeth, just then realizing he'd been making a fool of himself. "All I mean was that I'll have no trouble going up the trails through the mountain, that's all." He looked away.

"Why would I think anything different?"

"No idea. Do you think we'll reach them, though?"

She took a deep breath. "A lot of magic is time-based, meaning that it has to happen at a specific period during the day or night. If I were to bet, this one will be at night, so let's hurry because we can still make it."

Larzen glanced at the winding path that didn't even seem like it would go anywhere near where they had to go. There had to be some easier way to get Griffin's attention. "Can't you command some birds? Get them to stop them?"

"Command birds?" She grimaced.

"You can enchant animals, can't you?"

She was thoughtful. "Right. I have an even better idea. I'll get some birds to fly us up there, then we can talk to them. How's that?"

He was stunned. "You can do that?"

"Of course not." She rolled her eyes. "Where are you getting these ideas from?"

"Well, you set Griffin's dogs after Zora, I mean..."

"I ... what?" She laughed.

Larzen hadn't witnessed it, but had heard it from the girl's guard. "You sent Griffin's dogs—"

"Well, no."

"You're gonna deny it?"

"It's so absurd I'm not even gonna spend my energy on it, Larzen. I can affect animals, but not command them." She sounded sincere, or at least as sincere as Riadne could sound, which was not a lot.

"Then who did it?"

Riadne shrugged. "What do I know? Don't dogs misbehave sometimes?"

"Not like that, and someone must have opened the kennel."

She frowned. "Do I look like I carry kennel keys or something?"

"Well, you sent an assassin to kill or scare the girl, what am I supposed to think?"

"Hum... right. Evil Riadne is commanding assassins against innocent girls. Evil, evil, Riadne."

"You deny it, then."

She waved a hand. "Again, I'm not going to spend my energy denying something absurd. You can think whatever you want."

"I thought you wanted to convince me to trust you."

She raised her voice. "Well, I'm not gonna argue against idiocy."

"So you're saying you didn't send the guy with the dagger either. Who did it, then?"

"Want to hear my opinion?"

"I'm asking, so I'd assume yes."

"Nobody," she said. "Think about it. Do you really believe

the girl would have disarmed a man and stabbed him twice? I think the dagger would have gotten stuck, wouldn't it?"

"I don't stab people enough to know, Riadne, but perhaps you do?"

"That's a minor detail. But check it out, the next day, the girl goes to Griffin." She then made a high voice, as if mocking Zora. "Help me! Evil Riadne, I mean, Evil Alegra, is trying to kill me. Oh, mighty Griffin, be my hero and protect me."

Larzen snorted. "I doubt that's how it went."

"No, that's exactly how it went, because next thing I know, Griffin wants to see me. Here I am thinking... Well, nevermind. And then he's like, 'Don't you dare get near sweet, innocent Zora,'" she said with a thick voice, this time mocking his brother. "'You evil, evil, murderer.' That's what he said. And I was pissed. And you know what? It's pretty low and dirty. She wanted Griffin, whatever, take him, but she didn't have to make up lies against me."

"Well, you did enchant her horse."

"But there's a difference!"

"And you still saved her."

"I don't want to brag, but I just can't help being so magnanimous, you know? And that's why you should trust me."

He stared at her. "I am trusting you. A lot. A gigantic whole lot more than I think I should."

She smiled. "Doesn't it feel great to be so magnanimous? It means you're the bigger person."

Or maybe the foolish person. But he didn't want to say that and for now was willing to give her his trust, even if he had no idea why.

The path still wasn't steep but it was getting thinner, with bushes prickling his feet, and it looked as if there would be small rocks for them to climb. As long as it got them to Griffin eventually, it wasn't the end of the world.

Suddenly, Riadne turned to him. "You act so morally superior. Weren't you conspiring with the Dark Valley girl? What was even the point of throwing her at Kiran?"

Why was she so insistent on knowing that? And he truly thought that the answer, unfortunately, was obvious. "I don't see what's so hard to understand about it."

She thought for a moment, then snorted. "You thought he'd replace me? Me?"

Riadne would soon be gone from his life, and he decided to blurt out the truth. "Oh, no, not him. I was thinking about a princess from a kingdom of gold. I was thinking that the princess would realize the king she was about to marry was not what she thought. I thought the princess would maybe look at the king's charming younger brother. Well, it happened, but not with the charming brother. For some reason she turned to the grumpy brother. And it was for the best, as it all turned out to be a lie. There was never any princess."

Her brown eyes widened and locked on his as she caught a breath. She looked even younger than her nineteen years of age, her expression soft, almost innocent, the princess he'd once thought she was. "You..."

His heart skipped a beat and he realized he was treading in dangerous territory, so he'd better shut it all down. "Don't get ideas, Riadne. It was for Linaria's gold."

Her eyes hardened, again showing him the real Riadne, and she had a malicious smile. "Well, you're in luck, then. The real Alegra, Linaria's princess, is in your power, and I'm pretty sure all she wants is someone to put her family's heads on a tray. You can have the whole kingdom."

"Too gloomy for my taste."

She smirked. "Gold is never gloomy."

"I doubt your brother would let me."

"Why worry?" She had a bitter laugh. "In a short time, who knows, months, a couple years, he'll be a mess of broken bones and pain and die. Nothing to worry about."

She couldn't be serious. "How can you joke about something like that?"

Riadne was inches from his face. "How? You ask me how? What am I supposed to do? Crumble on the floor and cry? How do you think I can wake up every day? It's not just him, it's me too. It's my end."

"It's really true, then?"

"You thought I was lying about it? Why do you think I wanted you three to kill each other? You heard me? Or did you just hear the parts that interested you?"

Larzen wasn't a crumple of broken bones, but he felt as if his chest was a crumple, thinking about Riadne dying, her smile fading away. "There has to be a way out, there has to be. Perhaps I can help you. And what do you mean broken bones?"

"It's... the curse. Why it's so horrible and painful. But I'd rather not think about it."

"I... am sorry. Truly."

She looked down. "It doesn't change anything." Her eyes were then on his. "I live one day at a time. And today, you know what we have to do, right? Get up this mountain, so let's keep going. Tomorrow's problems are tomorrow's problems."

If it was really true, he had no idea how she could go on living, laughing, being so much fun to be around. Perhaps the trick was really to live one day at a time. Today, all they had to do was reach his brother in time, and that was what he was going to do.

FINDING calm when so much was at stake, when they were being chased, was not easy, but it was what Zora tried to do. When her thoughts quieted, she heard a woman's voice calling her from a distance.

At least Griffin trusted her, and she wasn't sure if it was a good thing or a bad thing. The voice was coming from the side of the mountain, a little below where they were. Zora latched on the rocks to move sideways, until they came to the end of a trail and found a stone door. It had a square frame with engraved flowers. On the door, there were circles and triangles similar to the ones she'd seen at the temple ruins. She wondered how to open that door, figuring perhaps that the drawings had some clues that she couldn't understand.

Then, on the bottom of the door, she noticed smaller engravings. Crouching, she realized that it had a sentence in Continental, partly covered by dust. She reached her hand to wipe it away, but Griffin stopped her. "Let me do it."

She bit her lip. Perhaps she could tell him that she was perfectly capable of wiping dust from a door, but he'd done it to be nice.

It had a sentence:

The circle of blood circles with one of these.

There were four stone squares protruding from the side of the door. One had a sun, one had a moon, one had a star, and one had little dots looking like rain.

"It's like a riddle." Zora frowned. It couldn't be. "But it's too obvious."

"What's obvious about it?"

"The circle of blood. I think it's the cycle of blood, you know?"

His face was blank.

"Women," she added. "We bleed. We have a cycle."

He frowned in confusion.

Zora rolled her eyes. Men. Of course he had no idea what she was talking about. "Nevermind. But it's the moon."

The button was a lot harder to press than she had imagined, and she had to push it with all her strength. The ground below her shook, and as she was crouching, she almost fell back, except that Griffin caught her. Then the door moved up, revealing darkness beyond it.

After they stepped in, Zora noticed that she was in a cave leading to the border of an inner canyon, opening up on a slit on top, from which sunlight came in. Along the edges, there were more platforms like those, leading to cave systems. A river ran in the bottom. Strangely, the place felt warm and stuffy.

A thin staircase without a handrail edged the stone wall below them, leading down. Considering there was nothing behind them, that was where they'd have to go. Zora descended it with a cold feeling in her stomach, avoiding looking at the abyss below. It ended on the opening of a huge cavern, with two clear natural water pools over flat rock. Stalactites adorned the ceiling. No stalagmites, though. In fact, the floor was smooth as if it had been artificially flattened. This was not a completely natural chamber, and her heart raced with the realization that she was about to find the mysterious cup. The sound of water dripping somewhere echoed in the cave.

Zora glanced at Griffin. His eyes met hers, a glimmer illuminating them. Her heart raced a little more. She continued looking at the walls, trying to find a platform, something, and walked towards the back of the cave, where there was a wall covered with a thin layer of dripping water. Her eyes found something on the ground. It was like some kind of transparent red rock, with something inside it.

Around it, she found more of those strange circles and triangles. Like before, there was also a text in Continental.

When the stars come up, water from the chalice can break the circles holding darkness in the boys and the land. When the time is right, in the quiet of night, drip it in the circle and break the chains.

By the strange rock with the cup there were some deeper grooves forming a spiral. If her understanding was right, she'd have to take water from one of the pools and drop it in that circle, using the cup. She tapped her finger over the rock where the cup was. Solid. But then, the text said it had to be done at night, which was still many hours away. *Darkness in the boys.* That had to be Griffin's curse. It was incredible that the solution was so simple. Now, *darkness in the land*? Did she dare hope again? Could this cup reverse the magic of the Dark Valley?

What was strange was that everything pointing to this cup could have been found before, without the need for the competition. Well, not really. Only after she won that she heard voices and had this intuition as to where to go.

Griffin's hand landed on her shoulder. "I guess we need to wait until it's night."

Zora turned to him. "Yes. Hopefully I'll figure out a way to get the cup then." But something was bothering her. "I'm worried Alegra and Larzen will find us."

Thunder roared in the sky.

He shook his head. "I wouldn't worry. I don't think they can climb. Even if they can, how are they going to find this place?"

"This place is magical and she has magic."

"Fair enough." He pointed up. "But there's a rainstorm coming. That should slow them down enough. I mean, slow her down, if she's really that insistent. I can't see my brother climbing a mountain."

His words did little to appease her uneasiness, but there wasn't much they could do.

He got up. "I'll block the entrance. That should keep them away, if they find us."

"How?"

"There must be some loose boulders somewhere." He crouched by a water pool, slowly dipped his hand, and smiled. "Zora, you won't believe it, it's warm. You know what I'm thinking?"

The image of both of them undressed in that pool crossed her mind. Hopefully that was not what he was thinking. "No idea."

"Baths, of course. If you want, you can go first while I block the entrance. Don't worry, I'll turn around and won't look."

Zora glanced at the water. "Hum... warm still water. It's not like there will be thousands of germs in it ready to cause infections."

"I don't think it's still." He pointed to the ceiling, dripping above it. "And it was just a suggestion. I'll risk the germs. Yell when you're ready and I can come back in."

He disappeared through the opening and up the narrow stairs. Zora glanced at the water again, so crystalline, reflecting the rocks in the ceiling. She undressed quickly and got in. It felt so good to have that water caressing her body, relaxing her, removing the gunk from her journey. She didn't fear that

Griffin would go back on his word and catch her undressed, but even so, she didn't spend as long as she would have liked, as she didn't want to keep him waiting by the stairs.

Lukas trembled on the bed, his skin hot from the fever. A healer had given him a draught for the pain, but it didn't seem to be working. Tris sighed. The only reason he was being treated was because he was pretending to be her brother, the crown prince of Linaria. The Gravel king didn't even see them, but ordered a healer to take care of Lukas, and now they were in a remote wing in the castle, in a room for isolating patients, which was oddly similar to the room where they'd been kept, with walls and rotating compartments for food and buckets.

The healer said Riadne was sick too, and didn't let Tris see her. She'd have to find a way to convince him, as perhaps Lucas's sister would be able to explain what was wrong with him. He lay sideways on the bed. This was different from seeing someone she loved suffering, but it still hit her hard, with painful memories of Krimm being hurt in front of her while her father smirked, then her brother dealing the fatal blow. Nobody deserved to suffer that. Nobody deserved to see that. But this was just someone who was ill.

"You'll be fine," she whispered, trying to comfort him, while hoping he would indeed be fine, hoping this wasn't serious.

He shook his head. "Help me." He moved his hands to the buttons of his shirt, but the trembling was so much he couldn't open them.

Tris helped him remove his shirt and noticed that his back

had two strange dark marks, black bruises, as if he'd been hit recently. But he hadn't been hit by anything.

Removing his upper clothes seemed to alleviate some of his pain. His face was calmer as he reached out his hand and grabbed hers. "Tris. Tris. Please."

With the other hand, he pulled a dagger from his belt and gave it to her, then he pointed to the center of his chest. "Please."

How dramatic. And terrifying that he'd go as far as that. Well, no, she wasn't going to stab him in the chest. "You'll be fine." She hid the weapon behind her, meaning to hide it very far from him, just in case.

He shook his head and his face went from a grimace to a bitter laugh. "Sorry. I..."

She ran her fingers through his hair, now damp with sweat. "It's fine." She smiled. "You can tell me all later."

"Didn't... have time." He pointed again to his chest. "Please."

His voice was weak. She'd also asked the healer to give him a sleep draught, so that he could get some respite from whatever horrible pain he was feeling. Her thoughts turned to her brother, and how he had finished Krimm off. Had it been mercy? Strange kind of mercy, when he'd promised to help her, to help Krimm escape. Escaping life wasn't exactly the same. And here was Lukas, *asking* to be killed. Hopefully he'd be better soon and rethink his death wish.

She looked at the wounds on his back again. Strange. It was as if there was something stuck there, like two black blades. She paid more attention to the skin. No, nothing had been stuck on his back. It was sticking out. Then a desperate yell came out of his mouth, which kept ringing in her ears.

19

———

RAIN

G riffin also bathed in the pool, then extended the hammock on the ground.

"We'd better rest while we wait for night to fall."

Through the opening of the cave, she could see some drops of rain falling into the abyss in the middle of the mountain, while thunder roared above them. But that part of the cave was dry, or as dry as any place could be when surrounded by humidity and warm water.

Griffin lay down and stretched his arm, as if suggesting she lie on it. The gesture felt intimate, but Zora didn't refuse his invitation. Not only was she tired, she also enjoyed being close to him, even if she wasn't sure where this would lead and wasn't sure she wanted to open her heart just yet. It still felt good.

He ran his hand through her hair.

"You lighten the tips?"

"Lots of people do in the valley." She chuckled. "After all, we fight the dark."

He moved his hand to his hair. "Like mine?"

"Yours is different. And it shines, so... it's brilliant and spreads light. I like it like that."

He smiled and touched her hair again. "Yours is soft, pretty. I like it too."

She didn't get the feeling that he wanted to discuss hair, but rather wanted an excuse to keep running his fingers through hers. The gesture was relaxing. That, together with the hum of the rain outside, made her close her eyes. Despite her nerves, and her fear that perhaps the cup wouldn't work or that Alegra would somehow sabotage them, she relaxed, enjoying that moment of bliss.

"Zora?"

His voice called her attention, as she opened her eyes and peered into attentive dark eyes.

He asked, "Are we just gonna keep cuddling and pretend nothing's happening?"

She stiffened and moved away from his arms, lying a little further from him. "You're right."

He snorted. "Very mature, Zora."

She turned to him. "No, you're right. If nothing's happening, we shouldn't be lying down like that."

"And you're gonna tell me with a straight face that nothing's happening?"

She shrugged. "Nothing happened."

Griffin sighed and closed his eyes. "There's tomorrow for us to think about. And the day after, and the day after. I get it that you don't want to kiss me while you're still not sure—"

"That's not it!"

"What is it, then? Are you still disgusted because of what I am?"

Zora frowned. Where was he getting those ideas? "I'm not disgusted. I've never been, never will be."

"Why won't you kiss me, then? Don't tell me you don't want to." His voice was gentle, more curious than angry.

Somehow his presumption didn't even annoy her. She wasn't sure what to say. "I... need to trust you. I... don't want to..." What was she even going to say? Have her heart broken? Do what they did in her vision?

He leaned on his elbow, resting his face on his hand. "That's fair. I don't mind just cuddling, if that's how you want to take things for now, but, like I said, there's tomorrow to think about, and I need to know where you stand."

This was a huge question. She tried to be playful and smiled. "Right now, I'm lying down."

His face was still serious. "Zora, I'm not gonna go back to Gravel, not with my brother and his army after me. It would be foolish to do it now. I intend to cross the border and keep on going, leave everything behind." He closed his eyes, as if in pain. "It's not gonna be easy, and I swear, had it been a few days ago, I would think this wasn't for you, that you deserved something better, someone better."

Better than him? He had to have lost his mind.

He continued, "It's possible that we will be poor, that our lives will be hard, but I think we have something between us that's worth more than all the gold in the world. Will you come with me, stay by my side? Start a new life with me? And again, it won't be easy." He then added softly, his words a caress, "But I think it will still be worth it."

His words were whirling in her mind. *Our lives. Something between us that's worth more than all the gold in the world.* For the first time she truly believed that his looks, his touches, even his kiss, were more than just some fleeting entertainment. For the first time she thought that he was someone with whom she could dream about having a life together. He'd even said it.

Start a new life. And this would be after getting the cup and undoing whatever curse that had to be undone. He didn't want to leave her behind, probably as much as she didn't want to part from him.

Crossing the border and moving on rather than returning was a wise decision to avoid Kiran's guards. Starting a new life would be hard, obviously, but they could make it work. They knew how to read, had many skills, they would find a way to make a living elsewhere. Zora had never wanted a castle or even a real prince. She just wanted someone to love.

The only sad part was not saying goodbye to her parents, her family, but returning now would be foolish and irresponsible. Perhaps they could come back later, when things were calm, perhaps she would still get to see her niece and nephew, it was just a matter of giving it some time. In a way, it was as if their parents had given her their blessing when they packed their things and gave them a single hammock.

"Uh, oh. Now you're worrying me," Griffin said with a cheeky smile that contradicted his words. "Not only you're taking forever thinking, you're crying."

Zora rubbed a finger under her eyes. Damn tears, always showing up when least called for, this time probably because of the relief and emotion. "No, I was just thinking about my family."

His smile was gone, replaced by that concerned look of his. "I'm sorry."

"It's fine and it's for the best. As long as Kiran is intent on killing you and still has a grudge against me, even I shouldn't go back to the valley on my own."

He blinked slowly. "I know, and it's all my fault. You'll miss them, won't you?"

"Yes. But it's how life goes, right? And I think they knew I was leaving. Maybe we can come back and visit in a few years."

"Hum... *we*. Are you teasing me with hope?"

Zora smiled and rolled her eyes. "As if you didn't know what I was going to say before even asking."

"From time to time, it's a good idea to check if you're not delusional." He looked down, then back up. "And again, it might be hard."

"Like the bread we've been having?"

"Better. If we find a river or lake, away from Gravel, I can catch some fish."

Zora smiled. "Well, then, see? We have food already, and a hammock. All we need is a roof."

Griffin chuckled and took a deep breath. "For me this is new, to dream about the future, and it doesn't matter if it's hard or easy, just the possibility of having a future..."

He meant getting rid of his curse, and Zora still had a nagging fear that perhaps things could go wrong, but his calm expression, so filled with certainty, ceased her doubts. "Because you're sure this is going to work."

"I'm positive."

"Because of the vision?"

"That's part of it."

"Which you're not gonna tell me what it is."

"Of course I'm gonna tell you." He then raised an eyebrow. "When you tell me yours."

"Well, I guess it's never, then."

"So stubborn." He pinched her cheek, then gave her that wide, awe-inducing smile that gave her goosebumps. His fingers trailed her face down to her lips, then he extended his arm again.

Zora rested her head over his shoulder and could hear his heart pounding as he hugged her tight.

"Together, then," he said.

"Yes."

Zora chuckled then looked at those bright dark eyes which had a brilliant glimmer. She kissed him on the corner of his mouth, which turned into a smile, then his lips were on hers, his arms pulling her even closer.

Of course there was always the risk that things wouldn't last, there was always the risk that perhaps he wasn't being truthful, but Zora was tired of holding back, of suffocating her feelings and strangling her heart as if it would make her happier, when it didn't. She wanted all his kisses and hugs and wanted to enjoy every moment of it and allow herself to let her feelings flow like the water running outside. And this was like rain falling down after being locked in dark clouds, something that couldn't be stopped. Releasing her feelings, accepting them, that felt freeing.

Griffin ran his fingers lightly over her arm, the touch making her shiver. His touch was delicate and yet somehow affected her entire body. Zora ran her hands over his arm, his back, his chest, unsure when the shirt had come off. His lips moved down from her lips to her chin and neck, kissing sensitive parts, giving her thrills, and still moving down. After holding back for so long, it felt good to be in such a daze, letting her feelings guide her, just relaxing and surrendering to his touch, to the comforting feel of his skin against hers. Everything warm, comforting, perhaps sometimes too hot, a fire brewing inside her. A fire casting away darkness.

Time slowed down or perhaps stretched as they spent it between kisses and caresses. It wasn't as if he was asking her to do something for him, but a shared moment, her body coming close to his in the same way her heart already was.

Zora was on her back, Griffin kissing her, when he broke apart and knelt, his knees around her legs. His eyes never left hers, with that glimmer that now could light a fire. Slowly, he unlaced his pants.

It was like in the valley, when gongs were used for warnings, and a gong rang in her head alerting her about some danger. But it all felt so good. His pants were about to come off, and it was as if someone had thrown a bucket of water on her, the vision coming to her mind, and terror creeping up on her. She wasn't even close to ready to do whatever he thought they were about to do. Whatever perhaps she made him think she was about to do.

He stopped. "Zora, are you all right?"

She sat up—and realized she had no shirt on. Or undergarments. "I, I don't want to, I'm sorry. I've never..."

His eyes widened. "Oh. I'm so sorry, I... I have no excuse for my behavior. I thought... No, I wasn't thinking, I just—"

"It's fine, here I am..." She looked at herself. How had this happened? Her cheeks were burning, but she was more surprised than embarrassed. "Undressed. Lying down."

He bit his lip. "You're gonna think I have no manners." He paused. "Maybe I don't have manners. I'm not used to this. I assume I'm supposed to court you, right? Like for a few weeks. Or months." He was thoughtful. "But then, if you add up all the time we spent together, that is the equivalent of a month or two seeing each other occasionally. Not that I'm making excuses. Well, I am making excuses."

She placed a finger over his lips. "It's fine."

"You want to wait until we're married?"

Married? Well, he had spoken about starting a life. Not

that they had discussed any of that. But that wasn't really the main issue. "It depends when. It sounds silly, but I'm scared. It's scary, Griffin, and I..."

"I think I'd be scared too, if I were a girl. It's normal."

She looked down. This was so horribly embarrassing and awkward.

He lifted her chin and looked in her eyes. "Hey, I said I was fine with just cuddling, didn't I?"

"I like the kissing part."

He smiled. "I like it too." He then pulled her in for a kiss, a slow, chaste kiss, or as chaste as it could be when she had no clothes on. When they parted, he looked at her. "This is perfect. And I have time. We have time. Whatever makes you comfortable."

Zora looked down. She hadn't gone so fast with Seth, but when they did get to that point he was always asking, demanding, it was always about what she had to do to him. But he was her past and she couldn't let one idiot poison her present. This time, perhaps it had been four days of repressed feelings bursting forward like a ball exploding.

"And I'm sorry," he added. "Truly. I got carried away, I..."

"That was my vision," she blurted, perhaps glad to get that off her chest. "Us. Doing it."

His eyes widened. "That was what scared you more than a shadow creature? Cause I've seen you fighting them."

"Well, yeah, I have experience with them."

"How did that lead you to the temple?"

She shrugged. "Not sure. A hunch."

"Perhaps the basin is right. You were asking where the cup was, weren't you?"

"Maybe it shows other things. Your fears, maybe. Maybe it had nothing to do with the cup."

He glanced to the end of the cave, where the cup was, then back at her. "Not only fears, Zora. I saw you crying and pleading for Kiran to stop when I entered the arena. I saw it exactly how it happened. Perhaps I was afraid of seeing you suffering or hurt, but it also showed me something that came to happen."

"And what did you see this time?"

One corner of his mouth lifted. "I have to tell you?"

"I just told you mine!"

He looked down and laughed. "Well, if you thought *your* vision was scary... I'm not sure..."

"It has something to do with my vision?"

He was laughing and nodded.

"But it's scarier?"

His laughter didn't stop.

Zora didn't even want to imagine what could relate to what she had seen but be even scarier. It made her hair stand on end. "It's not funny, Griffin."

"It isn't."

"Yet you're laughing."

"Just give me a second." He took a deep breath. "It isn't funny. I don't know if I'm nervous or relieved or what. Laughter can be weird sometimes. And I'm not laughing at you." His eyes met hers. "The first thing I felt this time was that I was being taken to a scene, I was part of it, and that was different and somewhat disorienting. Then I saw you screaming in pain, and I just wanted it to stop, I didn't want to see you in pain again, but I also wanted to know what it was, wanted to know if maybe I could avoid it. But then you stopped. A baby cried, a boy, with brown eyes. I carried him to you. He was wrapped in a red blanket. Don't ask me who wrapped him or how it all happened, I just know I showed him to you. Your smile was like nothing I've ever seen before, even if I love your smile. You looked at him and said, 'He's got your eyes.' And there was so much happiness and love in your voice, I could almost touch it, I could feel it like a pleasant buzz in my body. And I looked at him. Let's be realistic, I have pretty average eyes, but I looked at him, and I saw what you must have seen, the most beautiful eyes ever. And there was so much hope, so much of something I can't even explain. I think it's true. We'll have a family."

Zora could feel the pleasant buzzing sensation he had described, she could feel that something between them, and could imagine herself holding his son. "Worth more than gold." His earlier words came to her, overwhelming her with emotion. "That was what you meant."

"Part of it. The rest is a feeling, a sense of calm when you're around. I'll be honest, I never thought about having a family. Well, how could I? But the feeling from the vision felt so palpable, real, it made me want it. You want a family, don't you?"

"Yes." She wasn't going to deny it.

"Maybe part of me has always known it. I know I upset you, and I regret the way I treated you before, but maybe that was the reason I couldn't bear to see you hurt."

Zora glared at him. "You also told me to go and find a husband."

"I said I was confident you'd find a great match. It meant I thought you were attractive."

"You didn't even know me."

"These things are not based on knowledge, but feeling. What about you, 'I don't want to serve men?' I mean, I should take back the idea of ever marrying you, since you think it's so demeaning."

"It's not like we're engaged." Not that she'd mind, but he should at least ask. "And it's not that I think love is bad, or even marriage is bad, it's just that it shouldn't define who I am as a person. I'm more than that."

"But that was not what I meant." His voice was soft.

It was hard to get angry, but she had to get it out of her chest. "You didn't want me to compete."

"I didn't want you getting hurt."

"The challenges were not dangerous. At all."

"Because you were there!" he yelled. "There wasn't going to be anything dangerous while you were competing." He sighed. "We're not gonna argue about this, are we? Again?"

"One day we'll have to sit and have a long conversation about all that."

"We will." He then lay down again and extended his arm, and Zora rested her head on it. He ran his fingers through her hair. "We have time."

They spent some time like that, close together, and there was something so magical and powerful in that. It felt good to kiss him, to begin something, to hope for the future. It could always be possible that things wouldn't last, but she wanted to live this moment, enjoy this feeling. And she felt safe with him, knowing he respected her limits and wasn't going to try to coerce or guilt-trip her into doing something she wasn't ready for.

After some time, the opening got darker.

"I think night is falling," she said. It was strange that she didn't want to get up, didn't want to leave his embrace, but on the other hand she was also eager to finally use the cup.

They got dressed, Zora lit a lamp, then went to the opening of the cave, to look at the sky. The grey clouds were turning black. Griffin put an arm around her. This would be a new beginning for them. Together. The idea of crossing to other kingdoms was scary, but seeing more of the world was exciting. As to her valley, if her hunch was right, perhaps she would free it tonight, freeing her to go wherever she wanted, knowing that her family and her people were safe. One day she'd come back.

When all the sunlight left the sky and they could barely see the walls on the other side of the abyss, she turned back to the cave and walked toward the cup, the flame of the lamp casting moving shadows on the walls.

She knelt by the translucid block, her heart pounding in her chest. When she reached out to touch the cup's encasing, she realized it was no longer solid. Her hand submersed in a strange, viscous red liquid, and she touched the cup. It looked like a wine cup made of red glass. There was nothing distinctive or special about it. Griffin stood by her, his eyes wide. He was putting so much trust in her, so much trust in this one small object... But then, it had always been his hope.

When the stars come up, water from the chalice can break the circles holding darkness in the boys and the land. When the time is right, in the quiet of night, drip it in the circle and break the chains.

She looked at the cup. The text said water, so it wasn't the viscous liquid that had been solid a few hours before. She took some water from the other natural pool, not the one where they'd been into. She brought it to the rock with the spiral grooves. Now, how should she do it? When she enchanted objects, she imagined the properties of the ingredients being absorbed by the material. She decided to pour the water and imagine freedom to the boys, meaning the royal line and especially Griffin, and freedom to the land, meaning her valley. So much hope.

She poured the water slowly on the edge and saw it move

in circles to the middle. The cup in her hand became liquid and fell on the ground. This had been it. Whatever had to be done with the cup was done, as it didn't exist anymore. She glanced at Griffin, perhaps hoping to see something happening, some change.

"Do you feel different?"

"No." He paused. "But I think the difference will come only in the next new moon. Something happened, Zora, I know it."

It almost felt naïve to put so much hope into something so simple, as that nagging feeling that perhaps the cup wouldn't work was now gnawing at her insides.

Zora ignored her apprehension and asked, "What do we do now?"

"Let's wait for the morning, then we can circle the mountain, and go to Kentosa, maybe."

Kentosa. It was a prosperous kingdom, but had been threatening Linaria. Well, they could maybe keep on traveling. Zora had another fear. "What about Alegra and your brother?"

"If they show up, great, I can say goodbye, maybe see what they want, talk to my brother. But I can't see how they'd come here with this storm."

"It stopped raining. And she still has magic."

He rolled his eyes. "Even then. They're not gonna climb a mountain at night, and if she wanted to stop us from getting the cup, they're too late." He pointed to their bags. "Let's eat something."

"Hum, let me guess... hard bread?"

"You don't sound excited, you're hurting my feelings." He laughed, then stepped close to her and leaned his forehead on hers. "It will get better, I promise."

"I wasn't complaining. I'd choose this over a banquet without you."

"Because you're worth more than all the gold in the world."

His words left Zora speechless and out of air. They had nothing and yet they had everything. So much hope for a future they knew nothing about. She closed her eyes, basking in the pure bliss of that moment, until the sound of rocks rolling snapped her alert.

"Did you hear that?"

He nodded. "Get your sword."

"It might be Larzen."

"And then, it might not."

Zora took Butterfly. Having her sword in her hand always made her feel safer. Griffin had his sword Thunder, its blue shimmer quite noticeable in that dark cave. The noise could be some animals in the caves. Hopefully they wouldn't spend the night with their swords in hand, expecting something dreadful that might or might not happen. But then, who knew what kind of animal dwelled in that place? The thought sent shivers down her spine, but between her and Griffin, they could deal with most threats.

He seemed to have guessed her thoughts. "It's probably nothing." He smiled. "And together we're a mighty team."

There was something so amazing about that smile, and even more amazing when it was all for her. He was right. Together they could defeat anything, and she felt so incredibly lucky to have him by her side, to stand together, to fight together, to be ready to face any obstacle together.

"Worth more than gold," she said.

But then she turned and watched the cave. There would be a lot of time to stare in his eyes and see his smile. For now they had to get through whatever was coming.

There were no more sounds, but something didn't feel

right. She said, "Maybe we should leave this place. Go outside."

"I'll have to remove the boulders, but yeah, it might be a good idea."

"Cover me, and let me know if you see anything." Zora crouched and put their things in a bag as fast as she could.

When she glanced at him, he was examining the blade of his sword. "Griffin!" she tried to make him focus again.

"Strange... magic," he muttered, while still staring at the sword.

"This is not the time." She tossed him a bag.

The impact of the bag must have snapped him awake because he took it, then said, "Let's run!"

Whatever strangeness happened to him was gone, and maybe it was just an impression. When she got to the edge of the cliff, she could swear she was hallucinating. She couldn't be seeing what she thought she was seeing.

20

BEFORE THE DAWN

A human shadow was descending the stairs. With a swift stroke, Zora cut it in half in its midsection. Her hand was trembling. "Griffin? Did you see that?"

"Maybe this mountain has some magic like your valley. I'll go first up the stairs."

No, it wasn't like in the valley or they'd be swarmed with creatures at this point, with all that darkness and only a tiny lamp.

They climbed up, and Zora had to turn twice to kill human shadows that followed them. In front of her, Griffin did the same. The only illumination was the faint light from the moon and stars coming from the opening, painting the cave in tones of gray. Nausea rose up in her stomach. Something terribly wrong was happening, and she had no idea what. They came to the upper cave by the entrance and found three human shadows waiting for them. Zora dealt with two, and Griffin destroyed one.

He then dropped his sword and proceeded to move a couple heavy boulders from the front of the door. She wasn't sure those rocks would have stopped Larzen, but now they certainly slowed them down. Three more human shadows came from a side opening, and she struck one, then two more, then finished one, and finally finished the last two when they were almost on her.

"I can't open the door," Griffin's voice came from behind her, sounding strained.

Zora turned and examined it. There was no handle, no buttons, and pushing it didn't do anything.

"Let's try to go up," she said. "There has to be another exit."

He nodded. "This way," then led her to a side passage. It was a thin corridor, but they came to a large chamber. There was an exit on the other side, but as they ran across it, human shadows sprang from holes she hadn't seen before. There were how many? Ten, fifteen, all running in their direction.

Zora didn't waste time, she ran forward with her sword, slashing and cutting, getting two, then three creatures at a time, even if it was hard to see them in that semi-darkness. So many. It was almost as if Griffin wasn't fighting with her. When she glanced towards him, he stood still, his sword down. But he wasn't being attacked. At that moment, a human shadow's claws reached her arm, drawing blood. Zora cut off its arm, then stabbed the creature. Slowly, it disappeared.

She ran back to Griffin. His eyes were his normal dark brown, except that he stood still, as if confused.

"Griffin? What's wrong with you?"

"Zora?" He sounded surprised, then fell down.

Please, not again. How were they going to escape if he was unconscious? And what if the effect of the cup killed him or something worse? She crouched, meaning to take his pulse, when she heard fast steps. A shadow wolf. She beheaded it when it jumped. These creatures always had a final leap, which was the perfect moment to kill them.

Three more human shadows appeared, and she dealt with them swiftly.

She turned to check on Griffin and this time he was standing, sword in hand.

"What happened?" she asked.

He lunged forward, as if ready to strike her. She ducked.

"Griffin? It's me."

Instead of replying, he tried to stab her again, his sword casting a blue glow around it, but she blocked him. His eyes were distant, cold, glassy, and that wasn't Griffin, or she'd be unarmed and dead by now. But his eyes weren't glowing green either.

"What are you?" she asked.

He pulled back then turned, trying to strike her at the end of his circular motion, but she blocked him again.

There had to be a way to get through him. "Griffin. Please."

A human shadow was behind her and she turned to strike it, then turned back to defend herself from weird Griffin, who attacked again, and made her step back. The edge of the precipice and the stairs were getting close, but then a creature came up from behind her, and she had to turn and attack it. When she turned back, weird Griffin hit her sword, which flew down the abyss.

Butterfly.

Her first and only sword. The sword with which she had learned to fight, the sword she had used to kill four shadow wolves at once, the sword she'd used to save Griffin. Griffin, who stood in front of her, not himself. How had that happened?

She felt tears running down her eyes as she contemplated

death coming for her. At least she'd had a moment of bliss, she'd had someone who thought she was worth more than gold, even if for such a short time.

Some bats flew in the cave creating a distraction and she ran past him, toward the corridor. She'd need to find a way to open that door and run. Run? If it was night outside? Even if these creatures were not like the ones in the valley, they'd certainly survive at night. And she had no sword.

False Griffin was after her, and yelled, "Zora!"

She turned. Perhaps he was back. "Is it you?"

He pointed his sword at her. Something ran towards them, like a human shadow, but not quite, carrying a torch in its hand. It was Larzen—who kicked Griffin from behind. He lost his balance and dropped his sword.

"Take the sword and come with me," Larzen yelled.

"And leave him?"

"He's not himself," he said.

Zora took the heavy sword. It was better than having no weapon. Weird Griffin got up but stood still, and she followed Larzen to another opening, which led to another chamber, this time long and with natural pools.

Someone stood by an opening far away.

"I told you to stay behind," Larzen yelled at the other person.

"You're welcome." It was Alegra's voice.

Some five more human shadows appeared in front of them, while some five more came from behind. Zora understood the point of the heavy sword. It took some effort, but with one movement she cut three creatures, then finished the other two quick enough. As she glanced behind, Larzen shook his torch, which seemed to keep the creatures at bay. He was lucky because there were bats between him and the creatures. Zora passed Larzen and swung that huge sword again, killing two human shadows, then two more. The final one advanced towards Zora, but she stabbed it before it reached her. The bats were really helping them, flying in front of the creatures. She glanced back and saw no sign of strange Griffin. Her chest squeezed, fearing he would be hurt, guilty for leaving him behind. No, she wasn't leaving him.

"We have to get him," she pleaded.

"He's not himself anymore," Alegra said. "Now escape. You can't help him if you're dead."

Zora ran towards the opening. It wasn't a door, but just a thin fissure in the rocks. When they were outside, a shadow wolf pounced on them, and Zora almost missed it, struggling with the heavy sword, but she stabbed it when it was almost on her.

"Hurry, hurry," Alegra said.

Right. How silly of Zora to waste her time dealing with deadly creatures.

The princess led them to a tiny cave, a small hole, actually. "In, in."

Zora followed. The cave was taller than the hole, and they could stand up inside it. She kept watching the opening, until Alegra punched the ceiling and a pile of dirt fell over the entrance, blocking it. Other than Larzen's torch, they were in complete darkness.

Alegra lit a lamp. "We'll be safe here until morning," she said.

"What about Griffin?"

The princess was silent and looked down. Larzen was silent too.

"What about him?" Zora insisted.

Larzen closed his eyes as if he were in pain. "That wasn't him."

"I know, but..." She wasn't even sure what to ask, so many questions circling in her mind, so many fears strangling her heart.

"He's possessed," Larzen said. "But he's alive." His voice was kind. "Let's take it easy. To start," he pointed at Alegra. "I don't think the two of you have been properly introduced."

"I know her!" Zora said.

"I'm not Alegra," the red-haired young woman said.

Zora frowned. "Are you... her twin or something?"

"No. I'm the person you met in the castle, but I was an impostor, pretending to be the Linaria princess. My real name's Riadne."

Impostor? Riadne? More confusion to add to the tons of things Zora didn't understand. "Okay. You knew that this would happen? That was why you were following us?"

Larzen shook his head. "No, at first I just wanted to find Griffin and put some sense in that empty head of his. Make a decent plan for him to escape Gravel. And you too, if you wanted." He looked down. "But then... we got some books and found out some things."

"What things?" Zora was shaking.

"You should rest," the false Alegra, Riadne, said. "We'll tell you all tomorrow, when the sun shines again."

Zora shook her head. "Don't do this to me. Tell me. What's wrong with Griffin? Will he be all right? And why weren't his eyes glowing green this time?"

"Let's sit, then," Riadne said. "My legs are killing me, and I don't want to look up while talking. There's a lot I need to explain."

Zora wanted to run, to fight, perhaps to break something,

but that wasn't going to help anyone. Riadne and Larzen sat with legs crossed, and Zora had no choice but to do the same. The cave was so tiny that their knees were almost touching each other's.

"We could start with the good news," Larzen said. "You freed your valley."

"How?"

"Well," Riadne said. "The walls should no longer be standing, at least not standing as strong. And the Dark Valley won't have the magic allowing creatures to survive in daylight or making them spawn even in the smallest dark places."

Zora braced herself for the "but" that she knew was coming.

Instead, Riadne asked, "Do you know how the Dark Valley was created?"

"Can you just tell me what's going on?" Zora wasn't in the mood to listen to a long story.

"I'm trying," Riadne replied, and Zora decided it was easier just to let her say whatever she wanted to say. The false princess continued, "It happened four hundred years ago. I'm still not quite sure what happened, but someone opened up Gravel to the shadow realm. There were dark creatures everywhere, but they didn't survive in sunlight, and didn't appear in small spaces. But it was a problem, as you can imagine. The Solanas were... a people who advised the king. We also have magic. I'm one of them, but we lost most of our knowledge. The solution they found was to isolate the shadow realm connection, leaving it in only a small place in the kingdom."

Zora sucked in a breath. "Condemning the people in the valley."

Riadne shook her head. "It was empty, then. The people who moved there were volunteers who would remain just to make sure shadow creatures wouldn't overrun the walls and escape. I'm not sure how it became a place where people lived permanently or how they convinced everyone that the blame for the Dark Valley was in its dwellers. That part of the story is Gravel's; it has nothing to do with the Solanas. All my ancestors did was contain the dark magic, that was all. The cup was a fail-safe."

Riadne's people had created the curse of the valley? "You're the flying witches?"

She had a sad sigh. "How I wish we could fly. We just die."

Larzen listened, but didn't seem surprised. He probably knew all that already.

One question was burning in Zora's mind. "What does it have to do with Griffin?"

"I don't know if it was a deal gone wrong between the Gravel king and the King of Shadows or what," Riadne explained. "I read that the Gravel king wanted to make sure his line would stay forever in power, and this king tricked him. Another theory was that it was revenge because we contained his magic in a small valley. The King of Shadows was going to possess the heir to the throne. What the Solanas did was find a way to delay it long enough that a solution could be found. The heir would only be possessed once he matured. I guess he died before that, and the curse continued in some of the king's descendents, not necessarily the heirs."

"So your people didn't curse the royal line? You tried to stop it?"

Riadne nodded in silence. "The green glow you're describing could be Solana's magic. It was probably stopping Griffin from being possessed."

It didn't make much sense. "But I saw him. He acted... Like an animal."

The false princess took a deep breath. "I don't know much about his curse. What I know is that an animal would mean he was no longer in full command of his body, but it wouldn't mean that the king was in his place."

Zora looked down. It made sense. Weird Griffin this time didn't have that crazed look; he could even duel, even if not as well as the real prince.

Riadne continued, "I believe the Solanas needed more time to research, more time to find a solution. They delayed it to gain time."

"Why didn't they find a solution, then?"

Riadne's eyes were sad. "The king slaughtered them, apparently because he wasn't happy they couldn't cure his son fast enough."

Zora put her hands over her mouth. "Like in the temple ruins."

Riadne nodded. "Yes. But the thing is, the cup was meant to reverse this spell that contained the darkness, that pushed it back. Once you used it, nothing contained it anymore."

Zora shook her head. "Griffin had always thought it would be his salvation. That was what his ancestors always thought. He was so sure of it." More sure than she could even explain. She faced Riadne. "You tried to warn us."

She shook her head. "I had no idea about any of this until a day ago. We were late, far behind, and there was no way we could have reached you. I swear we tried. Larzen even trusted me, when he had all the reasons in the world not to. Accept it as fate, Zora. At least we got here in time to help you."

That felt so useless now. "Why did you save me?"

It was Larzen who replied, "Well, I don't think my brother would be happy if he woke up tomorrow and you were dead."

The idea of Griffin being himself again when the sun came up lit up a hope in her heart.

"Larzen." Riadne's voice was soft, but there was a warning in it.

"What?" He looked at her.

The false princess looked down and closed her eyes.

"What is it?" He insisted, his voice urgent.

Zora felt empty, dreading what the false princess was about to say.

"I..." Riadne took a deep breath "Don't think he'll be back tomorrow. Not to this body at least."

Hearing it said out loud was like getting stabbed in the heart.

"You can't know that!" Larzen protested. "Where's my brother?"

"I don't know!" Riadne said. "The spell keeping him was broken, now he'll be fully possessed."

"You mean he's gone?" Zora was shaking. "There's no way to get him back?"

Riadne paused. "Maybe. I don't know." She bit her lip and looked at Zora and Larzen. "But I do know one thing: magic can always be countered and reversed. Especially if it's unnatural and powerful. It can be reversed."

"Any idea how?" Zora asked.

Riadne shook her head.

Zora closed her eyes. The pain was so much that even her tears had dried. "If only I had known, if only we had tried to find out more."

"You can't undo the past," Riadne's voice was surprisingly kind. "And blaming yourself won't help."

"I also knew nothing about it," Larzen said as he stared ahead of him, his eyes lost. "I had no idea what Griffin was going through, what he feared, why he even wanted that cup. Why wouldn't he open up? But maybe it was my fault."

Riadne sighed. "Again, self-blame doesn't help."

"One son every generation. It could have been me." It was as if he was talking to himself.

"Not every generation," Riadne said. "That's a wrong translation."

"Then what?" he asked.

"Every mother."

Chills ran down Zora's spine and her eyes met Larzen's.

He turned to Riadne. "Every mother? Then Kiran is possessed too."

"You have different mothers?" The false princess was surprised.

"Yes. Kiran's mother wasn't the same as mine and Griffin's."

Riadne frowned. "Oh. That might be a problem."

It didn't make much sense. "Who's possessing Kiran, then?" Zora asked. "And it didn't seem that he had any curse. I mean, he wanted to host a challenge right in the night... uh, Griffin would get weird."

"I don't know," Riadne said. "Perhaps it manifests differently in him, if he's really possessed."

Larzen's eyes were wide, then he pinched his nose and looked down.

Riadne continued, "I know very little about it. For instance, I had no idea about Griffin's curse either. There's much that I still need to learn." She then tensed and stared at Larzen. "My brother. He's in the castle."

"He should be safe," Larzen said.

"How can you know?"

"He was in an isolated wing, Riadne. And Kiran, or whatever he is, doesn't even know your brother is there."

Riadne glared at him. "You better be right, Larzen."

"I am. I wouldn't put either of them in danger." Then he turned to Zora. "Riadne here has a long story, but I doubt you're in the mood to hear it now."

"Later. Right now I feel dead inside, that's what I feel."

They were silent for a while, the air heavy.

Something else came to Zora's mind. "By undoing the magic of the valley, does it mean there will be creatures everywhere tonight?"

Riadne took a deep breath and nodded.

It couldn't be. "In every village? In every city?" Zora closed her eyes, unable to absorb the horror of her actions, the amount of people who would be killed.

"It's not gonna be like in the Dark Valley," Riadne said. "These creatures will come from caves and forests. Most people will be safe inside."

"Most. Not all. They had no warning." Zora's voice was cracking with pain, regret, and so much more.

Riadne shook her head. "It's not your fault."

"We could have waited for you!" Zora said.

"We could have been faster. We could have learned about it earlier. If my people's books hadn't been hidden and destroyed, maybe we could have known this truth much earlier, maybe reversed this curse. So many *coulds*." Riadne's voice was gentle again. "We can't change the past. It is what it is."

Something else annoyed Zora. "I had these visions, heard this voice. A woman, she looked like the Sun Goddess. I don't even believe in any goddess. But this voice guided me."

Riadne paused, then said, "It could be Astrea, our spirit guide."

Zora was horrified. "She guided me to do this awful thing?"

The false princess took a deep breath. "There could be a bigger reason. We don't know."

So many questions, so much pain, so much regret. The cave was already tiny, but Zora was feeling like it was going to crumble and suffocate her. What fate was this? The air was heavy as minutes ticked by.

After some time, Larzen broke the silence. "So, what do we do?"

"We shine our light," Zora replied without even thinking.

"What?" he asked.

"It's silly." She snorted. "It's a stupid chant. For courage and hope. What's the point of hope?"

"To make you feel better?" Larzen suggested. "What's the chant? Now I'm curious."

Zora rolled her eyes. "Yes, it's going to solve all our problems."

"Hope can get us through until morning," Riadne said, then added, "It's gonna be a long night."

Well, telling them her chant wouldn't hurt anyone. It certainly couldn't hurt Zora, as she was beyond the point of feeling any pain.

"All right. What do we do? We shine our light. What if shadows come? We fight, we fight, we fight. What if fear shows up? We always trust our might. And what do we do meanwhile? We hope, believe, and try." Of course, the words were almost meaningless when said without the energy they needed.

But then she remembered the way she used to do it with her students, and the words rang in her head. *What if shadows come? We fight, we fight, we fight.*

"We fight," she said, looking at Larzen and Riadne. "We fight." There was a small sliver of hope lighting up in her chest. "This King of Shadows, it, he, whatever, must come from somewhere, right? I mean, if he can come here, possess Griffin, and wreak havoc in our world, I'm pretty sure I can go to his world."

Larzen tilted his head. "Maybe."

The idea was perhaps stupid. Why hadn't anyone done this before? Perhaps because they hadn't tried. Perhaps because people in the Dark Valley were too busy fighting shadow creatures and people outside were not bothered. An idea was coming to her mind.

"I'm going to find this king. And if he doesn't give me Griffin back, I'll rip out his heart with my bare hands. If he has a heart. But I'll figure a way to get Griffin back regardless."

Larzen raised his eyebrows. "That's a plan."

"Larzen, this is no laughing matter," Riadne said.

For the first time, Zora wondered if there was anything romantic between them.

"Who's laughing?" He asked. "I'm not. Nobody tried to get this king in his own kingdom. Maybe that's what we need to do. Maybe that's the answer." He turned to Riadne. "We'll need your help."

"We?" Zora was surprised.

"I also want my brother back." He closed his eyes and sighed. "My brothers back. Riadne?"

"Well, once we survive this night, once I have *my* brother back." She gave him a pointed look that reeked of fury. "We'll see. I live one day at a time."

Zora had lived one day at a time too, and she understood it. It was about surviving. But this time she wanted to more than just react to the way things were. She was going to plan her future and plan her actions.

For most of her life, Zora had been guided by hope. It was what had kept her going. When Seth betrayed her, she learned the power of anger, and how it could be such a strong motivator. Even if it didn't take her in the best direction, anger lit a fire in her.

Zora then remembered the hope in Griffin's eyes, his certainty, his vision. It had to mean something, it had to have the potential to become true, the potential for them to have something worth more than all the gold in the world. At the same time, she was more than angry or pissed, she was furious at this Shadow King. How dare he possess Griffin? She was going to latch onto hope, hope that she would find Griffin, and latch onto her fury. Together, hope and fury were more than a flame in her heart; they formed a scorching blaze that would burn down this Kingdom of Shadows with everything in it.

THE STORY CONTINUES

I believe in happy endings, but this isn't the ending yet.

There's more coming, and we'll follow our characters as they try to fix the mess they're in.

The series *Kingdom of Curses and Shadows* concludes with in *The Dawn and the Prince*. Find it here:

The Dawn and the Prince

ABOUT THE AUTHOR

I love to give life to characters and connect with readers. I'm originally from Brazil and I live in Montreal, Canada.

You can check my ramblings at my blog and also sign up for my newsletter and get an exclusive short story which is a prequel to *The Cup and the Prince* at:

dayleitao.com

SUMMARY OF BOOK 1
THE CUP AND THE PRINCE

Zora lives in the Dark Valley. It's a secluded place in the kingdom surrounded by walls, and its inhabitants aren't allowed to leave. In this valley, shadow creatures spawn in the dark, even in the smallest spaces, and they survive even in daylight. Everyone carries a sword and knows how to fight, including 17-year-old Zora, who is a school teacher (equivalent to an elementary school teacher), teaching some kids (9- 11 year olds) about everything, including self defense. Her parents are doctors.

Zora's boyfriend, Seth, is one of the best rangers in the valley. Rangers light up the valley and fight shadow creatures. This year, one representative of the valley will be allowed to participate in the Royal Games and go to the castle, and it's Seth. They are in his bedroom, saying goodbye the night before he leaves for the games, and he wants her to give him a parting "gift". Zora is a virgin, quite terrified of doing it, and reconsidering her decision. A shadow creature attack interrupts them, and after the attack she learns he was planning on never coming back and also cheating on her. As revenge, she gives him a sleep draught and steals the letter and the rod that the champion should carry, so that she'll take his place in the competition.

Zora leaves the valley and heads to an inn in a nearby town, where the royal delegation is staying. There, she has an altercation with a stranger and threatens him with her sword, just because she felt he was dismissive of her because she's a girl.

The stranger is prince Griffin. He just started an affair/relationship with Alegra, who's a princess from a nearby kingdom, and betrothed to his older brother, Kiran, who's king. He's feeling guilty and confused, but his attraction to Alegra is stronger than his guilt. He isn't angry at Zora for having attacked him, just perhaps intrigued.

STAVOS, an assistant to the crown, takes Zora to the castle. There, Zora learns that the young man she attacked is prince Griffin, who is taking part in and helping organize the games. He claims the games are too dangerous for her and that she should participate in the festivities and find a good husband. Zora is angry that he's underestimating her. Griffin's older brother, prince Larzen, intervenes, so that Griffin reluctantly allows Zora to compete. Larzen tells Zora he knows she is an impostor and asks her to help him with flirting games so that he'll help her with the competition. Zora agrees.

Zora shares a room with Loretta, who's friendly. After eating, Zora goes to the library to do some research and meets Griffin again, who's polite but asks her to quit the competition. She refuses. Later, she finds herself locked in a room in the library, and about to be late for the games. Someone opens the door for her and she barely makes it to the presentation of the champions in time. She learns that the winner will have to defeat a lion and feels sad for the animal.

THE NEXT DAY, Larzen asks Zora to flirt with a young man in a garden. She goes to the garden but mostly challenges the young man. Larzen then shows a dungeon where Seth is being held, and says Zora had better do what he asks or he'll release Seth, who can tell the kingdom that Zora is an impostor.

Thanks to Larzen's tips, Zora wins the first challenge. In the ball afterwards, she befriends Mauro, a strong and tall competitor who doesn't have an eye. Zora finds out that she flirted with Kiran, the young king. Kiran and Alegra announce their engagement. Even so, Kiran asks Zora to dance and is flirty with her. Later, a drunk Griffin asks Zora to dance, but he's so drunk she takes him to the garden where he pukes and collapses. She takes him back to his bedroom and makes sure he feels well. He's mumbling and she finds out that he was interested or having something with Alegra.

GRIFFIN WAKES up with a pleasant feeling, remembering someone taking care of him. He wakes up and Alegra is there. He tells her to leave, but she sings and then he gets confused and attracted to her. In his confusion, he thinks she was the one who took care of him, but he doesn't understand why she's still engaged to his brother.

He has a dungeon with magical objects and a basin of truth. He asks if Alegra loves him. He sees Zora instead, quite distraught and in tears, begging someone to stop something. The vision shakes him, and more than ever he wants her out of the games.

. . .

THE NEXT COMPETITION includes horse riding, but thanks to Larzen, Zora got some lessons. In the arena, Alegra stops by each competitor and touches Zora's horse. When she mounts the mare, it goes crazy and Zora almost falls, but thanks to the horse misbehaving, she does well in the challenge.

Griffin calls Zora to his office and asks her if she used dark magic in the horse. She denies, and when she suggests it was Alegra who did it, he changes the subject. But he believes Zora, and asks her to come to him if she feels she's in danger.

IN THE SECOND BALL, King Kiran dances again with Zora. He invites her to work for him and be his "magical advisor" while subtly insinuating that he wants her as his lover. Zora doesn't confront him but doesn't say *yes* either, and leaves right after that.

In the hallway, someone with a knife attacks Zora, but she takes the knife and the assailant runs away.

The next day, she goes to Griffin to tell him about the assassin. He's quite concerned and assigns her two guards. He also suggests that she change the key to her room. Zora is impressed at how thoughtful he is.

GRIFFIN MEETS Alegra near some ruins, and asks her to stop trying to harm Zora. He thinks the princess is jealous of the king. He also thinks she might have sent the assassin. Alegra sings and he gets confused and again attracted by Alegra.

. . .

ZORA GOES for a ride with her friend Loretta and her two guards, Natasha and Isabelle. By some ruins, she sees Griffin's and Alegra's clothes on the ground and realizes what they are doing, horrified that she trusted the prince. When she comes back to her room at night, Alegra is there, key in hand, saying that those matters concern her too. Zora leaves the castle and goes to the city with Loretta and her guard Isabelle, to stay at an inn, now that she feels unsafe in the castle.

The next day, Griffin finds Zora training and showing her guard a motivational cry that she teaches her students. He asks Zora to be careful. Larzen finds her at the inn and reminds her she has a competition in 3 hourse. Without time to train or plan, she starts thinking that maybe the guards were told to distract her. She also starts to wonder if Griffin is the one who sent the assassin.

ZORA BARELY PASSES the next challenge. She also learns that Loretta left the city, and feels alone, now that she doesn't trust anyone around her.

The next day Zora goes to a picnic with Larzen, Griffin, Kiran, and Alegra. Griffin starts looking at Zora differently. Zora goes into the ruins with Kiran and agrees to be his "potion girl", despite knowing that he wants more than just her magical skills. She's doing it to anger Alegra and Griffin, who had warned her against Kiran. Alegra is caught alone with Griffin, uses her magic singing on him, and asks him to humiliate Zora. When everyone's back, Griffin asks Larzen if he's sleeping with Zora and she leaves the picnic, determined not to flirt with anyone anymore and stop playing Larzen's games.

After another challenge, Zora goes out to celebrate with

Mauro (the champion who just got eliminated) and his friends. She returns with the guard Isabelle, and is almost attacked by three dogs that turn out to be Griffin's. Isabelle calls the prince, who calms down the dogs and asks Zora to talk to him. In his office, she confronts him about his relationship with Alegra, says she's not going to tell anyone, and asks him to stop trying to kill her. Griffin is confused, doesn't remember much, and doesn't answer things properly. Zora leaves his office and finds out King Kiran heard everything she said. She is forced to confess she's seen Griffin and Alegra together. Kiran doesn't look upset, and says he'll help Zora win the games.

ZORA AGREES to brew a potion to make Griffin slow and confused, so that he'll lose his challenge against her, which is probably going to be sword fighting. Griffin is outstanding at sword fighting, and Zora knows that she'll have no chance otherwise. Before the challenge, Griffin takes the juice with the potion, and Kiran asks Zora to sit with him in the stands. She gets nervous because she wanted to get ready to fight Griffin and because the effect of the potion might fade.

Zora sees them bringing the lion and realizes they are about to make Griffin fight the animal while partially incapacitated with her potion. She begs Kiran to stop it. It's just like Griffin's vision; she's in tears, distraught. Kiran doesn't stop the challenge and Zora jumps in the arena and saves Griffin, but then the king orders soldiers to attack and kill Griffin, who's now unconscious on the ground. Zora stands in the way and is hit on the shoulder by an arrow. Surrounded and outnumbered, she knows she has no chance, but she doesn't step away from Griffin, determined to die defending him if necessary.

Alegra comes into the arena singing and everyone stops, so that she saves Griffin and Zora. Mauro helps Zora carry Griffin out of the arena, take a cart with a horse, and escape the city.

On the way, Griffin wakes up. He learns that Zora saved him, realizes his vision and the fear she felt were for him, and kisses her. She likes the kiss and realizes she'd been wanting to kiss him for some time, but she pushes him away, afraid that he's still in love with Alegra and that he'd want nothing with Zora because he's a prince and she's a commoner.

We get Alegra's point of view. Her real name is Riadne and she's not sure why she used that much magic, and how she'll go through with her plan to have the brothers destroying each other.

Griffin is feeling better and agrees to go to the Dark Valley, where Zora can get medical attention from her parents, as she's wounded from the arrow. He then realizes what day it is, and that night is about to fall, and gets worried. He tells Zora that there will be a monster tonight, and that the monster's him.